The Lucky Ones

The Lucky Ones

A Novel

JULIANNE PACHICO

SPIEGEL & GRAU

NEW YORK

Published in the United States by Spiegel & Grau, an imprint of Random House, a division of Penguin Random House LLC, New York.

SPIEGEL & GRAU and Design is a registered trademark of Penguin Random House LLC.

Some of the stories in this work have been previously published: "Lucky" in *Lighthouse Journal* and subsequently in *The Best of British Short Stories 2015;* "Lemon Pie" in different form in *Shooter Literary Magazine;* "Honey Bunny" in *The New Yorker;* "The Tourists" as a pamphlet by Daunt Books and subsequently in *The Best British Short Stories 2015;* "The Bird Thing" in *The White Review.*

LIBRARY OF CONGRESS CATALOGING-IN-PUBLICATION DATA
Names: Pachico, Julianne, author.
Title: The lucky ones : a novel / Julianne Pachico.
Description: New York : Spiegel & Grau, 2017.
Identifiers: LCCN 2016033951 | ISBN 9780399588655 (hardback) | ISBN 9780399588679 (ebook)
Subjects: LCSH: Colombians—Fiction. | Civil war—Psychological aspects—Fiction. | Guerrilla warfare—Psychological aspects— Fiction. | Colombia—Fiction. | New York (N.Y.)—Fiction. | Psychological fiction. | BISAC: FICTION / Literary. | FICTION / Cultural Heritage.
Classification: LCC PR6116.A315 L83 2017 | DDC 823/.92—dc23
LC record available at https://lccn.loc.gov/2016033951

Printed in the United States of America on acid-free paper

randomhousebooks.com
spiegelandgrau.com

2 4 6 8 9 7 5 3 1

FIRST EDITION

Book design by Dana Leigh Blanchette

For E,
who read everything

"Here," he said, not really joking. "The bullet
we didn't shoot you with."

—GABRIEL GARCÍA MÁRQUEZ,
News of a Kidnapping

Inside a single moment, you can live many lives.

—FRANCISCO GOLDMAN,
The Art of Political Murder

CONTENTS

The Lucky Ones

Lucky

2003

VALLE DEL CAUCA

Her parents and brother are spending the holiday weekend up in the mountains; they're going to a party at the Montoyas' country house. Before getting into the car her mother asks her one last time, Is she sure she doesn't want to come? Isn't she going to be bored all weekend, with only the maid around to keep her company? And she says of course not, don't be silly, and in any case the impossibly long drive on that endlessly winding road always makes her carsick (she shakes her head, sticks out her tongue, and makes a face like she can already feel the nausea). She's been there several times anyway, remembers what it's like: She's seen the automatic shampoo dispensers in the bathroom that fill her hands with grapefruit-scented foam, the shiny mountain bikes that have never been ridden propped up on the porch, the indoor fishpond and the seashell-patterned ashtrays. Her brother will run around the yard screaming with the other kids, weaving and ducking around the water fountains and angel statues, begging the gardeners to let them feed the peacocks, hold the monkey, cuddle the rabbits. She always gets so bored, sitting in a white plastic chair and batting away flies while the adults drink beer out of green glass bottles and talk, talk, talk for hours about things she either doesn't care about or doesn't understand. When she hears the word *guerrilla* she'll picture a group of men dressed up in gorilla suits, roaming the jungle while carrying rifles, wearing black rubber boots with yellow bottoms, and she'll have to choke back laughter to prevent Coca-Cola from snorting out of her nose. The sinewy meat and burnt black corn from the grill always get stuck in her teeth and hang down from her upper molars like vines for Tarzan, and she'll inevitably end up prodding them with her tongue for the rest of the weekend. Mariela Montoya will be there too, of course, most likely wearing an oversized T-shirt, glowering in the corner, sucking on the tip of her long black braid, and they'll turn away from each other gracefully without even a kiss on the cheek, let alone a greeting. *Hi, Mariela,* Stephanie will never say. *It's been so long. How have you been?*

So no, she tells her mother again, but thank you very much, and she brushes strands of hair away from her eyes, smiling sweetly.

"Fine, then," her mother says, a little sharply. "You're lucky Angelina was willing to cancel her weekend off and stay here instead. Was that church thing of hers tomorrow or next week?" She says this last part to her husband, who shrugs without looking up, still fiddling with the car radio knobs. One of the announcers is saying in a highly amused voice, *Communist rebels? Those words don't even mean anything anymore. You might as well call them cheese sandwich rebels.* Her brother makes a face at her through the car window and she makes a face right back.

"Well," her mother says. "Since you're going to be here all weekend—just keep something in mind." She glances over her shoulder at the hedge, leaves barely rustling in the wind. The sweat stains in the armpits of her pale green blouse look like tiny islands.

"If the phone rings," she says, "or the doorbell sounds—let Angelina deal with it. And make sure she tells any men who ask that we're not in the country anymore. Could you do that for me?"

"What kind of men?" she asks.

Her mother tucks a strand of hair behind her ears—brown like hers, but gray at the roots. "You know what kind I mean," she says in her soft accent.

So they want their revolution? the radio asks. *Listen, I'll tell you what I'd do to them!* Her mother's head flicks sharply toward her husband, and he quickly switches it off.

After they drive away she finds her mother's cigarettes almost immediately, hidden at the bottom of one of the woven baskets Angelina brought back from her village marketplace. She smokes one under the trees by the pool, taking quick little puffs, watching carefully for Angelina at the window. What she didn't tell her mother is that she has plans to meet up with Katrina in the city center mall on Monday. Katrina's chauffeur will take them there and drop them off at the entrance, where they'll hover just long enough to make sure he's gone. Then they'll cross the highway together, ducking fast across the busy intersection, laughing and running past the wooden sticks of chicken sweating on grills and giant metal barrels of spinning brown peanuts, the clown-faced garbage cans and men in zebra costumes directing traffic. The plan is to head to the other mall across the street, the one with the upper floors still closed off with yellow electrical tape from when the last bomb went off. On the first floor is the food court that serves Cuban sandwiches and beer in lava lamp containers. That's where the members of the football team will be, dark hair slicked back and glistening. She and Katrina are going to sit at the wooden picnic tables and yank their jeans down as far as they can go, tug at their tank tops to reveal the bra straps underneath, peach and pink and black. She has this way of crossing her legs at the ankles, tilting her head to the side, and smiling as though whatever is being said is the most interesting thing in the world and there's nowhere else she'd rather be. She'll accept their smiles, their eyes scanning her up and down, their low murmurs of approval, even the breathy whispers of *Hey, beautiful,* with the same icy sense of destiny that she accepts everything else in her life.

Later that night, instead of going through catalogs for college applications in the United States, she sits on the couch rereading one of the Arthurian fantasy novels from her childhood. It's the kind filled with knights kneeling before queens and saying things like, *My lady, perchance you have misunder-*

stood me. Rereading kids' books is one of her sneaky, most secret treats, saved for holiday weekends or summer vacations, something that someone like Katrina has no need to ever know about. As she reads she never needs to raise her eyes to know where Angelina is or what she's doing—the sound of her black plastic sandals slapping against the floor tiles is like a noise made by the house itself. Without looking she knows when Angelina's opening the silverware drawer, lighting the candles to chase away flies, setting the last of the dishes on the table. The radio in the kitchen crackles loudly with static, which drowns out the newscasters' gruff voices.

She's turning pages rapidly, eager to arrive at the climax (the knight finally encounters the magician who blessed him with shape-shifting skills—or did he curse him?), when she feels a stubby finger gently tracing her scalp. "We really need to fix your hair, *mija*," Angelina says in that same shrill voice Stephanie's been listening to her whole life. "It's bad to have it in your eyes all the time like that."

"That won't be necessary," she says, not looking up from the page.

When Angelina's hands linger close to her face, she uses the book to push them away, ducking irritably from their overwhelming smell of onions and stale powdered milk. She turns a page as the sandals slap slowly back to the kitchen.

During dinner she drips a giant spoonful of curry sauce onto her plate and swirls around the lettuce leaves and onion slices to make it look like she's eaten something. When she pushes the chair back from the table, Angelina is already there, reaching for her plate with one hand and squeezing the flesh on her lower arm with the other. "My God, but you're skinny!" Angelina says in the same high-pitched shrill. "Eat more! How are you going to fight off men?"

"Could you please not touch me?" she says, jerking her arm away, but the tiny nugget of pleasure that's formed inside her just from hearing the word *skinny* is already giving off warmth.

Angelina says something else, speaking in a low voice this time, but her words are muffled beneath the trumpets of the national anthem blasting from the kitchen radio, in its usual slot just before the news.

"What?" she says, but Angelina's already abruptly turned away, her white apron swirling through the air like a cape.

"Don't worry about it, *mija*," Angelina says, not looking back. "It's nothing."

She doesn't wake up till midmorning. Because Katrina won't be coming by until Monday, she doesn't shave her legs and wears a baggy pair of yellow basketball shorts instead of jeans. The day is already uncomfortably hot. She heads outside to the pool and smokes a cigarette under the grapefruit tree, careful to stand in the shade to protect her skin. It never feels like a holiday weekend to her until she's smoked, until she gets that jumpy feeling in her stomach that makes her want to stand very still.

Back in the kitchen, she opens the refrigerator and drinks directly from the pitcher of lemonade, careful not to bang her teeth against the ceramic. As she puts the pitcher on the counter there's a loud blast of the doorbell. It echoes through the house, followed by six blunt buzzes, as though it's a signal she should recognize.

"Angelina!" she calls out. She waits but there's no sound of sandals slapping against the floor tiles, heading to the front door.

The buzzing is long and sustained this time. "Christ," she says. "Angelina!" When she was very young she would stand in the middle of a room and scream Angelina's name over and over again, not stopping until Angelina came running, apron flying out behind her, but that's not the kind of silly, immature thing she would do now.

She takes another long swig of lemonade to hide her cigarette breath, just in case it's one of her mother's friends. It would be just like her mother to send someone to check up on her. As she walks down the hallway it's hard to decide what feels worse, the damp cloth of the T-shirt sticking to her armpits or the sweaty bare skin of her collarbones. At the front door she runs her fingers through her hair, tucking it carefully behind her ears. Sometimes when she's standing in the sunlight, if she tilts her head just right she can almost pass for blond.

The first door is made of heavy dark wood, covered in stickers Angelina gave her years ago, with a yellow bolt that slides open easily. She stands behind the second door, the one made of white crisscrossing bars, forming diamond-shaped gaps that reveal the front yard and crackly bushes, the dried-out banana trees and hedge surrounding the property. Behind the hedge is the gravel road winding down to the main highway, past the neighbors' houses with bulletproof windows and security guard towers, and beyond that are the palm trees and fields of sugarcane, the eucalyptus forests and the mountains.

Standing a few steps away, in the front yard, is a man. He's grinning in a way that makes him look slightly embarrassed, rocking on his heels, arms behind his back. There's a lumpy purplish-red scar running down his face, from the bottom of his eye to the top of his lip.

"Well, here I am," he says. "Let's go."

He's wearing a shapeless brown poncho, which hangs off him as if empty. His feet are bare and caked in red clay, his legs thin and hairless.

"Sorry I'm late," he says. He brings an arm forward, a dirty plastic bag hanging from his wrist. "It took me a lot longer to get here than I thought. I came as fast as I could."

She stares at the plastic bag, which sways, hitting the front of his thigh. "Lord, am I thirsty," he says. "Does that ever happen to you, when you have to walk a long way?" He licks his lips. "Never mind, don't worry about answering now. We'll have time to talk later."

"Can I help you?" she says, taking a step back.

The man's face suddenly becomes a mass of deeply ingrained lines. "She didn't tell you I was coming?" His voice comes out high-pitched and sad in a way that sounds deeply familiar to her, like something she's been listening to her whole life, though she cannot say why or how.

"Daddy!" she calls out over her shoulder, her voice echoing down the hallway. "There's somebody here to see you!"

"Princess," he says, the lines in his face growing even deeper. "Come on. Don't do that. You know that I know they're not here."

She stares at the scar on his face. It's shaped like a fat river leech and shiny, as if covered in glue. Looking at it makes her suck in her breath. She takes another step back, tucking her body behind the door so that only her head is poking out. Without taking his eyes off her, he kneels and starts ripping grass out of the ground. It's a habit she recognizes in herself, sitting on the edge of the football field at school, tilting her head back so that her hair falls down her back like a waterfall. The material of his poncho is rough and scratchy-looking.

"I just don't understand why she didn't tell you about me," he says. "It doesn't make any sense." His voice gets more high-pitched the longer he talks.

"Look, I don't even know you," she says. It creates a sudden fluttering in her chest to use a loud voice like that, to be rude without caring. It reminds her of the time she saw her father slap the hands of the street children reaching for her leftover ice cream on the park picnic table.

"Don't know me?" He rubs a hole into the ground, sticks his index finger into it, and wiggles it around before covering it up again. "Don't know me," he repeats. "How about that." His mouth turns downward, an exaggerated sad smile like a clown's. "Well. At least it's a beautiful day for us to run."

His head snaps up and he looks directly at her, narrowing his eyes in a way that makes her stomach leap and hit the back of her throat.

"Are you ready," he says, "to run?"

"Sorry," she says. "I'm sorry I can't help you." Her mouth tastes the same as when she's carsick. She's closed the door to the point that she's looking at him through the thinnest crack possible, her torso leaning forward in an L shape.

"Hey," he says, rising quickly to his feet, blades of grass drifting down from his robe. "*Mija*. Seriously. How lost are you? I'm here to help *you*—"

"I'm sorry," she says again, right before closing the door completely, not finishing her sentence: *I don't have the key*. She's staring at the Bert and Ernie sticker now, plastered there by Angelina years ago, their smiles bright and beaming as they drive their fire truck. The jumpy feeling in her stomach is still there.

Angelina's room is at the back of the house, next to the washing machine and the stacks of cardboard boxes filled with champagne. She forces herself to walk there as calmly and slowly as possible, the doorbell blasting and buzzing. The pale green door is covered with a giant sticker of Baby Jesus, dimpled elbows raised, smiling heavenward. On the floor, lined neatly against the wall, is a pair of black plastic sandals. She places her hand on the center of Baby Jesus's face but doesn't knock. "Angelina?" she says, softly at first, then louder. "Are you there?"

She checks the rest of the rooms in the house, just to be sure. She checks her parents' bedroom, her brother's, her own. She makes sure the back doors are locked and tugs experimentally at the bars over the windows.

With Angelina gone, she has no choice but to prepare lunch herself. She props the fridge door open with her torso, scooping the rice and lentils out of the Tupperware containers with her hands curved like claws. The doorbell is still going, one long, sustained note. By now the annoyance is bubbling inside her like the suds fizzing at the top of a shaken Coca-Cola bottle. She's already rehearsing the words in her head, picturing herself standing furiously in front of Angelina, arms akimbo, head tilted just like her mother's that time she addressed the electricity repairman, the one she suspected of stealing from them. *How could you do that,* she'll say. *Unacceptable. You know that I've never been left home alone before—completely un-fucking-acceptable. Good luck finding another job; I hope your bags are packed and ready. Are they ready?*

It's only that evening—when Angelina still isn't back, when she cannot get through to her parents, when their cellphones ring and ring—that she starts to get the feeling that something is happening.

The first thing she does is phone Katrina. She'll know what to do—she'll send her chauffeur along with the bodyguard; they'll come and take her away. But the telephone is silent when she presses it against her ear, the plastic heavy in her hands. She flicks the light switch a dozen times, pushes her thumb down on the TV power button as hard as possible, but the screen stays black and silent. She turns on Angelina's radio, the ridged wheel imprinting her fingertip as she rapidly surfs through the hisses and crackles. She finally finds a program that seems to consist (as far as she can understand) of a fuzzy voice ranting endlessly about the need to drive out all the rebels, smoke them out of the mountains, exterminate them all, punctuated by short blasts of the national anthem. It creates a tight feeling in her chest. She switches the radio off, pries out the batteries with a kitchen knife, and puts them away in the drawer with the silver bell Angelina uses to ring to announce dinner. She spends the rest of the day in her bedroom, curtains shut tight, watching Disney movies on her laptop. The battery dies seconds before the Beast's magical transformation into a handsome prince, and after that she just lies there without moving, knees tucked near her chin, ears tensed for the sound of car wheels on the road, keys rattling, the doorknob turning.

The next day is Monday, the holiday—Katrina's chauffeur never arrives. By midafternoon she heads outside to check the generator, more in hope than expectation. It's located in the garage, behind a barred door that prevents stray dogs and street people from sneaking in and sleeping there. She wraps her fingers around the bars, studying the thick braids of red and green wires, the forest of rust-encrusted switches. The gardener is the only person who knows how it works, when the power goes out due to bomb attacks in the city center. He'd head to the back of the house, wiping his hands off on his denim shorts, and two minutes later, as if by magic, the lights would fly on again. (What is his name again? Wilson? Wilmer?) Her brother would whoop, bolting to the computer room, her parents smiling in relief as the soothing tones of BBC broadcasters returned, and she would blow out the candles and pick the wax off her algebra homework with her nails. Now, as she stands there by herself, she takes a last long, slow look at the impenetrable cluster of wires and switches before trudging back to the house.

The computers in the office seem like medieval relics. The screens stare at her, blank and impassive as children asking for coins at traffic lights. In the end, she closes the office door, shutting it tight with her hip. It's not like there's anything in there that's useful anyway; most of the room is used to store cardboard boxes full of junk: her parents' skis from Yale; faded blue-and-pink tapestries covered in dead-moth wings; the wooden toucans and leopards she played with as a child, their eyes colored in with washable markers; Christmas presents from Angelina that she opened politely before stuffing them away—brightly patterned shirts and alpaca shawls she'd never dream of wearing, not even alone in her bedroom.

If necessary, they'll come for her. She's certain of it. Some kind of international peacekeeping army. Professional rescuers, speaking Norwegian, light green berets and cars with blue diplomatic license plates. Pale smiling faces pressing against the white bars of the door, extending their arms as she runs to the kitchen to get the keys out of the wicker basket on top of the fridge. They'll take her away in a shiny black car with squeaky plastic seats. Embassy members, the international community.

She won't just be left here. She won't be forgotten.

Mostly she wanders through the house, drifting from one room to another. The days blend lifelessly together, thick fuzz growing over each one like the dust accumulating on the unspun fan blades. She spends hours reading her fantasy novels, lying stomach-down on the bed. She reads childhood favorites, like a novelization of *Star Wars, Episode IV: A New Hope* with half the pages missing, ending shortly after the scene where Luke bursts into Leia's cell: *My name is Luke Skywalker, and I'm here to rescue you.* She stares at the page for hours, the words blurring until they could be saying *cheese sandwich, cheese sandwich* over and over again.

She never puts anything away. She starts eating the canned food her parents reserved for parties, strange things like silvery fish floating in red sauce and olives in slimy black liquid, and leaves jars of sticky jam and cans of condensed milk licked clean and shiny on the kitchen counters. She rummages through old school papers from eighth grade, Ms. Márquez's world history syllabus and Mr. B's English reading list (she never got around to reading *A Connecticut Yankee in King Arthur's Court*, barely made it through the first few chapters of *The Scarlet Letter*). She finds ancient notes Angelina wrote to excuse her from P.E. swimming class, every misspelled word painfully scrawled out in shaky capital letters. She rips open pink and purple envelopes she never gave to her father to mail to America, pen pal letters covered in Lisa Frank stickers for friends who moved away, people who left years and years ago (during third grade? fifth?), names that haven't crossed her mind in years: *Hi, Flaca! Hi, Betsy! How's New York? How's Washington, D.C.? Miss you lots and lots, forever and ever.* She lets them fall to the floor slowly. *Time to get ready,* a voice whispers in her head: a vague memory of someone speaking to her, somebody walking away on a playground (who? when?). The moment is just there, barely fluttering on the edges of her mind, and it's easy as anything to chase it away, like when she swats at mosquitoes buzzing at her face.

While walking through her parents' bedroom she keeps her eyes strictly averted from her mother's clothes in the open chest drawers, the stacks of books on her father's bedside table (it's best not to worry about where they are, what happened: Don't wonder, don't go there, just don't). She heads straight to the bathroom instead, opening her mother's makeup drawer, spilling peach-colored powder all over the sink, smearing herself with eye shadow, ignoring Angelina's high-pitched cries in her head: *Mija, what a mess! What do you think you're doing?* In her brother's bedroom she lingers by the *Transformers* poster on the door but avoids the framed photograph on the wall of the entire family: her parents, her brother, herself, and Angelina (don't think about it, don't, don't, don't). She pulls dusty games out of the hallway closet, Monopoly and Clue and Candy Land. She finds a puzzle from third-grade geography with Ms. Simón, each piece a different department, the capitals represented with tiny red stars. She picks out the familiar names first: Valle del Cauca, Cauca, Antioquia. And then the more exotic ones: Guaviare, Putumayo, Meta.

Once the pieces are sorted, though, she never tries to fit them together. Instead she leaves them scattered on the floor— she has to take an enormous step over them every time she heads down the hallway, like a giant who can cross an entire country with a single stride.

Every once in a while a frothy panic will start to rise in her stomach, making her hands shake, and when that happens, she can't control herself; she dashes to her room and peeks out through the window, holding the curtain close to her face like a veil. He's always there, still in the scratchy poncho, sitting on the grass by the bristly hedge. Leaning against the banana tree. Pacing, mouth moving as if talking to himself, arms swinging exaggeratedly as if mocking army marches. Standing still before the tiny crosses on the far left side of the front yard, where she and her brother and Angelina buried generations of dead pets, cats and dogs, ducks and chickens, killed by possums and tropical diseases. If she squints her eyes, he multiplies into blurry doubles, triples, quadruples. There are dozens of him, an army. Pressing their scarred faces against the door, wrapping their sticky brown fingers around the bars, calling out again and again in a voice muffled by the glass against her ear. *Hey. Beautiful. Let me in.*

One night she feels both brave and desperate enough to go outside by the pool. It's so quiet she can hear the water move, gently lapping against the concrete walls. She hugs the grapefruit tree and strains her eyes as she looks toward the mountains, almost convincing herself that she can see the fires, as small as the orange dots burning at the end of her cigarettes. She wills herself to smell smoke and gunpowder, hear the explosions and gunshots of incoming American forces, foreign backup support. Closing her eyes and pressing her face against the scratchy tree trunk, she can almost hear the helicopters, the clang of the metal doors as they slide open, the thud of the knotted rope ladder as it hits the ground by her feet. *Stephanie Lansky, we're here to rescue you!* But when she opens her eyes there's only the scratchy gray fungus draped over the tree like a fisherman's net.

Later she stands outside Angelina's room, hand resting on Baby Jesus's face. She looks down at the sandals, waits for the picture to form in her mind. Angelina dressed in her white apron (what else could she be wearing?), carefully unlocking the front door, heading outside. Dawn is breaking, the earliest morning birds are singing. Or maybe it's still dark, the sky speckled with stars. Angelina's humming, hands in her pockets; Angelina's frowning, face wrinkled in her classic sour scowl. No matter what she imagines, the picture always abruptly ends the moment Angelina rounds the hedge corner, apron swirling through the air. Walking busily, purposefully, on her way to—what? Toward whom?

Sometimes she thinks she hears the slapping sound of black plastic sandals hitting floor tiles and turns her head sharply. But there's never anything there.

One morning she awakens abruptly to the sound of someone banging on the door, the same insistent sound ringing out again and again. It takes her a second to realize that she's lying down instead of standing, fantasy book resting heavily on her chest. She struggles out of bed, dragging the bedsheets along the floor, dressed in her mother's fancy silk nightgown and saggy pink underpants (she ran out of clean pairs of her own panties long ago). Pale dust motes float through the air, following her down the hallway as she stumbles forward, still dazedly clutching the book to her torso like a shield.

Once again she just barely opens the door, so that only her face can be seen. He's holding a walking stick, beating the bars like a monk ringing church bells in one of her Arthurian novels.

"Oh," he says, his face framed in the diamond-shaped gap, "you came!" His eyes widen in what is unmistakably delight. The whites of his eyeballs are lined with yellow; the scar on his face looks redder and puffier than ever. There's a low-pitched rumbling in the distance she hasn't noticed until now, the sound of a low-flying plane or helicopter. He's dressed in the same poncho, but the plastic bag is gone, his feet are no longer bare; instead he's wearing a pair of shiny black rubber

boots with yellow bottoms. The sight of those boots make
goosebumps break out on her neck; sour liquid leaks from her
tonsils.

"Be a good girl," he says. "Open the door."

"It's locked," she says. She's turning away when he presses
his face against the bars and reaches out, fingers fluttering urgently toward her.

"*Mija*," he says. "Time to go."

"Could you please not touch me?" She uses the book to
roughly push his hands away. The buzzing of the aircraft returns for a bit, circling overhead, is replaced by a single engine. He says something else, speaking in a low voice, but his
words are muffled beneath the sound of shots rattling out. She
flinches.

"Don't worry about it, *mija*," he says. "It's nothing."

This time she looks directly at him. But he's already
abruptly turned away, the hem of his poncho swirling through
the air like a cape.

The tiles feel cool and steady under her feet as she backs
away. The book clatters loudly against the floor as it falls. She
watches herself head toward the back of the house to the
washing machine and boxes of champagne, bedsheets trailing
behind her. She's standing in front of the Baby Jesus sticker,
spreading her fingers on his face before turning the doorknob.
The door opens easily. It only takes a few seconds to take
everything in: the bed with thin pillows, the window with
faded curtains, everywhere the strong smell of soap. She opens
the closet, but there are only rows of white dresses hanging
headless and limbless, a pile of neatly folded aprons, a single
black cardigan, no shoes to be seen. There are thick gobs of

candle wax on the windowsill by the altar. On the floor by the bed, propped up against the wall, is a framed photograph of the two of them, her and Angelina. It's an old photo: She must be around six or seven years old. They're standing behind a birthday cake on a table, her arms around Angelina's waist; her hair is hanging in her eyes and she's smiling sweetly. Angelina is looking straight into the camera, mouth flat, expressionless. What Angelina is thinking or feeling at that moment, she couldn't even begin to say.

She sits down on the bed, letting the sheets she's dragged from her room drift to the floor. The sharp smell of mothballs makes her sinuses itch.

She thinks, *I have got to figure this out.*

She thinks, *If only I had more time.*

She doesn't know it yet, but there's something waiting for her. It could be a future or it could be something else. It could be the plastic gearshift of a car pressing stickily against her knee, a man's wet fingers on her legs trembling as he helps her pull her saggy underpants back up from her ankles, mumbling over and over again, *I'm sorry, so sorry, I didn't mean to hurt you.* Or maybe she's in an enormous orange tent next to the raging, overflowing river on the border, one orange tent among many, where she wakes up at the same time every morning to stare at the silhouette of a lizard crawling across the fabric and think about how she needs to head to the Red Cross tent to get into the line early. Maybe she's running through a field, grass stinging her legs and an aluminum taste in her mouth, the thudding footsteps and clink of machetes against belt buckles behind her getting louder.

Or maybe it'll be something else. It could still happen. She could be lucky. She could be sitting in a wood-paneled class-room in Europe or Australia, her pen moving slowly across a notebook, her eyes never leaving the professor as he speaks at the opposite end of the table.

It's still possible. But for now all she has is her slow rise from the bed. She has this walk toward the refrigerator, the reach for the wicker basket hidden on top, the round ball of the key chain in her hand and the rattling metal. As she watches the many keys dangle from her fingers, she thinks about how there's not a single one that she recognizes, not one she can pick out and say with confidence, this key opens that door, that key opens this one. This home was never really hers, and nothing in it was ever really hers, and the tightly clenched muscle squeezing out blood in her chest has never really been hers either. For now there's only the cool metal in her hand that rattles loudly as she lifts it toward the dirty silver lock.

"Oh!" he says. The door makes a loud scraping sound against the ground as it swings open. "You clever girl." He lets out a deep sigh that could also be a groan of pain. Behind him the hedge rustles and she turns her head sharply. It could be the flash of a white apron or the metallic shine of a machete. It feels like noticing the shadow of her own half-closed eyelid, something that has always been there and should have been seen at least a thousand times before.

Lemon Pie

2008

GUAVIARE

Something is going to happen today. He just knows it. Call it a hunch, a gut sense he got from how roughly Pollo rapped the metal spoon against his plate this morning, trying to get the gray lump of oatmeal to fall off. Or maybe it was the way Julisa's shoulders hunched up as he marched brusquely past her toward the latrines with the shit-encrusted shovel, or the random, loud giggle César let out before abruptly falling silent as he sat on the overturned bucket, blackening his rifle with a tube of printer's ink.

But he can't think about it. Not right now, not with class about to begin, students lined up neatly before him on the forest floor. Sitting calmly, expectantly, the same way they do every morning: dark tapestries of ants marching steadily over them, salamanders scampering through the surrounding fern leaves and scattering tiny drops of water. Waiting patiently in place, the same way they've waited every morning for the past five years, eight months, two weeks, and five days (today counts, even though it's still unfolding, even though it technically hasn't happened yet; today always counts). They are waiting for him to begin, same time (nine A.M. on the dot, an hour and a half after breakfast), same place (sandy beach on the riverside, within sight of the armed guard on duty—today it's César, currently struggling with the solar panels to recharge his clunky cellular phone). Five days a week. Here they are.

"And good morning to you too," he says to the vine-covered ceiba tree, raising his voice to be heard over the screeching chorus of crickets and birds. "Late again?" he says to the flattened-out leaves on the ground, green and brown and yellow, chosen deliberately for maximum diversity in terms of their size, shape, and texture. "How embarrassing. Ah," he says to the row of sticks and branches, covered in scratchy gray lichens and powdery green moss. "Wonderful to see you; I'm so glad you're feeling better. That flu has really been making the rounds, hasn't it? Everybody, make sure you grab some hand sanitizer before we break for lunch, okay?"

Everybody nods. Attentive, focused, the same way they always are. Hanging on to his every word.

He begins the same way he does every morning: peace fingers pressed against his lower lip, chest out, back straight, standing steady as a general. The students wait with bated breath. The fern rustles slightly in the wind; a row of smooth river stones keeps the leaves pressed against the ground.

"Hamlet," he says. "Here we go."

Their homework was to read Act I, up to the part where Horatio informs Hamlet of his father's nightly patrols. *"My father—"* he says, trudging back and forth on the sand, rubber boots leaving deep imprints. *"Methinks I see my father."* He wiggles his naked toes, the front of the rubber boot cut away so his U.S.-size-ten foot can fit. "What's interesting about Hamlet saying this?"

One of the stones volunteers that it's ironic that Hamlet says this (*in my mind's eye, Horatio*) without realizing that Horatio really *has* seen his father. "Good, good." The yellow leaf thinks that *Do not mock me, fellow student; I think it was to see my mother's wedding* was pretty funny. "Yes—what an image! The funeral meats on the table barely grown cold! That Hamlet, such a snarky little dude!" The twigs giggle at his use of the word *dude,* but he lets them get away with it, even offers them the flicker of a grin. They all enjoy it, he knows they do: his undeniable gringo-ness, his casual teaching lingo, his speck of Southern California lighting up this corner of the Amazon jungle like a tiny golden flashlight in an ocean of green.

"A big theme we're going to see in the next couple of weeks," he says, scratching the bites on his arm, "is the theme of Hamlet's madness. His *antic disposition,* as he calls it." He twists his head so that he can cast a quick glance at the child-size notebook on the ground behind him, double-checking his notes. "That's what makes the fact that Horatio sees the ghost particularly interesting. Can you genuinely be crazy if someone's having the same hallucination as you?"

This is by far the biggest pleasure of teaching *Hamlet—*

how easy it is to remember direct quotes. At night, locked up in the shed, he tries to remember as many as he can, writing them down in his notebook in whatever order they come to him, so that Hamlet's mournful oration for Ophelia (*the cat will mew and dog will have his day*) is written alongside the pipe speech (*you cannot play upon me*), which is scrawled beneath the near entirety of *to be or not to be* (he has it almost perfectly memorized; it's only after *what dreams may come* that it gets a little fuzzy). So many memorable lines! The joy of using words straight from the source material! He learned his lesson from *The Scarlet Letter* (his first class a year and a half ago, when he was just starting out and didn't know any better)—he gave up after the opening chapter, which was all he could remember ("Hester Prynne represents purity—that's basically all you need to know"). *As I Lay Dying* wasn't too bad, not with those occasional gorgeous gems: *My mother is a fish* and *my father used to say that the reason for living was to get ready to stay dead a long time*. *Mrs. Dalloway,* that definitely had its moments too—*life; London; this moment of June*. But *Hamlet*! This is what he's been waiting for all fall semester, writing out as many quotes as he can remember by candlelight at night, in the teensiest tiniest handwriting possible, as César's flashlight shines through the cracked shed door during bi-hourly checks. This is what they've been building up to. This moment.

"So," he says to the fern the size of an armchair. *"A little more than kin, and less than kind."* He's backtracking a bit, quoting an earlier scene, but they don't mind, they can roll with it; they always do. Behind him he hears Julisa's voice, shouting something. When he turns to look, though, it's César who's staring straight at him, locking him in a brief second of direct eye contact. Then César jitters the safety of his gun a couple of times, and as he turns back to the class he can still hear the faint click-click-clicking drifting through the air toward him, like an audible dust mote.

The tree is making a remark about *I am too much i' the sun.* "Sun—son! Excellent. Keep paying attention to that kind of wordplay." Somewhere in the branches above a bird screams the high-pitched shrill of a gym class whistle.

In an hour and a half they'll break for lunch, and they'll all say goodbye in a chorus of voices (*See you tomorrow, Mr. B! Hasta luego!*). He'll walk away with a huge smile on his face and a light tickling sensation in his chest—the faintest feeling of warmth.

After lunch (rice and lentils, with the unexpected surprise of a fish head on the side), there are a variety of different options he can choose from. There's Spiderweb Inspection or Boot Cleaning. Toucan Watching or Facial and Vocal Exercises (these are especially important during the weeks of randomly enforced silence, when his cheek muscles start to droop and his voice transforms into an old man's creak from lack of use). Aerobics and Strength Training he saves for midafternoon, to prevent stomach cramps (his current fitness goal is to hold the plank pose long enough for two verses and a chorus of "Eleanor Rigby," sung silently in his head). Sometimes there's even Magazine Reading, depending on whether he can bear to pick up the 2005 copy of *Semana* he's had since day one, week zero, month zero ("Here you go, *profe,*" Pollo said, dumping it in his lap) or the rotting 1990s computer manual stained with rat droppings.

For the time being, he settles for watching a session of Parasite Squishing, since César has already gone ahead and gotten started on Pollo. César takes a perverse personal pride in being the best Parasite Squisher in the camp, and even now it's hard not to admire his commitment as he hunches intensely over the red-rimmed holes in Pollo's arm. He watches from a respectful distance as César pinches Pollo's skin as hard as he can, eyes tearing up with the effort, forehead sweating, gasping for air. Pollo just sits motionless, eyes closed. After enough squeezing and massaging, a stream of watery liquid bursts from the hole in Pollo's arm, followed by a hardened black marble that emerges with a thick slurp that is both delicious and horrifying.

"You should do that for a living," he says as César wipes the hole in Pollo's arm with a ragged scrap of cloth. Pollo's eyes are still closed, lips curled inward.

"We're not done yet," César says, eyes wide and bright. "We have to get the mother."

A minute later she follows, enormous and sluglike, in an eruption of blood and pus.

Pollo heads immediately to the hammock—it's always a good idea to lie down for a bit after an intense session of Parasite Squishing. César's eyes are still bright, flicking slyly around the camp. "You next, *profe*?" he says with a grin.

He turns away as César laughs, the high-pitched giggle following him through the camp like an irritating fly.

It feels like a good time to transition into Thinking and Picturing—it always works to kill an hour or two, provided

he's strict with himself about not opening his eyes and checking his watch. Usually he does it sitting cross-legged on the
ground, but today he sits on a bench at the rickety wooden
table. Behind him he can hear César tearing open a packet of
Frutiño juice powder with his teeth, his tongue lapping greedily against the aluminum surface. Raspberry flavor, most
likely.

Yesterday he was working on his apartment bedroom, so
today he backtracks and focuses on the entrance. He starts
with the door, scanning it up and down, his mind's eye a camera, a superbly efficient piece of bomb-detecting antiterrorist
technology. The rickety silver doorknob. The faint scratches
on the reddish wood. The gold-bordered peephole he never
used. He takes his time, moving slowly, reconstructing the details as fully as possible (it's amazing how well you can recon-
struct something you haven't seen in five years, eight months,
two weeks, and five days if you really try). The multicolored
rug he bought in Taganga, constantly speckled with dirt and
dead leaves. The cream-colored tiles, delicious to walk on in
bare feet during the summer, holding a glass of ice-clinking
passion fruit juice. The faint yellow walls, tiny cracks in the
paint branching out like miniature trees, surrounded by black
mold confetti. There are his posters: *Return of the Jedi* and
Blade Runner, wrinkled by the long-ago journey in his suitcase from California, and a vintage black-and-white poster in
Spanish of *The Martian Chronicles* purchased at the local
Unicentro mall. And there on the table: a hardback copy of *A
Connecticut Yankee in King Arthur's Court.* His next assigned
reading for eighth-grade English.

Was that really it? There wasn't anything else? Stained coffee mugs? Scribbled syllabus notes for class, attendance lists, flyers for parent-teacher conferences? Empty plastic water bottles with the sides caved in, crumpled Éxito receipts, torn tickets from salsa concerts?

He takes a deep breath but it's happening. The camera is getting frantic, darting rapidly around the apartment from item to item, scene to scene, his vision jittering. He shuts his eyes, tries to slow down, returns to examining everything one piece at a time. But it's too late. Everything is blurred, and before he can help himself he's there.

In bed. Blinking fuzzy eyes open, stomach sour from last night's aguardiente drinking session and Marlboro chain-smoking with Ms. Márquez (eighth-grade world history, his most reliable hook-up ever since Ms. Simón from third grade moved away in '99, a weepily dramatic scene he doesn't care to dwell on, not now, not ever). He's in the shower, standing under a low-pressure trickle of blessedly hot water. (Whenever he washes himself now, peeling off his clothes for a session of River Bathing, it's impossible to tell if the yellow color of his skin is jaundice or dirt.) He moves through the apartment faster and faster, reliving the first moments of the last morning, a manic sped-up cartoon. The way he skipped breakfast, didn't even have coffee because he knew he could buy it from the lady with the thermos at that one traffic light, chug it like a tequila shot in its disposable plastic cup. The way he opened the cupboard door, lingered briefly over the bananas and tangerines, opened the fridge next and took a quick swig of orange juice. Didn't even glance at the Styrofoam box of leftover lemon pie from the French bakery, the glass bottles of *ají* sauce and Poker beer. (*Ají* sauce! Imagine what he could do with *ají* sauce now! His mouth waters and he swallows hard, shifting his position on the bench, doing his best to ignore the sounds of César behind him sucking his teeth.)

What does the apartment look like now? Bananas rotted, tangerines shriveled into nothingness? *A Connecticut Yankee* covered in mold, pages curling? Would they have sent somebody by to pack everything up, put it all away in boxes and into storage? Somebody from the school or police or the international embassy? Who would have done it? Who would have cared?

He keeps going. He's using up about three weeks' worth of Thinking and Picturing at this rate, but his cartoon character legs keep carrying him out the door, down the apartment steps, a whirring Road Runner blur. Smiling. Greeting Freddy the doorman, *Qué más? Nada mal, un poco de guayabo, jaja!* Gray early morning light, redbrick apartment buildings. Into the car, the Volvo he bought from Mr. Rover, the eighth-grade English teacher he replaced in the fall of '93, the year he arrived.

You're going to love Colombia, Mr. Rover said as they walked across the parking lot. *It's a very . . . special place.*

Special how?

Oh, you know. Mr. Rover paused by the Volvo, their untucked shirts flapping in the breeze (one of the benefits of working at the American international private school, as opposed to the British or German or French one, was the casual dress code—it even got mentioned in the recruiting brochure).

Special like a girlfriend you know you shouldn't be with. At a certain point you get a bit crazy from the constant paranoia— always on the lookout. Always worried you're going to "dar papaya."

Dar papaya? The car keys jingled as Mr. Rover dropped them into his hand.

You haven't heard that expression? He must have frowned or made a face at this, because Mr. Rover immediately said, *It means, don't put yourself in a position where others can take advantage of you. Easier said than done down here.* And then Mr. Rover laughed in a way that was maybe happy or maybe sad or maybe even a little bit angry.

Enough of that, then: back to the original memory (it's important not to get too sidetracked during Thinking and Picturing, not to go spinning off into the stratosphere of endless, dangerously random thoughts). Now he's turning the ignition key, on his way to work. Down the street. Walls with jagged teeth of broken bottles on top, automatic gates. He likes living on the edge of Cali, away from the hustle and bustle of the center, the legless bums and toothless women selling chewing gum, the children juggling and tumbling at traffic lights. It's a true pleasure, driving past the fields of cows and horses, men on white bicycles holding on to the backs of buses, the two-lane highways that are constantly turned into three when a car tries to overtake a milk truck.

At the intersection he has to decide which of the two main routes to take to school: the first, his usual route, a nerve-racking drive through the heavy suburban traffic; the second route longer but often quicker, a more isolated road through rural countryside. Despite the indifferent green numbers on his dashboard flicking closer to nine A.M., he chooses the second, turning right off the Pan-American Highway, hitting the gas pedal.

He doesn't think about it, doesn't let phrases like *if only* and *I should have* and *of all days* creep into the scene. Instead he likes to linger on this moment, on Rod Stewart singing "Maggie May" on the CD player, that epic acoustic guitar solo. On his tongue, fuzzy and sour in his mouth, the anticipation of aspirin in his desk drawer. The split feeling in his stomach, one half shivery from the knowledge that he'll arrive for first period ten minutes late, the other half hazily calm with the knowledge that today will be easy, a breeze, he's taught *Connecticut Yankee* so many times he could do it in his sleep, let alone hungover. The green numbers on the dashboard say 8:37.

It's hard to know at what point it became What Happened.

Maybe it was when he saw the soldiers standing on the side of the road, their tiger-striped fatigues and M16s slowly coming into view as he approached.

Or maybe it was when he obeyed their waving arms and pulled over, saw their knotted bandannas, noticed the way one soldier's hair fell to his shoulders in black greasy locks.

Or when the soldier leaned in close to the window, motioning with his rifle for him to pull up behind their truck, and he saw the word EJÉRCITO stenciled in clumsy black letters (worse than a child's handwriting) above the soldier's shirt pocket.

The black rubber boots. The Fidel Castro hats. The way they passed his school ID card among themselves, chattering

so rapidly that he only caught one word: *gringo*. His slow re-
alization that no, actually, these were not soldiers from the
Colombian army.

And now he's opening his eyes, blinking in the dim sunlight, the greenness of the moss and leaves and ferns closing in
around him with the density of a fog, and because he's fucked
it up this much, he might as well fuck it up even more. He lets
his eyes drift down to the black plastic watch on his wrist.

Not even ten minutes.

Dinner is rice, lentils, and soggy fried potatoes. Julisa doesn't
bring him any chocolate or coffee to drink, and when he asks
her if he can have some, she just says, "No."

"Did we run out?"

"No."

"Then why . . ."

He loses energy midsentence, lets his voice die an abrupt
death as if by sniper fire. Somewhere in the air is the faint
scent of fried fish, and if only Julisa were to take a step forward, stand closer to the flickering candle, he bets he would
see it: smears of grease around her mouth, thin slivers of bone
stuck between her front teeth, the dark stain of coffee dregs
on her tongue.

"Because I said so, *profe,*" Julisa says, reaching for his
plate. Her glittery hair band sparkles in the candlelight as she
walks away.

He turns toward Pollo. "Any news today?" he asks.

"No." Pollo is eating while standing, holding the plate

close to his lips, rapidly shoveling in the food. "Tomorrow, *profe.*"

"Yesterday you said today."

"Tomorrow. We'll have news tomorrow."

"Why the change?"

"Who knows?" Pollo's jaw makes a twisted motion, as though swallowing an enormous piece of gum. A random memory swims across his eyes, a slow-motion cinematic flashback sequence: that one girl slyly looking at him, sticking a huge wad of bright pink gum under her desk. First row, third desk. Head tilted back, hair streaming down her back like a waterfall, brown turning to blond if the sunlight hit it the right way. What was her name again? Something Lansky? What happened to her; where did she go?

"Do you think orders will come soon?" he says, speaking loud enough to chase the image away. "From *el comandante?*"

"Who knows?" Pollo slurps up the last of his lentils. "It'll be better in summer next year anyway. The roads and trails will be clear. It'll be easier to release you then."

Summer 2009. In two days, it'll be Halloween 2008. Halloween will be five years, eight months, three weeks exactly.

Julisa reappears, carrying the padlock. Her acne looks puffier than ever, angry and swollen beneath her skin.

"What?" he says. "So early?"

"Orders."

"What orders?"

"Just orders."

"From who? You?"

"I already said," she says, voice still flat. "They're orders."

He scratches the bites on his wrist. "Well, I have to go to the latrine first."

"No."

"Why? *Because I said so?*" He mimics her voice, as high-pitched and mean-sounding as he can make it, as nasty as a group of girls gossiping in a bathroom stall. Julisa doesn't say anything, just keeps standing there holding the padlock. Clenching his fists is a good way to stop his hands from trembling.

Inside the hut, as he listens to the clinking sounds of Julisa outside looping the steel chain around the door handle, it hits him like a sharp intake of breath. It's finally happened.

Today—five years, eight months, two weeks, and five days—is officially over.

Tomorrow, just like yesterday—and the day before that—and the day before that—won't begin yet for hours. And hours. And hours.

"'*Seems,*' madam?" he says. "*Nay, it is. I know not 'seems.'*" The students listen respectfully, while in the distance César lets out a loud phlegmy cough. Getting locked up early last night meant he had even more time to scrawl down quotes in his notebook. Discussion today was originally supposed to focus on the ghost ("Real or imaginary? From heaven or hell? Go!"), but it's fine, they'll get to it soon enough. They've got time.

"*These indeed seem,*" he says. He rubs his sienna-colored beard. "*For they are actions that a man might play. But I have that within which passeth show, these but the trappings and the suits of woe.*"

The students applaud, and he gives a modest half bow.

"So," he says. "What do we think about Hamlet's relationship with Claudius?"

The yellow leaf tentatively says it's interesting how it's Gertrude that Hamlet listens to, not Claudius, when he finally concedes to staying in Denmark instead of going away to college. (Where was Hamlet going, again? He quickly twists his head around, consulting the notebook on the grass behind him: Wittenberg.) "Good point," he says. "Notice Hamlet's concern with appearances versus reality. This says a lot about his relationship with Claudius. *That one may smile, and smile, and be a villain.*" He scratches his hand, feels something wet. One of the bites is leaking clear liquid from the center—it's gotten bigger, now the size of a fifty-peso coin. Was that the same size as a nickel? How big were nickels, again? He lets his hand drop, flopping toward his leg.

"*O that this too too solid flesh would melt, thaw and resolve itself into a dew!*" he says to the wide-eyed fern, who's been trying to hold back laughter all morning and will likely giggle later with the twigs during lunch break. He keeps going, voice steady: "*How weary, stale, flat, and unprofitable seem to me all the uses of this world! Fie on't, ah fie! 'Tis an unweeded garden that grows to seed.*" He makes a mental note to rearrange the desks: The fern and twigs are getting too cliquey anyway, sitting next to one another all the time like that. It'll be good to shake things up a bit, make them interact with different social groups. Keep them on their toes.

"Pay attention," he says sharply to the river stones, who are getting distracted by a shiny black beetle crawling across the sand, "to the motifs of rank and grossness. This kind of language will keep popping up again and again. Things rotting, not being right. *Something is rotten in the state of Denmark.* Some of you might even want to consider it as a potential essay topic. Yes, there will be essays," he says, voice rising over the chorus of moans from the leaves, who are inevitably the most inclined to complain. "We'll get to those next class. Any other questions?"

He stands there. Waiting. But nobody has anything to say this time. Even the branches overhead are silent, barely rustling in the faintest of breezes.

At times like this, it's hard not to let the camera zoom out, see what it really looks like. A row of sticks and stones on the ground. Twigs, leaves, painstakingly arranged to look neat and ordered. An emaciated man, white spots on his nails, brittle teeth, sunken cheekbones like thumbprints in clay. Pacing by the river, waving his arms around, ranting and rambling to thin air.

A person might think that there was something wrong, seeing somebody behave like that. A person might even be worried.

"All right, then," he says loudly, and this time it's hard to keep his voice from trembling. "Have a great lunch."

Lunch is rice and lentils with a surprise: a long, stringy piece of fried tripe. As he raises the fork toward his mouth, Pollo says, "We'll be leaving soon."

He looks down at the backs of his hands. The insect bites are in patterns like Pangaea, slowly splitting apart into separate continents. One has a tiny sliver of raw, exposed skin in the bull's-eye center, bright red and shiny.

Pollo's still talking. "It's true. To the main camp in Meta. Orders from *el comandante* himself."

Despite himself he looks up at Pollo, who's chewing on the inside of his cheek like a cow. He's never seen *el comandante* in person, but of course he knows who he is—they all do. There's a photograph of him somewhere in the *Semana* magazine from 2005: a troop surrounded by dense rain forest, somewhere in the department of Meta or Vichada or maybe even here in Guaviare. Green-brown fatigues, Castro-style hats. *El comandante* in the center: the youngest, the blondest, and the only one grinning from ear to ear. His face is vaguely familiar in a way that can't be placed, like trying to remember a scene from a film watched long ago during childhood. Blond hair under black beret, the dirty, scorched yellow of *el comandante* a striking contrast to the shiny rows of sweaty black skulls surrounding him.

He swallows hard and puts his hand in his lap. "I don't believe you," he says.

Pollo's eyebrows shoot up in exaggerated surprise. "Julisa!" he shouts. "*El profe* thinks we're lying!"

"Of course he does," she says, crouching over a bucket of sudsy water. Her hair tie today is a sparkly pink, a disturbingly bright color amid the mud of the camp. The acne bumps by her jawline also look pink today, rather than their usual flaming red. She shoves the pan she's been washing in the bucket and straightens up. "He loves us too much to leave."

"No." *Too good to be true*—what's the translation? *Don't*

get my hopes up—how does the correct grammar go? How
could he have lived here for fifteen years and still not know the
correct way to say things? He settles for gently touching his
bites one at a time, his fingers tap-dancing across his wrists.
It's hard to tell if his skin is wet or cold.

"We're not lying, *profe*," Pollo says. "Why would we lie?
We're trying to help you. We're telling you things you ought to
know."

Julisa wipes her hands on the back of her sweatpants. As
she passes by the table, she says, "You'll like the new camp,
profe. There'll be lots of sticks."

He looks sharply at her. Her mouth is twisting—a smile?
She keeps walking toward the tents without looking back at
him, not once.

Actually, the insect bites aren't like a split-up Pangaea. More
like buttons on a highly futuristic computer board. He touches
the reddest and blotchiest one, near his thumb knuckle. This
one—for blowing up the world. That one—for deploying de-
fenses. For calling in reinforcements, playing warnings over the
loudspeaker. Women and children first.

Dinner is rice and potato slices. Pollo gives him an extra-
big serving, "to make you fat and strong!"

"Why, am I going somewhere?" In the background César
lets out one of his giggles.

"Yes," Pollo says, the edges of his lips quivering. Is he actually smiling too? "For a long, hard walk."

The potatoes are cooked well too: soft and white and
crumbly, instead of hard in the middle like usual. He cleans
the plate with his index finger, which he then licks like a little
kid eating an ice cream cone.

The ransom—maybe the school finally paid it.

(If he's not strict with himself, these kinds of thoughts will sneak in.)

International pressure. Scandalized parents. Fund-raising among the students. Media circus.

(Careful. Careful.)

Or maybe he has a great-uncle somewhere. Someone he's never heard of before, living in Utah or Nevada, with an enormous trust fund. Someone who'd fall into the category of *loving, dedicated relative* as opposed to *estranged, fucked-up alcoholic.* Somehow they've managed to get in touch with the Red Cross, the CIA, the FBI, some other random international agency. His head whirs with the possibilities, each forming a distinct picture in his mind. Maybe—maybe—maybe—

When Julisa takes him to the shed, he brazenly asks what day they'll be leaving. "Soon," she says, keys rattling as she removes them from her pocket. "Everything's arranged."

"Because you said so?" he says, and to his surprise Julisa actually laughs, an abrupt sound that she quickly covers up with her hand, like she's an embarrassed schoolchild caught in the act.

That night, he only comes up with a few notes for Act II. He lies down on the bare plank bed and waits for César's flashlight to shine through the cracks of his shed during the hourly check. Instead of scratching his bites, he clenches and unclenches his fists as though he's cupping a live creature— a broken baby bird, a fluttering insect—letting it take quick gasps of air.

For Halloween he treats them to a screening of the first *Alien* movie. Of course it's the tree who has to snidely ask, *But what about* Hamlet, *Mr. B?* as he struggles to set up the DVD player (i.e., place the notebook on a dry patch of ground within everyone's field of vision). *We're still on Act I—aren't we going to fall behind? When do we get to start Act II?*

"Glad you asked," he says coldly, flipping open to a blank notebook page that will represent the flickering blue screen. "If you guys prefer, I can take this right back to Ms. Márquez's room. That way, world history class can watch *The Mummy*, and we can talk about examples of iambic pentameter instead. How does that sound?"

He smiles as the rocks and leaves hiss.

He gives a brief lecture before pressing play, surprising himself by how talkative he is speaking without notes, the words bursting out of him as he bounces on his heels, furiously scratching his hand.

"Pay attention," he says, stalking past the river stones, "to the visual motif of bodily fluids. To the theme of maternity. The body versus the mechanical. Please notice," he says to the tree, who's still looking a little sullen, "how vital elements of the plot are left unexplained. What is the giant spaceship? Where did it come from; why are the aliens there? Who is the famous Space Jockey, frozen in his piloting seat for all time? Is it a flaw," he says, spinning around to face the respectfully silent sticks, "that the film leaves essential questions unanswered? Can we, as the audience, accept certain elements of mystery, or is it unforgivably frustrating?"

The film is a big hit. A yellow leaf comments during the wrap-up discussion that the director *is really into wetness.*

"Great observation—the dripping acid blood, the water on the ship." The leaf with freckle-like dark spots says it's interesting how the ship's computer is called Mother. *"You bitch,"* it quotes, and everyone giggles nervously, the swear word hanging in the air. The sticks are excited by the role of the Company and its attempts to acquire the alien as a biological weapon. "Yes—the glories of unrestrained capitalism. You'll learn all about that in college, assuming the Marxists here don't get you first." He can't help but laugh hysterically, and the students look at one another, frowning. *Keep it together, Mr. B. Don't get all weird on us now.*

He gobbles down lunch as fast as he can, rice and potato chunks (hard in the middle this time, but that's okay), scrapes his plate clean. The bite on his hand is now surrounded by dozens of tiny red dots, like a photograph of new galaxies forming. He tentatively touches them, jerks away from the deep stinging pain. He can feel Julisa staring after him as he rises and heads back toward the river, but he doesn't care at this point. Let her stare! To hell with scheduling! He needs to rest up for his long, hard walk. Movie marathon all afternoon!

They're all thrilled to see him again. *Mr. B, you're back! Yay! You're the best! You're our favoritest teacher in eighth grade!* "You mean *favorite*," he says, loading the sequel. "Happy Halloween, everyone."

Everybody cheers when *Aliens'* title screen comes up, and they keep cheering throughout: for the marines, for the epic scenes of aliens getting dramatically shot to bits, for Ripley kicking the alien mother's butt in her mechanical body armor. *Alien 3* he almost doesn't bother playing, but fuck it—Ripley's role as the only woman in a male penal colony will provide potentially interesting fodder for a discussion on gender. *Alien: Resurrection* he doesn't dare mention; it's best if they remain unaware of its existence. He lets them sit on the floor, the couples with one's head in the other's lap, allows them to use their bunched-up sweaters and backpacks for pillows. He graciously gives them permission to eat popcorn, mango Popsicles, chicken-flavored potato chips, scattering crumbs all over the tiled floors for the janitors to sweep up later. The girls braid one another's hair; the boys jiggle their legs as much as they want. On the edge of the classroom, a boy with dirty-blond hair sits with his legs sticking straight out in front of him. A girl with a long black braid bends over his shoe, writing something on it with a Liquid Paper pen. He stares at them both, brow furrowing, as though he's witnessing something important, a key moment he ought to remember (What were their names again? Who were they, exactly?), but then he's distracted by the surrounding cries, the high-pitched whoops of his other students as they touch his arm, tug at his shirt: *Mr. B, this is the best Halloween ever!*

Later, eating vanilla cake and ice cream he's brought in specially from the famous French bakery in Unicentro, they all agree that *Alien 3* is irrelevant, undone by its horrible third-act chase scene (*It reminded me of a Marilyn Manson video,* Katrina says, tugging at her earrings like the typical Goody Two-shoes she is, and everyone nods with wide eyes, as though the devil himself were mentioned). Stephanie Lansky comments that the first *Alien* film is more like classic horror, as opposed to an action flick. "Excellent observation, Stephanie," he says, and she flips her long hair over her shoulders, letting it fall down her back. *Alien* is the clear favorite among the three; Sebastián excitedly praises the scene where the marines *shoot the shit out of those sons of bitches*.

"Watch your language," he says, but overall he's pleased. He glances again at the blond boy; the girl with the black braid is still hunched over his shoe, pressing down the Liquid Paper pen. What year did he teach them? Why can't he remember? Something deep inside his hand is throbbing, like the core of a volcano, hidden under layers of muscle and tissue, causing goosebumps to prickle all over his arms and neck.

"But perhaps," he says loudly, "where the films fall short is in their contemplation of the aliens themselves—what are we to make of them?" He smiles at the sight of their furiously scribbling pencils, their rapidly flipping pages. Their intense, attentive expressions, which are nothing like Pollo's vacant stare, Julisa's gaudy hair bands and puffy acne, César's crazed smile. "What exactly is their ultimate motivation? Is their goal to just colonize as many worlds as possible, to keep spreading and reproducing through all corners of Earth, the universe, the galaxy?" A quick glimpse is all it takes to see it: The tiny sliver of raw, exposed skin in the bite's center has spread, expanding toward his wrist, peeling upward like lichen on a tree trunk. "What are they trying to do? What in the end do they even *want*?" With their fatigues. Their berets. With their long, slow jungle marches, slipping and sliding through the mud. "To just take, take, take as much as they can, as fast as they can? Too bad for anybody innocent who gets in their way? Too bad for people who only came to this godforsaken, goddamn country in the first place out of some misguided idea to *help and make a difference,* and because the salary on the brochure at the career fair looked good, and God knows I'm now going to regret that decision for the rest of my life?"

The blond boy isn't paying attention; he's blowing on the Liquid Paper message on his shoe so that it dries quicker, and the black-haired girl is brushing the tip of her braid against her lips. "Excuse me," he says, turning to address them. (When did they graduate? Why didn't he keep in touch with more of his students after they moved on to ninth grade?) "Do you think," he says, "that you could please be respectful, even for a moment? I live here fifteen years, learn the language, the dances, remember to always carry small change with me, and this is what I get? What the hell do they want from me? What exactly are they trying to achieve? You are *not*," he says to the blond boy, grabbing him by the shoulders and yanking him roughly away from the black-haired girl, "following instructions right now!"

The voice comes from behind, speaking loud and clear: "What are you doing?"

He doesn't have enough self-control to turn around slowly. Instead he spins with the frenzied energy of the guilty, of somebody caught red-handed. Julisa stares at him, eyes blinking, rubbery mouth slack. He lets his clenched fists open, and the crumpled leaves and snapped twigs fall to the ground. Nothing more than jungle trash.

Julisa takes a step forward. She reaches down and picks up a twig, holding it in her palms like she's cradling it. If he didn't know any better, he'd think she was about to start rocking it, lullaby-style. "Oh!" she says in a worried tone he's never heard her use before. "You hurt this one."

He stares at her. Still looking at the stick, she slowly closes her open hands into a fist.

"You need," she says, and this time the steeliness in her voice has returned, "to come back to camp."

Even from a distance he can see César with both hands behind his back, holding something. "Go inside," Julisa says, pointing to the shed. She and César follow, and once he's sitting on the plank bed, César lets the object drop.

It's a chain. César bends over and starts wrapping it around his ankle.

"What is this?" he says as César jerks at the links, tightening it.

"We're chaining you."

"Why?"

"Orders."

Even Pollo has shown up by now, lingering outside the doorway. He's never realized until now how smooth Pollo's skin is, practically baby-faced, like a brand-new brick of panela sugar before it gets scarred with knife cuts. Julisa, meanwhile, looks chipped, her cheeks pockmarked by acne scars, red bumps dotting her jawline. She's wearing a purple hair band today, which glitters with fake gemstones. The kind of thing an eight-year-old girl would wear; something not even a high schooler would be caught dead in. Middle school, even.

"What," he says in English, "the fuck."

"Only Spanish here!" César shouts, working the padlock through chain links. It's the same kind you'd use to chain a big dog, with a clip at the end to attach to a collar.

"What did I do?" he says when César finally stands up. His ankle is wrapped up tight. "Why the punishment?" *Penitencia*—did he use the right word? It's the one the students always chant during Trivia Wars, when the opposite team finally loses: *penitencia, penitencia*! A singsongy term, a word for children.

"Don't be mad, *profe*," César says, languidly stretching his arms overhead as though the effort of chaining him up has made his muscles sore.

But Julisa seems to understand. "It's not a punishment," she says before shutting the door. "And it's only for tonight."

The next morning, though, when the door is unlocked, instead of Pollo it's Julisa standing there, holding a mug of coffee. "You're staying in for the day," she says, passing it to him. "I'm locking the door."

"Why?" At the same time that she's opening her mouth, lips automatically forming the word *orders*, he says, "Can I go to the latrine?"

"No."

"Why not?"

She leaves him a bucket in the corner.

Lunch is rice with a spoonful of green beans. When he asks Julisa for more, she says no.

Dinner is a gruel of corn and potatoes.

"Why am I being treated like this? Listen, I'm sorry. I'm sorry I stayed by the river too long. It was a mistake; I lost track of the time. It won't happen again. I won't go there anymore, I promise. I promise."

Breakfast comes late. A single arepa and a cup of hot choc-olate filled with dregs of unmelted powder, which he slurps up greedily. "Have you gotten orders yet? For when to release me?"

"We're waiting."

Pollo is back for lunch. "Is he here?" he says as Pollo hands over the shallow dish of potato pasta soup, his voice coming out in a strange-sounding rasp. *"El comandante?"*

A line appears in Pollo's forehead. "What's wrong with your hand?"

He crosses his arms behind him. A strange feeling is rising in his hand, a desperate heat. "You know, Pollo," he says in the meanest-sounding voice he can muster, the voice of cafeteria-line whispering, of back-of-the-classroom bullying. "About *el comandante* . . . he's very *blond,* isn't he?"

Pollo stares back with his cowlike expression. All he needs are some green flies sucking at the corners of his eyes and the transformation would be complete.

"Very blond," he repeats as Pollo bends over to place the half-full dish on the ground. "Very strange. He looks very dif-ferent from you, no? From Julisa? What do you think that means?" His voice is getting louder now; he's almost shriek-ing. Something deep within his hand is throbbing, threatening to erupt to the surface and splatter everywhere. What is it that he's trying to get at? What is he trying to figure out? What is it about *el comandante* that's both familiar and strange? "Where did he come from, Pollo? Why does he get to make all the de-cisions while you and Julisa do all the work?" *Mr. B, don't get all weird on us now.*

"I don't know anything about that." Pollo begins backing away. "It has nothing to do with me."

"Pollo," he says, "how old are you?" But just like that, it's too late; the door clicks shut and Pollo's blank eyes are transformed into an equally expressionless wooden slab.

Dinner is cold rice with a teaspoon of canned sardines. He asks Julisa for water, and she lugs in another bucket before locking the door and leaving. When he takes a drink, his mouth fills with the soapy taste of dishwashing liquid.

At breakfast, when Pollo brings him coffee, he can't hold it back any longer: "Why does Julisa hate me so much?" He waits for the exaggerated widening of the eyes, the emphatic protest. *Hate you? She doesn't hate you, profe! We all take good care of you here! Why would you think that?*

But Pollo answers immediately, passing the mug to him: "Well, she's bored. She doesn't like it out here. But we have to stay because, well, you know."

Pollo's fingers twiddle in his direction.

"Sorry," he says. He holds the mug close to his chest. Presses it against his heart, trying to create warmth. Careful not to let the throbbing hand brush against his shirt. "I'm sorry that Julisa is so . . . bored."

"Profe," Pollo says, and there's a sharpness to his voice that he's never heard before. "She's been out here since she was thirteen. Why wouldn't she be bored?"

He doesn't say anything. Pollo stands there a second longer before turning away, shutting the door tight behind him.

Rice and beans. Rice and a single canned sardine. Rice, sardine, and a boiled potato. Rice and lentils. Rice and boiled potatoes. Soup of sardines, pasta, and potatoes. Rice with sardines, pasta, and potatoes. Lentils.

———

They come for him out of the sky. Their spaceship slowly descends through the jungle canopy, glowing yellow like the most beautifully cut slice of lemon pie there ever was. A perfect wedge. He waves them in, signaling like an expert air traffic controller. *Come in, just like that, there you go.* Orange-skinned, with red sores blooming all over his body, but smiling: the last survivor of a worldwide apocalypse, a desert island castaway.

They cast their bluish white searchlights over the campsite, slowly illuminating one item at a time: the wooden picnic table, the hammocks, the tin cups, the black rubber boots with yellow bottoms, the packets of Frutiño strawberry juice powder, the saltine cracker wrappers, the enormous blocks of unrefined panela sugar in plastic bags. They examine the rechargeable solar phone and the battered black laptop with an incredulous sense of wonder. *Who were these creatures,* they ask, mandibles clicking, *and what were they doing with such an extensive collection of Sylvester Stallone DVDs?*

He gives them a tour of the shed. Four steps this way, five and a half steps that way. He shows off his possessions: the blanket, the two candles, the black-ink pen (he doesn't mention the notebook, tries not to think of the riverbank). *Oh, how resourceful of you,* they say when he shows them the discarded rag he uses to store bits of potato for late-night snacks. *How very clever.* They express great interest in the 1990s computer manual, fishy eyes widening, waving their slimy tentacles around. *Oh my. How fascinating indeed.*

They try to share their own knowledge with him: their intricate experience of time travel, their ability to explore the depths of parallel universes and mirroring worlds. They show him a world where the green numbers on his dashboard flick to 8:38 and he drives right on by the roadblock, ignoring the waving arms of the soldiers instead of pulling over. They show him a world where he wakes up on time, not hungover, and makes it to school via his usual route. A world where he took a job in Bogotá instead of Cali; where he never went to Colombia at all, chose Indonesia instead. He stayed in California; he never left. Instead of studying literature he majored in business and accounting. His parents didn't drink; he never had anything to do with the foster care system.

Stop, he has to eventually say. *Please.* He covers his eyes. He sings the first line of the Fleetwood Mac song over and over again, *I don't want to know,* as obstinate and stubborn as a little kid on a playground, until they're touching him urgently with their tentacles, begging him: *It's okay. We're sorry, we didn't realize, we shouldn't have. Please continue to show us your world instead. Tell us: What's this?*

So he explains in great detail how everything works, making sure they understand. *This is the chain, and this is the lock. This is the way the lock clicks shut, and this is how the collar attaches around your neck. There are several things you can do with the links. You can drape them over your shoulder like a scarf, or wrap them around your neck like a turtleneck—be sure to leave yourself enough breathing room if you choose this option! The different places you can be chained to include the concrete block outside and . . . that's it. The concrete block is the only place.*

Yes, yes, the aliens say, sticky mouths falling open, furiously scanning everything they can with their photographic eyeballs, downloading the images of the shed and its contents into their computer-size brains. *Amazing, incredible.*

I know. It gets better. See this here? This wet patch of wood on these boards? I've tested it. With enough force it ought to crumble to bits. A couple of good hard kicks and that'll do it.

Oh my, the aliens say, blinking furiously. *But then you'll have a hole in your little house.*

Exactly. Except it's not a house, it's a shed. Make sure you get that right. Anyway, that's the point: I can kick open a hole, and then you know what I can do? I'll scramble up that mountainside in the dark. I'll get unchained somehow; I don't know. I'll run away and hide until the coast is clear, until it's safe. And then . . . then . . .

His voice falters, the picture barely forming. Him panting in the darkness, flashlights swirling behind him as he charges through the underbrush. Marching busily, purposefully, on his way to—what? Toward where?

Then what are you waiting for? the aliens say, and now all of a sudden they don't seem so alienlike anymore. Frowning, crossing their arms, tapping their feet against the ground. Julisa yawning in boredom, Pollo glancing impatiently over his shoulder. Him standing helplessly before the classroom, students staring at him incredulously. *Why not go now? Smash them over their heads; punch them in the stomach. Do it; take action!*

Because, he says. *Because, because, because.* His hand throbs, but he forces himself not to look. There's no need to see—no need to know. And just like that, the shed is silent and empty. Nobody here but him. Not even the light of César's flashlight shining through the cracks. No racing pictures, no spinning camera. His mind is empty, uncluttered. A perfect wedge of blankness.

He wakes early to the sound of far-off buzzing. Helicopters? Planes?

It's César at the door this time. Slurping on a cherry-flavored lollipop, he unlocks the door, pulling the chains off in one brisk, efficient motion. "Get ready," César says, slinging the links over his arms like a waiter's napkin. "We're going."

"Going where?" The voice saying the words sounds ragged, like a fairy-tale monster speaking for the very first time.

César's head jerks slightly, the side of his skull nodding west. Toward the mountains.

"We're marching?"

"Yes."

"Why?" The voice is still ragged but the words are coming through clearer now, less raw. "Where's Julisa?"

César traces the outline of his mouth with the lollipop, as though dreamily applying lipstick.

"Is the army—arriving?" Is that the right word? How long did you have to live somewhere before you learned the language?

César puckers his lips, now the saucy bright red of a sixteen-year-old girl, and points them toward the mountains. "Pack up, *profe*."

It takes him less than five minutes. Clothes, blanket, food

rag, candles. He leaves the *Semana* magazine and 1990s computer catalog. He is careful not to catch a glimpse of his hand, the skin now swollen and hardened into a shape like a mushroom cap. He doesn't look at the bite. The bite has no need to be looked at.

The table is gone, so he sits on top of his backpack. The sunlight makes everything look hyper-pigmented, an oversaturated piece of film. He can't stop blinking. César marches briskly back and forth between the tents, carrying out wrinkled stacks of clothing and crumpled plastic bags, dumping them onto the ground. The faint sound of a helicopter buzzes overhead again and gradually fades.

"Julisa," he says in that scratchy croak, when César emerges from a tent, his arms stacked with Sylvester Stallone films. "Where is she?"

"Don't worry about it, *profe*," César says. He lets the DVDs fall all at once with a giant clatter, the case lids breaking off and bouncing near his foot. He seems pleased by how much noise it makes, clapping his hands like a toddler. "Don't worry," César repeats, taking another lollipop out of his pocket. "These things don't concern you."

He's not listening. He's rising to his feet, swaying unsteadily. Staring at the pile of clothes on the ground, at something familiar. Something that's his.

He walks over to the pile. (Why are his legs so shaky? Why does his torso feel like water?) He bends over and picks up his notebook. The cover is smeared with mud, but the pages are uncreased, as though someone spent ages going through it, smoothing out the wrinkles, carefully making it look nice

again. He lets the notebook fall open. Someone has tucked a
single brown stick between the pages. His notes are faded but
still easy as anything to read:

Act II—emphasize Hamlet-Laertes connection!! FOILS.

Rosencrantz + Guildenstern → parallel universe of
Stoppard's play

"A king of infinite space, were it not that I have bad
dreams"

He stares at the stick, placed there with such care (tender-
ness, almost)—as though someone were trying to keep it safe.
He looks down at the stack of clothes by his feet: The dirty
green shirt could be anyone's, but the glittery hair ties are unmistakable.

He looks at César. "Julisa," he says. "Where did she go?"

César just blinks at him, an expression both familiar and
strange. It takes him a second to recognize it: *Mr. Beeeeeee, I
don't understand! It's too difficult!* Faces stricken with confused concern, waving around their copies of *A Connecticut
Yankee, Hamlet, Mrs. Dalloway,* small fingers curled over the
wrinkled paperback covers, pleadingly asking him for a direct
answer, a clear path to lead them out of the muddled confusion: *Explain it to me, Mr. B. Explain everything so that it
makes sense.*

I can't tell you, he should have told them. He looks at the
stick one last time before closing the notebook, shutting it
tight. *I can't tell you a single thing.*

"César," he says, still with that fairy-tale monster voice he doesn't recognize but must be his. "Why was I locked up?"

César is scratching his neck. "Orders," he says. "There was another prisoner at a different camp. He escaped." He pauses from scratching to study his fingers. "Ran away into the jungle. *El comandante* sent Julisa and Pollo to join the scouting party—if they find him he'll be shot." He scrapes his nails clean with his bottom teeth. "And you want to know something? He's also a *profe*." César grins. "Just like you."

His throat closes up. It's hard to get the words out, but somehow he manages: "Just like me."

César pulls a crumpled packet of Frutiño juice powder out of his bag and begins licking the aluminum in his usual style. "In just a minute," he says, lips dotted with pink grains, nodding in the direction of the hand, "I'll take care of that for you."

His hand throbs as if in response. César smirks toothily one last time, still licking the packet clean as he walks away.

The pictures come to him slowly this time: He doesn't even need to close his eyes. The other *profe*, whoever he is: scrambling up the mountainside in the dark. Panting in the darkness, flashlights swirling behind him as he charges through the underbrush. Swimming downriver, struggling to not get tangled in vines, to avoid the caimans' teeth. Sleeping while standing, leaning against trees, jogging in place when it rains to avoid hypothermia. The other *profe,* the one who is him and not him.

He's not alone either. Here they come, more and more of them, creeping in, slowly at first, then faster. Crowding his mind. Senators, engineers. Mayors of small towns, union leaders. Marching on muddy paths. Slipping, sliding. Minuscule figures seen from above, chains draped around necks, mud-stained rubber boots with yellow bottoms, tiny specks weaving through an ocean of green. Passing each other like Ray Bradbury astronauts drifting through space, just out of reach. If they could walk around with their space suit cords tied around their waists, at what point would the cords intersect? How long would it take for knots to form, tangles? How often did their paths cross and connect without them ever even knowing?

He stands up slowly. The notebook is still warm in his hands. He heads purposefully toward the riverbank with long strides, as if summoned by the recess bell. César is sitting on the bucket, licking the last of the juice powder. He can feel César's eyes following him but that's okay, he's welcome to come along if he wants to. All are welcome. All can join.

He sets the notebook carefully aside; he can do without syllabus notes for today. He leaves Julisa's stick in the spot that she chose for it, tucked between the pages. It's easy as anything to collect more twigs, lay them out in a straight line. He pulls leaves off the nearest branches, flattens them out on the ground. The tree sits there, immobile; the fern crouches, expressionless.

It's just like last time and the time before that, and all the times that came before these past few years, months, weeks, days. With one small difference. This time, he and his students aren't alone. The empty seedpods—the janitors—have come to visit, poking their heads into the classroom. The clumps of dirt he tears from the ground, those are the security guards who always waved at him as he drove through the gates. The

computer science and geometry teachers, lunch break cigarettes hanging from their mouths. The cafeteria cooks with
white cloth aprons. Ms. Márquez with her tight jeans and Fri-
day night salsa-dancing shirt, Ms. Simón clasping her hands
with pleasure at seeing him again so many years later. The
parents are arriving, crowding in, eager. The classroom has
become an assembly, a carnivalesque party, the entire school
congregating, everybody invited.

Julisa and Pollo—they've managed to make it too. There
they are, sitting cross-legged on the ground, eyes lit up with a
curiosity he's never seen in them before: calmly, expectantly
hanging on to his every word. Even *el comandante* himself is
here, sitting with his back to the tree and arms crossed behind
his head. Waiting patiently for him to begin.

It's going to be a good session today. Call it a gut sense, call
it a dream. This class, out of all of them—it's going to be his
masterpiece.

M+M

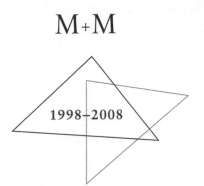

1998–2008

VALLE DEL CAUCA–META

—*You knew what they were going to do and you didn't tell me. Why?*

I know. I'm sorry.

—*You didn't say anything. You knew what was going to happen.*

Listen, now's not really the best time—

—*You didn't even try. What the freaking heck?*

I zip up my pants and stagger to my feet. Everyone else in camp is still asleep in the makeshift tents, plastic tarps hung over branches. From where I've been squatting over the latrine trench I can see how we're scattered over the hillside, hidden from the sight of any military aircraft in the tangled over-growth of coffee and papaya trees. The sun hasn't come up yet, the sky is still water-colored, so for now there are no bugs buzzing against my face, and everyone's boots lined up outside their tents are shiny from last night's rain.

—*You could have told me somehow, you know.*

Fuck off!

—*You could have found a way.*

I do a quick supply check while listening to the radio. Lanterns. Blankets. Plastic tarp. Ants the size of beetles crawl over my hand as I count the ammunition. Battered packets of antibiotics. Moldy rope. A knife. We'll bury equipment today to make marching faster; in two days' time the daily rations will be reduced to cans of sardines and blocks of panela sugar. Machete. Black garbage bag. A single plastic spoon. It's not raining, but it's still cold enough to make me shiver: the kind of dank, sticky jungle morning cold that I can never get used to, even after five years out here. Sweatpants. Spare shoelaces. And last of all the beret, which I pull over my head as tight as I can.

I sling the pack on and stand up. Not bad. Could be heavier, could be worse. The radio announcer is saying there was one dead, one wounded on the army's side in Saturday's clash. Casualties on our side are still being estimated but range between six and nine.

—*Hey. Did you know with that pack on, you look like a turtle?*

I shrug the pack off immediately; it lands with a squelch in the porridgelike mud. I sit down on it and shuffle off my boots, peeling off my socks to examine the white spongy growths on my feet. They burn when I poke them and smell faintly of salt. Slowly flexing my toes back and forth, I carefully go over the steps of our overall strategy. Listing them calmly, mechanically, just like an alien would, or a robot. An alien robot.

Top priorities: Get our strength back. Contact local peasants to guarantee us food for five to six days. Send some weapons ahead in a peasant's truck to lighten the load, if possible. Keep our presence a secret. Identify the scout from Putumayo who claims to be an herbalist; have him make poultices for the wounded. Clean the wounds that are infected. Those who died during the night—bury them in a well-hidden place by the river so that neither the soldiers nor animals can find them.

—*Jesus, you stink. Gross. What's that nickname that everyone calls you behind your back—Comandante Piggy? Or are they still calling you Blondie?*

Reinforce sentries. Punish anyone who fell asleep during last night's guard duty. Double-check rations. Our most urgent tasks remain unchanged, for two months and counting: Reestablish contact. Recruit combatants. Above all else: Stay strong.

—*So you're just going to ignore me? Seriously? You think you can cut me out that easily? Like Stephanie and Betsy and La Flaca and all the rest?*

I yank my socks up my ankles as brusquely as I can, jam my feet back into the boots.

—*You could have told me if you wanted to. But you didn't.*

Go away. Please.

—*They were laughing at me, all of them, and you didn't do a thing.*

Could you leave me alone for once? For today? For five minutes?

—*Do you ever think about it? What about on your very*

*first day—when they handed you a pair of black rubber boots
with yellow bottoms? Like you were a common peasant, wad-
ing around in the mud, instead of a future hot-shit com-
mander?*

God. Five years ago now. First day in the jungle, first day of
training camp—

*—Your first day at school. It was eighth grade and I was
chewing on the tip of my braid when you came in. You were led
through the door of Mr. B's classroom by Sebastián, your assigned buddy for the day, and one of the volleyball team girls
immediately covered her mouth with her hands and started giggling, exchanging glances with her friends as though already
thrilled by the idea of having a new boy in the classroom. It was
Katrina, or maybe Stephanie—the one whose fruit-colored
thong always peeked out the top of her blue jeans, mango or
raspberry or lime. You pulled the last empty chair back and its
high-pitched screech against the floor gave me goosebumps,
while Mr. B went on talking about Laertes's sword fight with
Hamlet like it was no big deal, whatever, we had new kids on
scholarships come join us all the time.*

*We knew you were on a scholarship right away. We knew
because your skin was the same coffee-candy color of our
maids and chauffeurs and gardeners—not like ours, peach-
pale tan, the shade of makeup always on display in the front
rack at the mall. But your hair was blond. Not brunette-blond
like Katrina in the front row, intensely raising her hand to Mr.
B's every question, focused on getting the best grades possible
for the academic transcript she'd mail to the prestigious boarding school in Switzerland. Not even a white-blond like Mr. B,
who was scribbling the chalk furiously across the blackboard.*

You were a dirty blond, the color of the scorched grass in August after being burnt for months by the sun. It always confused me: How could you be so blond and still be on a scholarship? It wasn't even until the end of class that Mr. B finally turned to you, stroking that epic beard of his, and said, Good morning, now why don't you go ahead and tell us your name?

"Good morning, *comandante*," the cook says. I'm sitting on a flat rock next to the fire, watching as he makes coffee. He holds the wooden spoon in a tight clamp with his only hand, the left one: His right shirtsleeve is empty, safety-pinned up high on his shoulder. I know for a fact that he's barely in his early twenties—almost the same age as me—but his face (like all our faces) is that of a tiny old man, shriveled by sunshine, bitter river water, tinned food twice a day.

The two lieutenants are also up and about by now: mustaches carefully groomed, owl-eye spectacles clean from splashes of water. They're standing downhill by the river, fiddling with the skinny antennas of their walkie-talkies. Their skin is the same color as mine, but their hair is dark and thick, as if someone scribbled on the top of their skulls with a pen, not leaving a single white spot.

"Here," the cook says, handing over a tin cup filled with just enough coffee to cover the bottom. "Just like home. Better than anything you'd get in Cali." He smiles broadly.

"I'm not from Cali," I say, in a voice that sounds too loud, even to me.

The cook blinks. His empty shirtsleeve sways as he takes a step back.

"Is that what people say?" I say. "That I'm from Cali? That's funny. Why on earth would I be from there? Ha-ha-ha." He looks away.

"I'm from right here," I say, gesturing around me toward the tents, the river, the trees dotting the mountains like iguana scales.

He stares intently into the pot. He's from around Pasto himself, his family killed by paramilitaries for electing a former insurgent as mayor. Or maybe it was the army that did it. Or the police. I can't remember.

The lieutenants have adjusted the antennas by now and are walking uphill toward us. They're coming to ask me about our plan, our goals and objectives for the day. The second they get here, I'll say, "Let's do this," before they even have a chance to open their mouths.

I'm always the one who gets asked. I'm the one who knows what he's doing.

—*You knew what you were doing. I could tell, that time in world history when you took the lighter from the football team boys. They were passing it among themselves, giggling and trying to keep it hidden from Ms. Márquez, testing to see who could hold their finger in the flame the longest before shouting* Puta madre! *and yanking their hand back. I didn't move when they tapped the lighter on my shoulder, bringing the flame close to my arm, and somebody, maybe Álvaro, said,* What do you think fat smells like when it's burning? *And somebody else, maybe Katrina, said,* No, no, you'll get in trouble. *I was trying not to watch, but somehow I knew when to raise my eyes and see when they placed the lighter in your hands. You held it in your palm for a second, as though testing to see how heavy it was. But when you flicked it on, it wasn't your finger hovering above the flame. We all stared. I pulled my braid out of my mouth. In the back of the room some-body (maybe Stephanie) sucked in her breath and said,* Ave Maria! *Under my breath I said,* What the freaking heck. *You were sticking your tongue out, pink and steady, the orange flame licking underneath. A second went by, then another one, and another. You slammed the lighter against the table with a sound as loud and definitive as a geography textbook getting banged shut and Ms. Márquez looked up from her desk and said,* Yes, Martin? Can I help you? *You shook your head back and forth, and even though your eyes were watery we could all see how wide you were grinning.* I'm good, miss, *you said.* I couldn't help myself. *I tried to cover my mouth with my hand but I wasn't fast enough; the laughter streamed out. Ms. Márquez said,* Mariela, that's enough. *That's when you looked at me, and I looked right back. A few minutes later she asked if everyone had a partner for the Interview a Historical Figure project, and when you raised your hand and said,* I need one, *you were looking right at me.*

I'm looking right at it: the abandoned farmhouse sitting on the hill's highest point. Creeping vines heavy with yellow flow-ers grow out of the collapsed wall, and when the next batch of coffee is ready that's where we'll head. A few people will drink while standing, leaning against the wall and staring at the sur-rounding mountains, but most will sit cross-legged on the dirt with their heads bowed, prodding at the parasite scars on their arms. On the lower side of the wall somebody has pains-takingly written one of my most famous quotes, spray-painted in streaky black letters: *Friends, are you ready to pulverize the enemies of us, the people?* We'll share cigarettes and maybe a bit of powdered milk if someone has a crumpled packet jammed deep inside a pocket somewhere. As the sun continues to rise, there'll be government observation planes droning overhead, but none of us will move: As long as we stay inside the farmhouse or under the thick overgrowth, we can't be seen. There'll be no meat today, but depending on how morale seems over the next couple of hours, I'll tell the cook to redesign my original rationing schedule. We'll assign groups of six—no, eight—a single can of sardines.

—*We were assigned William Wallace and Eleanor of Aquitaine.* I have an idea, *you said,* do you have a video camera? *I snuck it out of my father's bedroom and stuffed it into my backpack as fast as possible so that the maid wouldn't catch me, my heart pounding hard. You said we could work at your house, because you had a lot of younger cousins and we could get them to play the role of the Second Crusade and Scottish army. We took a city bus to get there, one of the blue and red ones that roar down the streets spewing thick clouds of black exhaust. I'd never been on a bus before and I didn't want to tell you that, didn't want you to guess how nervous I was, but maybe you knew anyway when I had to ask you,* How much does it cost? *and you said,* Thirteen-year-olds go for free before five. *I pushed the rusty turnstile with my hands and you pushed it with your hips, same as the other passengers. As we rattled along the road, you talked calmly about your last school, in the village with the famous marketplace; how the soccer field was just a strip of yellow dust and sometimes it'd get so cloudy you couldn't even tell where the ball was, how*

instead of textbooks you had stapled packets of blurry pho-
tocopies, and I kept nodding, making noises I hoped sounded
unsurprised. As we walked up the steep hill, passing under the
lines of white laundry flapping between the windows, we
passed a little girl hitting another girl over the head with an
empty soda bottle and you said, Linda, stop that or I'll tell
your mother. *You stopped in front of a house made out of*
orange-red brick with a tin roof and took a pair of jangly keys
out of your backpack. You live here? *I almost said, but was*
able to stop myself in time. The inside of your house was cool
and dark and there wasn't any furniture in the hallway. You
said, I have to feed Lassie, *and I watched you shake out a bag*
of pork rinds onto a plate and put it on the floor in front of a
scabby Dalmatian. You said, That's his favorite.

We sat down on a wooden bench in a stuffy room with only
one fan, which rattled violently. You said, So who would you
rather be, William or Eleanor, *and I said,* Either is fine. *There*
was a framed photograph next to the Virgin Mary candle on
the table: A short, dark-haired woman stood behind a birth-
day cake, wearing an apron. A brown-haired girl with light
skin had her arms wrapped around the woman's waist. Even
though the candles were all lit up and glowing, the woman's
eyes were serious, mouth flat, expressionless. I asked, Who's
that lady? *You said,* That's my mother. *I kept looking at the*
brown-haired girl, then at the woman. I said, Is your mother
here right now? *You didn't say anything, and then you said,* If
we go into my cousin's room, we can put on costumes. *The*
room was strewn with clothes and smelled like sour milk, and
you dropped your backpack on top of a mattress on the floor
in the corner. You picked a stiff white dress off the floor, the

kind a girl would wear to First Communion, and I tensed up,
already dreading the struggle to get my arms through the tight
sleeves, but instead you pressed it against your chest and said,
Perfect. *At first I thought you were kidding, but the way your*
eyes darted quickly over to me told me that you weren't. Then
you let the dress drop slowly to the floor. You reached for a
stick that was propped up against the wall, a broom with no
bristles. What do you need that for? *I said.* You looked at me
and smiled. This isn't a broomstick, *you said.* It's a sword.

We spent all afternoon filming our project. As William
Wallace you were perfect, leading the Scottish army into bat-
tle, charging furiously across the living room, sword raised
high. As Eleanor of Aquitaine I was prim but effective, shak-
ing hands with you in order to seal our unbreakable alliance
against the English. We invented our own history, something
that had nothing to do with time lines and facts and geogra-
phy. I mostly held the camera while you directed the dialogue.
You especially liked the way I zoomed in and out like crazy
during the battle sequences, just like that part in Saving Private Ryan. *You said,* Nice job. *You said,* If you have any money,
we can order pizza. *I ate six slices and you had four. When I*
went into the kitchen to get cups, I saw a giant metal bowl
sitting in the sink encrusted with fish scales and rimmed with
milk. It smelled terrible, as though it'd been sitting there for
days. When the chauffeur came to pick me up, the sun had al-
most set but you were still the only one home. You said, We
are going to get the best grade.

After Morning Drills and Weapon Cleaning is Lecture
Time. The recruits sit on the ground while I lean against the
ceiba tree, arms crossed behind my head, listening to the lieu-

tenant with the owl glasses. I have to turn my right ear toward him, the left one half-deaf from a long-ago grenade. The lieutenant is saying words that sound like his but I know are really mine; they've been said so many different times, in so many different press releases and official statements, that now they sound like they could be anybody's.

"We are revolutionaries," he says. He paces, boots crusty with mud. "Fighting for socialism. The paramilitary assassins of the so-called government try to paint us as nothing more than drug traffickers, but of course we can expect nothing better from them." The recruits are sitting up straight, hands clasped neatly in laps. They are hanging on to his every word—my words. "We know that we are fighting for justice," he continues. "To overthrow the oligarchy, just as our liberator, Simón Bolívar, did. Ours is a legitimate struggle against oppression."

I rip a strand of grass out of the ground and twirl it by my face, brushing my lips.

He says, "The other important thing to remember is that we're like priests. Celibate, but not because we want to be." (This statement always gets a snigger, especially among the new recruits.) "Poor, but not because of vows. And obedient, but not because of God." His eyes are getting wider behind his spectacles, like a teacher getting swept away by his own lecture. "We must be priestlike—because of the war and the massacres. Because of what the oligarchy has done and continues to do to our mothers and our families."

He doesn't say the next part, because I've never spoken it out loud to anyone: *Once a priest, always a priest. But a priest can leave the church and not be killed. Even the paramilitaries*

can go back to being ordinary citizens. But us? It'll never hap-
pen. They'll never forgive us, so we'll never forgive them.
What's the point?

He keeps going, my words sounding both familiar and
strange as they leave his mouth. He says things like "The best
food is hunger." He says, "If you don't work, you don't eat,"
and "You have to fuck them first before they fuck you." He
says, "After the revolution," in the same flat tone of voice I
used earlier when somebody asked me, "What time is it?" and
I said, "It's almost ten o'clock." He says, "The task of Simón
Bolívar has yet to be completed," like it's a homework assign-
ment. Every once in a while one of the new recruits fidgets,
but for the most part everybody is silent, listening. The best
classroom behavior ever.

I bite down on the blade of grass and let the other half flutter to the ground. He doesn't say, *At least we pay better than*
the paramilitaries, right? He doesn't say, *So many acronyms to*
choose from: FARC, ELN, EPL, even the paramilitaries (AUC)
and the army (FFAA) got in on the action, so you might as
well choose us. And he definitely doesn't say, *In any case, de-*
sertion will result in automatic execution. Without exception.

I lean my head back against the trunk and close my eyes.

—We started sitting next to each other at the wooden pic-
nic tables during lunch and watching the volleyball team girls,
the football player boys. You said, Do you think those girls eat
anything besides mango Popsicles and tiny bags of salt? *and I*
crumpled the bag of Doritos I was holding into a tight ball in
my fist so that no one would see it was my second and said,
Who cares, they're all idiots anyway. *You sat next to me in art*
class when we were making figures with wire and pliers and

asked me what I was making, and I said, A virus, you? *You said,* A cow. *I sat next to you in English class when we had to interview someone about My Hero from History. I said,* Kafka, *and you said,* Mary Magdalene. *In biology class we had to list the different steps of blood circulation through the heart, and you said,* Forget lists, they're dumb, let's write an epic poem instead. *You even made it rhyme. In world history when you went to the bathroom, Stephanie waved a torn-out magazine photo of a famous chubby soap opera star in front of my face and said,* Look, Fatty, it's your boyfriend! *But when you came back into the room she whipped it away as fast as anything, like it had never happened. After eating lunch we'd sit on the grass by the football field, or in the hallways leaning against the lockers. You'd sit with your legs sticking straight out in front of you and arms crossed behind your head, and I'd write your name on your shoe with a Liquid Paper pen, coloring it in carefully with different colored markers. In third grade I was famous for having the best bubble handwriting out of anybody, and everybody would pass me their note-books and ask me to write the title of their assignments, say-ing,* Do me next, do me! *After finishing your name on your shoe I did mine, our initials the same letter.* Wow, you said *when I finished,* I've been labeled. *I burned you a CD of my favorite songs, PJ Harvey and Nine Inch Nails and the Clash, and you said,* I liked how the songs didn't have any choruses, and also how they sounded like Satan. *We argued about Ti-tanic (you loved it, I didn't). I said it was sentimental, com-mercial, Hollywood crap, historically inaccurate rubbish. You said,* Well, sometimes all that really matters is a good ending.

You had this way of laughing where it sounded like you were just saying the words aloud, Ha-ha-ha.

After Lecture Time the recruits are taken up the hill for Training and Exercise. Explosives has been canceled because we don't have any new materials, not out here, and I can't seem to find the energy to organize a raiding party. Lots of things seem to require too much energy lately. Two scouts drowned in a river last week, searching for the escaped professor: the girl with her ridiculous hair bands, the boy with his smooth pudgy cheeks. Baby-faced, the pair of them. When the lieutenant informed me, though, the only thing I could think was *What a waste we didn't grab their weapons in time.*

The same lieutenant is here with me right now: shuffling his feet, clutching a notebook to his chest, ready to take notes as needed.

"The escaped prisoner," I say. "The professor."

He swallows hard as he informs me that there's been no trace of him—they think he might have gone downriver. There's a chance that the sentries posted at the narco-processing lab might be able to interrogate local Indians, find out if they've seen any trace of him.

"And the other prisoner?" I say. "The American."

The lieutenant swallows three times in a row before he speaks: The guard who was left watching him is now officially listed as a deserter; the camp was completely abandoned. And as for the American . . . there's no sign of him yet, but the rumor among the scouts is that he walked away into the jungle, talking to the trees, the sticks, the leaves. Some patrol members are even saying that they began to talk back. . . .

"Okay," I say. "That's enough." Details are unnecessary; facts are enough. "Radio Martínez in town and get him to check the whorehouses. If he finds the guard, shoot him. When we get reinforcements we'll double the search parties. Make sure you write that down."

His hands are shaking as he takes out his pen.

"Evening orders: Wood needs to be gathered, more latrines need to be dug."

The glasses ride up his face from how hard he's concentrating, moving the pen painstakingly over the paper.

I never write anything down. Not anymore.

I say, "We could use more cave deposits too. And send someone out with a machete to cut down some of the thick branches, build some benches. There's no reason we should be sitting in the dirt all the time like animals."

He nods, writing in an indecipherable scrawl while I wiggle my finger through the hole in my sleeve and stroke the bumpy scars on my elbow.

—*You started coming over to my house after school. I showed you my complete collection of* Asterix *and* Tintin *comic books and you said,* Cool, I like books with pictures. *We drank malt soda, cold from the fridge. (My family never drank malt; the few bottles we kept in the house were for the maids, a fact I never told you.) You knew how to take the bottle cap off with your teeth, a trick I'd always dramatically applaud. Once you slashed your lip open and my hands froze in midair, never meeting, but you just laughed as though it didn't even hurt you, as though nothing could hurt you, and kept laughing as you walked in circles around the kitchen, the red drops dripping on the white floor tiles and smearing be-*

neath your bare feet, like you were ice-skating on your own blood. You have the highest pain tolerance of anyone I know, *I said.* Are you an alien? A robot? An alien robot? *You smiled as though I'd given you the most extraordinary of compliments, as though I'd identified a secret superpower of yours that no one else had ever noticed. We'd eat packet after packet of plantain and yucca chips and get crumbs all over our school uniforms, eat vanilla cake from the Unicentro mall with our bare hands (I'd see the frosting stains on your shirt the next day). Sometimes we'd fall asleep on the squeaky brown leather couch on top of the empty packets, like we were street orphans sleeping in nests we'd built ourselves out of garbage. We snipped off locks of our hair, blond and black, which you then braided into a little voodoo person, just like you said they used to do at your village. We left it between the pages of Stephanie's biology textbook.* You really don't like her, do you? *you said when I immediately suggested her name, and I just pressed my lips together, not even bothering to nod. When she opened the textbook to the page about photosynthesis and saw the little figure, she let out a shriek that made the biology teacher almost drop his calculator, but we didn't make eye contact or even sneak grins at each other from across the classroom, because we were that good at being undercover, that sneaky and wise.*

One Saturday the chauffeur took us out to my father's country house in the mountains, a two-hour-long drive along endlessly winding roads with sharp curves that made our rib cages touch. Your eyes lingered on the collection of mountain bikes, the indoor fishpond with fat lazy goldfish, but it wasn't until I pointed out the landing field for the helicopter that you said, Wow. *You wanted to hang around and watch the keeper feed Carlitos, the ancient pet lion in his disgusting, meat-stinking cage, but instead I took you to my room, where we sat on my* Lion King *bedsheets and I showed you my complete collection of* Transformers *and* ThunderCats *action figures. You said,* Damn. *I introduced you to my pet rabbits, wiggling their noses frantically behind their chicken wire cage, and you wiggled your nose back and said,* Cute, what are their names? *You showed me weeds in the garden we could feed them and explained that when they pounded their little rabbit feet against the floor of the cage, it was a warning; when they rubbed their little chins against your finger, it's like they were saying,* You're mine. *You loved the swimming pool, dipping your toes into the clear blue water, gradually getting wet all the way up to the knee.* When can we go swimming? *you asked, and I said, just a little too quickly,* Oh, I don't have a bathing suit, maybe another time. *Instead I snuck you into my father's office to show you his collection of assault rifles and handguns and even a sword from the* War of Independence. *Your eyes got bigger and bigger as you stood in front of the glass case, your mouth twisting like it was hooked on some-thing, and as you turned your body quickly away I said,* What is it? *and you said,* Nothing. *You rarely spoke to my father, kept your eyes lowered whenever he walked briskly through the living room, talking on his cellphone.* What happened to his hand? *you asked me once, and I said,* Some kind of acci-dent, I think. *We climbed the mango tree in the garden so that we could design obstacle courses using the imported Italian angel statues and water fountains, using Xs to mark the spots where we'd bury treasure for future survivors of the apoca-*

lypse. You furrowed your forehead in intense concentration as you wrote it all down in my notebook. You asked, What does your father do for a living, exactly? *I said,* Business stuff.

"*Comandante,*" the lieutenant says. "Just a few more things." He coughs. "There's rumors, ah, that one of the new recruits has a Bible hidden in his mess kit. . . ."

"Burn it," I say, "and eighty trips to get wood." He nods, the pen dangling from his hand like an extra-long black finger.

"And before I forget," he says, his mouth twitching, "what do you want to do about the deserters? They've been chained up for three days now."

I look at him without speaking. His eyes get big and the mouth under his mustache gets very thin.

He says, "No trial?"

I say, "Make sure you assign execution duties to one of their friends."

—*On Sundays one of my family's chauffeurs would take us to the mall. I'd use my credit card to buy us iced coffees with whipped cream towers tall enough to smudge our eyebrows white, and we'd drink them by the racks of flowers on display from holiday parades. The crowds of shoppers and the long food-court lines would make me hot and sticky, and the sweat stains in my armpits would spread toward my chest, but I knew that with you it didn't matter, you wouldn't pinch your nose like Stephanie and Katrina and say,* Gross, Fatty, don't your parents ever buy you deodorant? How much hair do you have there, anyway? *Jittery from caffeine, we'd head into the music store and flip through the CD racks, the cases thwacking against one another, and listen to albums on the store's giant headphones, which made us feel like air traffic control-*

lers. I'd listen to the Smashing Pumpkins and the Ramones and Oasis, while you chose compilations of local hits, vallenatos *and* cumbias *wailing beneath strings and trumpets and accordions, the kind of music played on the radio stations I never listened to but my bodyguard did. One time you placed the heavy headphones around my ears and said,* Listen to this, I just love the violin solo. *It took me a second, but when I finally recognized it I started laughing hysterically.* You idiot, *I said,* you know that's originally an American song, right? *I found you the Rod Stewart greatest hits CD and played you the original version, "Maggie May," in English and said,* See, this is the one that's right; the one that you like is just a shitty Spanish cover. *But you frowned and shook your head, as though you refused to accept what you were hearing, as if it weren't possible for a single song to exist in two different languages at the same time.*

Then we'd head to the bathing suit section and you'd try on bikinis. Once the sales lady walked in on you in the changing room—how her mouth dropped open, round like a grape, and you said, At least I wasn't trying on a sexy corset. *At the end of the day the red straws of our coffee were so chewed up that the last sips we took sounded like phlegmatic wheezes. Then the chauffeur would pick us up, and back at my house we'd watch VHS tapes,* Jurassic Park *and* Mary Poppins *and Pixar films, most of which I could quote pretty much perfectly.* To infinity and beyond! *I'd shout, and this one time you asked,* What would that be like? *I said it'd just be black holes and stuff, but you said you wanted there to be infinite worlds, Narnia worlds, places like this one but not quite, almost the*

same but different. Different how, *I said, and you said you
didn't need anything complicated; you'd be happy with something simple, something small, like a never-ending birthday
cake that grew back a piece for every one you ate.* Martin, *I
said,* so beyond infinity, past the current borders of human
understanding and within the depths of unknown parallel
worlds, you want there to be cake? *Still grinning, you said,*
Yes, Mariela, that's exactly right, *and even when I said,* That's
the dumbest thing I've ever heard, *I couldn't help but grin
back.* To the cake and beyond! *you said. We were sitting next
to each other on the floor, your arm so close to mine it was
like I could feel secret signals being sent to me through your
hair. You put the book down and rubbed your chin against
me, just like the rabbits would, before leaning your head
against mine—if only I could have seen it from a distance,
blond against black.*

Dinner is oatmeal and cookies. "Man," somebody says,
someone who's been out here almost as long as I have, "remember how up north we'd throw whatever we found into the
oatmeal? Monkeys, macaws, palm hearts, hawks . . ."

"Yum," somebody else says, and there's laughter. From the
trees comes the sound of three gunshots fired in rapid succes-
sion; a couple of people look up, but not that many. I take my
boots off and examine the fungus on my toes again, scratch
my head to see how much dandruff falls off. I prod the rotting
molar at the back of my mouth, think about the one time
when all we had to eat was papaya bark, torn in strips from
the abandoned farms. Those were the days we'd find fallen
plantains in the mud and I wouldn't allow anybody to eat

them, wouldn't budge from the rule I'd made about not eating food found on unknown lands, due to rumors of the army inserting explosive mines or poison into scattered pieces of fruit. A shard of bark is still stuck in my gums, which I can't get out no matter how much I poke my finger around.

There's a scraping sound behind me and I turn my head: Somebody is walking slowly back from the trees, back from where the deserters were being kept. He drags the shovel against the ground with one hand and carries the execution rifle with the other. I keep my face turned away; I don't meet his eyes. I don't know his name—I try not to know anyone's name anymore.

Someone says, "I felt sick until I vomited, and then I felt better."

Somebody else says, "I never really got over how much a monkey arm looks like a baby's."

—*We were at my house, turning the pages of a* Star Wars *comic book, when you said,* Oh, by the way, happy birthday. *I said,* It's not my birthday, dummy, *and you opened your mouth into a smile so wide I could see the yellow stains on your teeth, the same kind I'd see in the mouths of men selling peanuts at traffic lights.* Well, *you said,* I got you a present anyway, *and I watched you pull something out of your backpack with the same quick flick of your wrist as the street magician we once saw through the tinted car window pulling scarves out of a hat.*

I didn't get any cake, *you said,* but I think you'll still like it. *I stared at the flowery bikini dangling from your hand.*

I picked it out myself, *you said.* Now we can go swimming! *Your arms reached toward me, the straps hanging from your hand. The fabric pattern was yellow flowers against a black background. I didn't touch it.*

I don't think so, *I said*. Thanks but no thanks.

Come on, Mariela, *you said*. What's the big deal?

I said no thank you. *I touched the tip of my braid to my lips.*

I got size XL. *You said it like it was the most natural thing in the world, as though it didn't bother you one bit. I looked at you and your face looked nothing like Stephanie's or the rest of them, but the words I said next still came out angry, like I couldn't help it.*

Great, *I said*. Thanks, Martin. Why don't you just write "Fatty" on the tag and get it over with?

Somewhere at the back of the house the maid coughed repetitively, like a machine gun going off.

And besides, *I said,* you're the one who wears the girly stuff, not me.

Your mouth stayed open in that same wide smile, but your eyes turned into small slits. The house suddenly sounded very quiet, as though we were the only ones home. I kept talking, thinking now that I'd let the anger out, it was going to fly around everywhere, smashing things, like a bat trapped in the house.

Well, *I said*. At least it's a change from me always paying for everything.

You lowered your arm. The bikini fell to the floor.

I'm tired, *I said*. The chauffeurs are on break today. Did you bring money for the bus? Or do you not have enough for that either?

You didn't answer.

Don't worry, *I said,* you can pay me back someday. Maybe when I'm in college in the U.S. Maybe your mother can send me the money.

You looked at me very quickly, head snapping toward me like the rabbits when they became alarmed, and for a second there I felt frightened. I kept talking, like my words would be enough to make the feeling go away.

Or maybe I can get you a job at my father's business, *I said.* Maybe that way you can earn enough.

Your father, *you said suddenly,* is a crook.

Excuse me?

You just looked at me. Your mouth didn't move, but your eyes said it all. The way they flickered, narrowed. Even if the newspapers don't say it, *you said.* Even if nobody says it at school. But everybody knows it. Don't you?

That's what did it. The words kept coming out of me, thick and fast. I don't know from where, as though I'd been saving them up for a long time and now they were leaking out, like Coca-Cola spilling over the couch cushions. You still didn't speak, not even when I said, Well, you probably just shoplifted it anyway, *or* It's a good thing the world always needs window washers, *or* God, do you have to keep sitting with that stupid common peasant expression? *I stayed there on the couch, not moving, as you wandered through the house, looking for the maid so you could ask her to unlock the front door for you. If I'd gone upstairs to my room and looked out the window, I could have watched you when you left, walking slowly down the gravel driveway, turning onto the street, your shadow long beneath the lights that flickered from the moths*

*banging against the bulbs. I could have waited to see if you
dug your hand deep into your pockets, searching for small
brown coins, or if you just kept walking, one slow step at a
time, the first step of many for the long walk that awaited
you, all the way to the other side of the city, past the condo-
miniums and parks, up the steep hills to your aunt's house
with the tin roof and brick steps. But I didn't see, because I
never looked.*

It's getting dark now. The sky is the color of gunmetal, and
in the distance is the rumble of thunderclaps. Somebody says,
"All it needs is shrapnel and we'll feel right at home." I find a
lighter in my pocket and flick it on and off slowly, almost pass
my hand through the flame but at the last second shove it
quickly away. Soon the bats will be flying in wide circles overhead.

The thunder stops but the rumbling continues. One person
stops talking, then another, and suddenly we're all silent, staring at the sky. In the distance a thin plume of smoke is rising,
the same color as the lichens growing on the ceiba trees. For a
moment it's quiet, and then the sound comes again: the low,
continuous burst of heavy caliber machine guns. The sound
of approaching army helicopters.

"They're using smoke bombs," one of the lieutenants says.
"Like in the canyon assault. I can tell from the color."

The smoke keeps rising. For now the air still smells like
dirt, the cicadas are buzzing, and the air is warm against our
faces, but without needing to say it aloud we all know it won't
last. Suddenly everybody is looking at me. Everyone's skin
looks gray and pinched, the expression of a twenty-day march,

of gathering everything up and leaving at a minute's notice, of burying important documents and medicine in plastic bags. Crossing rivers, walking all day without stopping, stepping in the footprints of the person ahead so that you don't leave too many tracks, the rear guard squad erasing prints with branches. It's like I can feel it already, the weight of the pack and the days, on my back and shoulders.

The shooting in the distance grows louder. Nobody says it, but I hear it anyway: *What do you want us to do?* They're waiting, but I don't speak. I don't say anything.

—*You didn't say anything. You knew what they were going to do, and you didn't tell me. You knew what was going to happen.*

I didn't.

—*You did. I saw you when I came into the classroom, even though everybody else was laughing. You were grinning too, tilting your chair back against the wall, arms crossed behind your head. Sitting with Stephanie and Katrina and Sebastián and all the rest. I was turning in your direction when they threw a bra over my head, and my eyes got covered by one of the D-cups and I heard Stephanie say,* Hey, Fatty, you left something here. *I pulled it off as I sat down, and that's when I felt it, something wet and squishy on my butt. I reached underneath me as the laughter grew louder, Stephanie and Katrina and you and everyone else shouting,* Eeew, gross! *Sat there looking at the bloody tampon in my hands, toilet paper from the garbage can still clinging to it, the stained note with "Fatty" written across it in your handwriting. That's when I looked at you. You kept your face turned away, eyes not meet-*

ing mine, but your mouth was open and you were laughing.
That was it. That's when it happened. Everything ended.

It didn't. A lot of things happened after that—

—Nothing did. That was it. But you know what? Who
knows? Maybe it's still too early to tell, but maybe it'll be
years in the future and I'll be touching your face on the jacket
of a hardback book, displayed on a front table covered in
bestsellers. Maybe your face will be on soccer match scarves
sold in marketplaces, or stenciled on walls covered in bullet
holes that by then will be ancient. At that point nobody will
know what your real name is anymore. But I know what it is.
I remember, because I wrote it down—

You wrote it down—

—in the back of my notebooks, on the very last pages. I
wrote it on the sweaty palm of my hand and on the sole of my
shoes. I used Liquid Paper, the thick bristles of the brush stuck
stiffly together, or permanent markers I stole out of plastic
cups sitting on teachers' desks. I wrote down your full name
and I wrote down mine. Then I wrote down our initials. And
then I wrote down the very first letter of both our names, the
one that we share, because I liked the way they looked sitting
next to each other, with only a plus sign to separate them.

Listen. When this—all of this—is over (whatever *this* means,
whatever *over* means), I'll tell you what I'll do. I'll come strolling down the mountainside. Maybe I'll bring the gun and radio
transmitter with me, but probably I won't. I'll go past the ancient indigenous temples hidden deep beneath the jungle canopy, the abandoned villages with adobe walls covered in bullet
and shrapnel scars. Maybe my legs will grow long and elastic

like the Rubber Man in that one comic book we read together, and I'll take giant steps over everything, since that's a good way to cover more ground and get there faster. I'll take a giant step over the fields of sweet-smelling leaves and processing plants filled with burning chemicals and black garbage bags. I'll cross over frothy churning rivers and fields of bored cows, the massacre sites and unmarked graves. I'll be getting close then. A couple more steps and I'll be there. At the school. When I cross the soccer field I'll step over the patches of grass that never grew back properly from all the time we spent sitting there and tearing blades out of the ground. The lockers in the hallway will have dents from the hours we spent leaning against them; the bathroom walls are still covered in the song lyrics you wrote down in Liquid Paper and permanent marker. And who knows, but maybe that's where I'll find you. You'll have survived. You were smart, you got away, you weren't there at the party at your country ranch when they came for your father, with their guns and their rifles and their *business stuff*. No, you escaped, you got away, you've been hiding out this whole time, hunting and scavenging, living off your wits, being resourceful. You were wise and tricky and sly, and that's why you'll be waiting for me in the classroom with the ceiling fan. That's where I gave them the bra I snuck out of your bedroom, handed over the bloody tampon I stole from the girls' bathroom trashcan. Where I wrote down the words on that note. But when I open the door and see you there, I know what I'm going to do. I'm going to take another step, my very last one, reach out, and pull you toward me. You'll feel soft and not at all like a weapon. I'll pull you close and I'll pull you hard. If I try to speak I won't be able to because my mouth and face and skull will be covered with your hair, black mixing with blond. I'll hold you—

—*you'll hold me*—

—and we won't speak. We'll be silent, and even if you start opening your mouth and moving your lips, I won't listen, I won't hear you when you say,

—*Why. Why didn't you tell me.*

Siberian Tiger Park

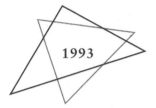

1993

VALLE DEL CAUCA

The first day back from Thanksgiving break, Ms. Simón says we're going to spend the morning making cards for Penelope's family. She writes a few sentences on the board for us to copy, in case we can't think of anything to say: *I am so sorry for your loss. Your daughter was a wonderful person. With much affection, [NAME], Class 3-B.* On the front of his card, Sebastián draws a picture of an Avianca plane on fire, flaming pieces disintegrating in the air. Tiny stick figures dangle from red parachutes or fall headfirst into the water below, arms outstretched. When Sebastián holds it up to show everybody, Mariela says, "They weren't flying over the ocean, dummy, they got blown up over the mountains."

Ms. Simón tells Sebastián to please make a different card.

Penelope usually sits next to Stephanie and in front of La Flaca and Betsy, but today her desk is gone. Instead of what's on the board, we copy what Mariela has written in enormous bubble handwriting, two seats away: *God bless you and your family and may the Virgin Mary keep your daughter safe with all of the angels forever and ever.* She's drawing an enormous flower, scribbling it in carelessly with her red marker until the ink is streaky and pale. While Ms. Simón wipes the board clean, we take our stencils out of our zip cases: hearts and triangles, circles and stars. We carefully color in our cards with our razor-sharp colored pencils until not a single white spot remains.

We Siberian tigers are suddenly orphans. Even though our mother is gone, never to return, we still must fend for ourselves. It won't be easy: Life on the tundra is hard, the winters long and ruthless. But we don't have a choice. One way or another, we must find a way to survive.

During recess, Katrina stands by the ficus tree and tells stories about the survivors to a group of fifth-grade girls. They're members of the basketball team: tall girls, older girls, with ponytails tied near the crown of their heads and long legs like those of the herons that lay eggs in the grass and attack people who get too close. There were just three of them, Katrina says: a crippled man, a seven-year-old girl, and a Labrador dog stowed away with the luggage in steerage. When the bomb went off they fell through the air for thousands of meters, still strapped in their seats, and were buried beneath a pile of debris for hours—tree branches, scraps of metal, suitcases filled with presents for family members in Miami. When the search party finally came, walking right past them in the dark forest, the little girl did the only thing she could think of. She squeezed her brand-new American doll as hard as she could, the one she'd been holding tight in her arms during the entire flight, and its high-pitched cries of *Mama! Mama!* led the search party directly to them.

"God help her," one of the fifth-grade girls says, almost sighing, and her friend reaches out and rubs her on the back.

(Penelope's sister lived in Miami—she was a business major in college. Penelope visited her during Thanksgiving every year.)

"Why didn't they just call out?" Mariela asks. "For help, I mean." She's hanging from one of the nearby branches, her flip-flops dangling precariously from her big toes. We're standing near but not exactly next to her, tearing leaves off the tree and shredding them into tiny pieces.

Katrina says they were definitely dehydrated; they hadn't had any water to drink for hours, let alone food to eat, so their throats were too sore to cry out. At least that's what it said on the news. "Does that make sense?" Katrina asks, her voice rising like Ms. Simón's when she's trying to get Álvaro and Sebastián to stop arm-wrestling. "Do you have any other questions?"

"Not right now, no," Mariela says. "But thank you for clarifying."

One of the fifth graders is staring at us, like they always do. We keep our eyes fixed carefully on Katrina, but the fifth grader reaches out and waves her hand in front of our faces to get our attention.

"I'm so sorry," she says. "Have you heard from her family? Is there going to be a church service?"

We look at one another, but none of us speak. All her friends are staring at us now too, turning in our direction. Now that no one is looking at her, Katrina is scowling.

"Did you hear what I said?" the fifth grader says. "Hello?"

We shuffle our feet, placing one shoe on top of the other. We pick at our nails and the frayed edges of our T-shirts. We look up at the sky and down at the ground.

Her smile has disappeared by now. "My God," she says. "It's like they're retarded." She curves her hand like a claw, swiping it through the air by our faces. "*Meow!*" she says.

We keep staring at our feet as everyone laughs, including Katrina.

"They're always playing that stupid game with each other," Katrina says, raising her voice to make sure they've heard her.

Then the bell rings and it's time to line up at the brick wall. The boys run over from the soccer field like a scattered flock of birds, Fernando hugging the ball close like an enormous white egg. As Katrina walks away, Mariela shouts out, "What about the dog?" but Katrina keeps going like she didn't hear a thing, touching her earrings like she wants to make sure they're still there, walking as close to the fifth-grade girls as she dares. They're marching in perfect rhythm with one another, arms draped over shoulders or wrapped around waists. One of them is still laughing with her head thrown back, ponytail hanging down.

We're straightening up, brushing off our arms and collarbones, when Mariela reaches out and plucks a leaf from a branch. "Forget them," she says. "Siberian tigers never meow." She pinches the stem until a white bubble forms and gazes at it in fascination. "Anyone who's not a total idiot knows that."

She places the leaf carefully between her front teeth. While standing in line she twirls it like a jaunty cigarette, until Recess Monitor Adriana tells her to spit it out.

In London we're orphans. Our faces are permanently smudged with coal dust, our knees rubbed red and raw from clambering up the side of brick buildings. We tap-dance down alleyways, sing the choruses from VHS copies of *Oliver!* and *Mary Poppins,* and leave our chimney sweep brushes behind in the library cubbyholes, crammed in with our backpacks and water bottles.

In the library Ms. Simón tells us (in a voice that is somehow both loud and a whisper) that we have thirty minutes to choose a book, and to please remember that our words and actions and behavior overall will be representative of Class 3-B. The cubbyhole Penelope usually uses is empty, until Álvaro shoves his rain jacket in it at the last second.

We find Mariela reading downstairs in the middle school section. She's sitting on the floor, leaning against a bookcase, even though it's an official rule that we have to sit at the tables. She sucks the tip of her long black braid, then brushes it thoughtfully against her lips like a paintbrush as she turns a page. We stand there for a while, shuffling our feet and nudging one another, until finally La Flaca is pushed forward.

"What are you reading?" she asks, raising her chin defiantly.

Mariela doesn't look up. Instead she just raises the book so that her face is completely covered. We stare at the title: *Jurassic Park,* spelled out in shiny red letters, a black T. rex skeleton in the background.

"What's it about?" says Stephanie.

"It looks good," Betsy whispers, looking at her feet.

This time Mariela lowers the book into her lap. The braid is back in her mouth, and she pulls it out, along with a thin strand of saliva, delicate like a spider's thread. "It has swear words in it," she says. "Wanna see?"

She points them out to us one at a time, jabbing her finger on the page. *Jesus Christ, hell, shit.* Is *Jesus Christ* a bad word?

"Of course it is," Mariela says. "You know what that means?" She leans in close, speaking in a dramatically hushed whisper. "It means . . . the Bible *swears.*"

La Flaca looks worried, but Stephanie laughs. Betsy manages a smile, eyes darting up quickly from the ground. Mariela tilts her head as if studying us one by one.

Later we stand in line and wait for Mrs. Thompson to stamp our books. We hold *Mary Poppins* close to our chests, novelizations of *Star Wars* tucked snug in our armpits, the spines of Arthurian tales sticky in our hands. As usual, Katrina's at the front of the line getting *Babar,* while Sebastián has the exact same picture book he always gets about the World Cup. Ms. Simón returns Penelope's books quickly, sliding them across the table when she thinks no one's looking. Even though the covers are facedown, the titles hidden, we know exactly what they are: an enormous animal atlas, *The Endless Steppe, A Day in the Life of the Siberian Tiger.* Books whose entire sentences we've memorized, whose lines we can recite by heart.

Mariela is still carrying *Jurassic Park.* "Hey," she says, drumming her fingers against Betsy's copy of *Anne Frank: The Diary of a Young Girl.* Betsy looks away, blinking quickly as if trying not to cry. "That's one of my favorites," Mariela says.

Mrs. Thompson doesn't let her check out *Jurassic Park* and says that maybe she would like *The Mouse and the Motorcycle* instead. That would be far more suitable for her age, wouldn't it? "Suitable how?" Mariela says, but Ms. Simón sends her back to the shelves. Betsy gets sent back too and returns with a Narnia book. "Another good choice," Mariela says, and Betsy smiles bigger than she has in days.

During Journal Time, it's impossible not to notice that Mariela's writing furiously, pen scurrying across the paper, flipping her notebook page with a dramatically loud crackle.

"Hey!" Stephanie says. Mariela doesn't stop though, doesn't even look up, so Stephanie has to lean over and tap on her desk. "What are you writing?"

Mariela pauses. She puts her pencil down, then stands up slowly: Holding her notebook with one arm, she picks up her chair with the other. Carries it casually to the spot left vacant by Penelope's desk, the enormous empty space. And just like that, before any of us can say *Wait* or *What are you doing?* or

wave our arms around in a frantic air-traffic-controller gesture to stop her—she puts her chair down and sits in it.

And just like that, it's as though she's been there all along.

"Look," she whispers, and we can't help but lean in close
to stare at the words scrawled across the paper, the bubble-
handwriting title. "I wrote it myself—it's a love poem." She
smiles, her mouth stretching like rubber across her face. "For
Mr. B."

"Oh my God!" La Flaca says. Betsy covers her eyes. Stephanie studies the page. "Wow," she says. "You made the whole
thing rhyme."

We all know Mr. B. He's one of the new teachers from
America. We've glimpsed him during the school-wide assembly: kindergarten babies sitting up front, seniors at the back,
us in the middle with the other third graders. We had to crane
our necks back to see the middle school section, but there he
was, standing by the other American teachers. Top buttons of
his plaid shirt undone, sleeves rolled up (what was he thinking
wearing a long-sleeved shirt in this weather?). Sunlight hitting
his hair so that his head lit up the dim auditorium like a flashlight. Scratching his beard and smiling like he was listening to
a joke that only he could understand. Everyone in the class
thinks he and Ms. Simón are in love (Katrina swore that she
spotted them together at the mall; Sebastián claimed they
climb into the same car at the end of every school day), though
so far nobody has provided any concrete proof.

"That's right. And you know what?" Mariela taps the bottom of the page. "I can copy Ms. Simón's signature pretty
much perfectly. Remember that letter she gave us, about do-

nating food for landslide victims? I've been practicing." She flips to the back of her notebook, and there it is, just like she said: rows and rows of Ms. Simón's loopy cursive signature. Even the capital *S*, one of the trickiest cursive letters ever, is done correctly.

"How are you going to give it to him?" Stephanie asks, at the same time that Betsy starts to giggle nervously, as if Mariela has already started creeping down the corridor toward Mr. B's classroom on her belly, army-style, a crown of leaves on her head and black camouflage ink smeared across her face.

"I have a couple of ideas." Mariela fiddles with her braid. "There's this special potion that my father brought me, all the way from England—you know, where Merlin's from?" She drums her fingers on Betsy's desk. "If you know how to use it correctly, it can make you invisible."

None of us say anything. Her fingers suddenly stop and hover over the paper, and she intently studies our faces. "Why—do you guys have any suggestions?"

We don't. Not right then. Not with Ms. Simón looking up, getting ready to open her mouth and say, *Mariela, could you please move your chair back to your seat?* Not with Katrina peeking up from her notebook, glaring as she watches Mariela smile at Stephanie, arms sprawled over Betsy's desk, head tipped toward La Flaca. Not the right time or place.

However, there are certain things we'd like to show her first.

First is the time machine. Mariela examines the gleaming engine parts approvingly, the black leather control sticks, the giant dial where you can set the day, month, and year. "Ancient Egypt," she says, running a fingertip across the steel doorway, wrinkling her nose at the dust. "I'd like to see some velociraptors—are they really as smart as they say?"

On the run from the Nazis, we show her the attic hiding room. Our flour sacks are full of family photo albums and rolled-up wads of cash. She listens intently, holding the candlestick up high. "Quick," she hisses, "this way!" She hurriedly guides us through the secret passageway, pulling the bookcase away from the wall with great heaving gasps.

The fifth-grade girls snicker as we run past them, staring at us with exaggeratedly open mouths. "God, what are they doing today?" one of them says.

(Following Mariela, listening to her instructions, we can ignore them more easily than ever. More easily than with Penelope, even.)

In Siberia, we try to show her the giant tundra, the icy river where we scoop fish out of the water with our enormous paws, the endless steppe where we go antelope hunting (antelope are, as everybody knows, Siberian tigers' favorite food). But she just shakes her head: "I have a better idea."

She herds us into giant pens, where we stand shoulder to shoulder. She swings the enormous gate shut, locking us in. Pacing, keys jangling at her waist, she explains: Here, we'll be the main attraction of a brand-new park. It's open to visitors of all ages and nationalities—that is, until things suddenly go terribly wrong. As she flips the switch that deactivates the electric fence, she instructs us how to flee from the gamekeeper's bullets, how to terrorize naïve park guests and stalk stray goats.

"That's not how Penelope would do it," Stephanie says in a low voice, but at the same time the recess bells rings, so if Mariela does hear her, she gives no sign.

"Hurry up, now," she says, tapping her foot as we scramble to put away our pencils, retie our sweaters tightly over our belly buttons. "This way please." We clamber to the top of the monkey bars and listen as she explains how her newly redesigned time machine works. In order to activate it, we now have to jump off the center of the monkey bars, holding hands. If we skin our knees on the ground, or split open the palms of our hands, or scream loud enough to cause Recess Monitor Adriana to come running over and get us all in trouble, well, that's not exactly Mariela's fault, is it?

(Penelope never used the monkey bars—she liked the swing set, where fewer people tended to congregate. There was less of a risk that way. No chance of the fifth-grade girls wandering up to us, mouths twisting in amusement. Saying things like *Wow, wait. Aren't you guys a little too old for Let's Pretend?*)

"Is it too much to ask for your attention now, please?" Mariela asks, in a voice that sounds just like Ms. Simón's, when we start flicking sticky yellow butterfly eggs off the bars or pinning dried cicada shells onto our shirts.

"What do you think 'Mr. B' stands for?" she says as we read over her epic poem, flipping through the pages of her latest draft. "Mr. Blow Job? Mr. Boobs?"

"That's *rude*," La Flaca says, looking up sharply.

"No it's not," Mariela says. "It's sex. It's natural. Is a natural part of life rude?"

"When you say it like that it is," La Flaca says.

Mariela just smiles and wiggles her index finger deep into La Flaca's ribs.

She stands next to us in line, arm draped over our shoulders or wrapped around our waists, while we look around nervously, making sure the fifth-grade girls aren't staring: The worst possible thing ever would be to have the word *lesbian* whispered in our direction. Mariela keeps reaching for our hands to hold in line, though, like she doesn't ever hear them, like she wouldn't even care. Mariela says we should come to her house for a sleepover. She says we just have to. We absolutely must. Will our parents let us? Can you ask permission? When can you do it; when will we know? We can sleep in her living room on the couch cushions. Her father won't check on us, not once. We can read her American comic books, make prank phone calls, and tell the maids to order all the pizza and cake we can eat. Did she tell us about the time that she answered the phone before the maid got to it, and as a joke she told the voice on the other end that her father had gone on vacation with the paramilitaries? "What's a paramilitary?" La Flaca says, but Mariela just scrunches up her empty packet of Dori-

tos and says that the voice on the other end of the phone did
not find that very funny, no indeed. And if her father's not
home, she can sneak us into his study and show us where he
hides one of his guns, in a cardboard box under some VHS
tapes. She once found photos of naked women in there too.
"Breasts and vagina," she says, pinching Stephanie's arm until
she winces. "I swear to God!"

"What are you guys talking about?"

It's someone else's voice this time, someone who's not us.
We look around in alarm, gripping onto the monkey bars so
that we don't slide off. It's Katrina, staring up from the ground.
"Can I come up too?" she says, curling her fingers over the
ladder.

"Sure," Stephanie says, still rubbing her arm. But Mariela
swings a leg back and forth so that Katrina has to back away
to avoid getting hit in the face by her flip-flop.

"Sorry," Mariela says. "Siberian tigers only."

(It sounds scary when she says it out loud like that—like
it's a secret she's not afraid of sharing. Something special
that's ours and no one else's.)

Katrina flips her hair over her shoulders, the same way as
the fifth-grade girls. "Who cares," she says. "You're a bunch
of kindergarten babies anyway."

As she walks away, Mariela shouts after her: "If you don't
start minding your own business, Katrina, I'm going to give
your name to the FARC!"

Later, filling her tray with french fries, Mariela says that
she doesn't care that Katrina's father was killed by the Ameri-
cans. No, she isn't sorry one bit. Men like him deserve it.

Wait, you didn't know about him? Oh, everybody knew. Are you saying you *didn't* know? He got gunned down by the CIA, just like Escobar, running for his life on the rooftop. Where have you been living these past few weeks—on Mars? Don't you know anything about what's going on in this country; can't you see for yourself what it's really like? Picking at her tiny cup of Alpinito yogurt, Stephanie asks, "What's the FARC?" but Mariela just frowns and doesn't answer.

You know what we should do, Mariela says. We should come to her father's ranch in the countryside. Come on the weekend; come *this* weekend! Remember her birthday parties in kindergarten? The way she invited every single person in the class? Everybody came; don't you remember? She scans our faces, touches our elbows, voice rising. Remember the swimming pool? Remember Carlitos? Baloo? Candy Bird?

We shake our heads and back away. Dig holes in the ground with our shoes. We don't remember. We can't get permission. We can't come; this weekend we're busy. She quickly looks away, pulling her fingers into a fist, mouth twisting like she's just bitten into an extra-sour piece of mango.

That afternoon she can't stop rushing us along. She pulls us past the open cage doors, points out the failed electric fence. "Look out," she whispers, "here they come!" There's the slaughtered security guards, the smashed-up army jeep, the trembling pond water. We're going to have to run for our lives. We're going to have to be extremely sly and sneaky if we want to have any chance of surviving at all. And as her eyes dart everywhere, we turn in circles, trying our best to see the same thing that she can—the danger all around us. As she ducks and crawls, throwing her arms fearfully over her head, we can't help but nervously glance over our shoulders. We search the sky, scan the football field, strain our eyes. We look everywhere, as though there's truly something out there that we need to watch for, and if we just stare long and hard enough we'll be able to see it—but of course we never do.

And then there's the morning that we come into the classroom and Mariela's desk has been moved. She's now next to Stephanie and in front of Betsy and La Flaca—Penelope's old spot. It's like looking into a mirror that shows an old reflection, except the person who's supposed to be there isn't. Mariela sits there calmly, hands folded on the wooden surface.

"Ms. Simón said it was fine," she says. "She gave me permission."

We stand there until Ms. Simón tells us it's time to take our seats now, please. We slide off our backpacks. Fiddle with our sweatpants strings, twist the scrunchies on our wrists.

It's time for News Sharing. Álvaro's brought an article about how the oldest tree in the Cali city center is getting cut down, because the politicians want to build a parking lot, or maybe a new office building. Sebastián has a story about the most recent soccer game, as usual. And then La Flaca surprises us by raising her hand.

"I'm moving to New York," she says. "In January." Her eyes are fixed on Ms. Simón's face as she speaks. "My grandma wants me to go to boarding school there."

Stephanie starts coughing, like she's swallowed too much water. Ms. Simón says that even though that's not official news, it's still good of her to share—we'll certainly all miss her.

As La Flaca lowers her arm, Stephanie leans over. "Since when did you know?" she whispers, and when La Flaca doesn't answer she waves her hand frantically around her desk, as though swirling the air will be enough to get an answer from her. "Since when, Flaca?"

La Flaca folds her fingers into fists and stares straight ahead.

It's Katrina's turn now: Last Saturday she went to the christening party for the mayor's new baby—he rented out the entire Club Campestre and she and her family were personally invited. She's talking about tasting her mother's champagne when Mariela leans toward us.

"I have news to share too," she whispers. She takes a newspaper clipping out of her notebook and smooths it out across her desk.

Now that she's sitting so close, it's as easy as anything for us to see it. It's a photo from the nightclub section, a dark room filled with people. Mr. B. is dancing on a tabletop, his face bright red, his blond hair a shocking flash in the darkness. He's surrounded by women in skimpy dresses, bare shoulders, and exposed backs, pale as ghosts. None are facing the camera, but we can all tell without saying it out loud: Ms. Simón is not one of them.

"See what I mean?" Mariela says. "Somebody has to tell her."

We just stare.

"It's the truth," Mariela says. "It's important that she sees it."

"Anyone else?" Ms. Simón says, and Mariela immediately raises her hand.

It's Stephanie who does it. She leans over and yanks the newspaper clipping off Mariela's desk. Crumples it in her hand before passing it to Betsy, who shoves it deep inside her pencil case. Mariela doesn't say anything, just stares at us, eyes growing wide.

"Mariela?" Ms. Simón says, frowning, but Mariela still doesn't speak, doesn't even shake her head, just stays in her seat as if frozen. Katrina raises her hand and says she still has photos to show from the party, if no one else brought anything to share.

"That's fine," Ms. Simón says, still frowning. She can show them tomorrow—it's time for geography now. "Everybody, please take out your puzzles; spread the pieces out across your desk."

Boxes rattle as they're pulled out of backpacks—Sebastián spills half of his pieces on the floor, Katrina's already picking out her edges. But Stephanie and Mariela still don't move; they remain frozen in their chairs, looking down at their laps.

During recess we play Hindenburg. Standing by the monkey bars, Mariela gives the directions: adjusting an arm here, a leg there, referring to her library copy of *DISASTER! The Hindenburg Story* when needed. La Flaca the stewardess is pushing the drink cart. Betsy is a passenger by the window. Stephanie is the famous acrobat who breaks his ankle rolling to safety but whose dog burns alive in the wreckage. There are no other survivors.

When it's time to move into position, though, Stephanie crosses her arms over her chest. "No," she says.

"Sorry," Mariela says, not even glancing over. "The dog dies. Stick your arms out," she says, tapping La Flaca's wrists.

"I'm not leaving without my dog."

In one swift motion, Mariela turns and picks the library book off the ground, flipping toward the glossary in the back.

"Ulla the Alsatian," she says. "Brought all the way from Germany as a gift for your children. Killed in the crash." She places the book back down and wipes her hands off on the back of her shorts, as though they've suddenly become sticky.

Stephanie looks up at the sky.

"Maybe," Betsy says, so quietly that it's hard to hear, "the dog is in the luggage." She pauses, saying the next part as fast as possible: "Maybe that's how she survives."

Mariela's shaking her head. "No." She's moved on to Betsy now, directing her into the passenger seat, where she'll sit and wait to be burned alive. "That's not how it happens. We have to do what's true. Don't forget your doll," she says to Betsy.

Do you die right away when a plane crashes? At what point do you understand what's happening? Is it the rattling of the overhead bins, the roar of the engines, the screams of the other passengers? What does it feel like, what are you thinking, how can we ever imagine?

Stephanie says, "It's just a stick."

Mariela pauses, her hand still resting on Betsy's arm. Betsy takes a step to the side so that they're no longer touching.

"You're pretending," Stephanie says. "It doesn't mean anything. It's a stupid game for babies."

She's still craning her neck back, looking at the sky. Betsy lets the stick fall to the ground. Mariela tugs her braid over her shoulder and brushes it against her lips.

This time it's La Flaca who speaks. "You know," she says, "it's gross when you do that."

"Do what?" Mariela says, but her hand freezes.

"That," La Flaca says. Stephanie starts swinging her leg, kicking the side of the monkey bar ladder, the metal ringing out like a bell. "It's really gross," La Flaca repeats, "when you do that."

Mariela looks at Betsy, but she's staring at the stick on the ground as though there's nothing else in the world she'd rather look at. Mariela traces her braid slowly against her teeth. "Well," she says. "So what?"

"It's true," Stephanie says. "You're always chewing your hair."

"Yeah," La Flaca says, her voice rising. "It's disgusting."

Betsy still doesn't say anything, and Mariela just stands there.

"And you know what else?" La Flaca says. "You better watch it with those Doritos. If you're not careful, we're going to have to start calling you Fatty."

"Fatty!" Stephanie cries out, as if delighted. Even Betsy smiles.

Mariela still hasn't spoken. Recess Monitor Adriana hovers by the brick wall in the distance, hands shading her eyes as she scans the playground. Everything must seem safe. The boys score a goal on the football field, cheers erupting like explosions. The fifth-grade girls sit on the grass, tilting their heads back so that their hair tumbles down like a waterfall.

Except this time it's not them who are staring. It's us:

Stephanie, La Flaca, Betsy, all of us here together. Standing here and watching, until Mariela finally pulls the braid away from her mouth and lets it drop.

"Time to get ready," she says as she walks away, leaving us alone to deal with it, all of it, for the rest of our lives.

Honey Bunny

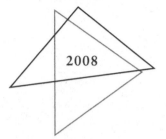

2008

NEW YORK, NEW YORK

He comes up to her on the dance floor. "Nice purse," he says almost immediately.

"Nice Charlie Brown sweater," she says. She actually means it too. She glimpsed him at the bar earlier, talking to his friends, and the black zigzag stripe running around his torso had made her smile, despite herself, into her cosmopolitan.

His name is Tony. He's a law student at NYU, originally from Maine, now living in Williamsburg. "So where are you from?" he asks as he passes the bartender his credit card.

She says it as the bass drops and the crowd of dancers lets out a cheer.

"You mean, like, Columbia University?" he shouts.

"Sure," she says. Her purse tonight is made of striped An-

dean cloth, yellow and red, with blue tassels. It's big and bulky.
People keep brushing up against it as they crowd toward the
bar.

"What was your name, again?" he asks.

She looks down at her nails, the perfectly curved white tips
of her French manicure. He keeps smiling, as if waiting for
her to go on. Instead she leans in close and whispers into his
ear, using as much hot breath as possible: "I've got some goodies, if you're interested?"

They stumble outside four hours later, blinking in the watery light like woodland creatures emerging from hibernation.
Eventually he runs his fingers through his hair and says, "You
taking the A train?"

As the subway car pulls out of the station with a groan, he
turns to her. "You have something on your nose," he says. He
reaches out, fingers fluttering by her nostrils like a blurry
peach moth, and she ducks.

"There's no need for that," she says, taking out a folded
square of toilet paper. The baggie is in the ladies' room at the
club, licked clean and crumpled, crammed in the disposal can
for sanitary pads.

"Sorry," he says, not sounding that upset. He crosses his
legs and wraps his fingers around his kneecap, as if cuddling
it. The wrist poking out of his jacket is still a New York win-
ter pale.

She dabs the toilet paper against her nostrils, sniffing
loudly. Sitting across from them is a group of three girls.
They're wearing flower-patterned dresses, shiny American
Apparel leggings, long dangly earrings, brown oxfords. One
girl is leaning forward with her head bowed, cradling a giant

green backpack in her lap like a baby. Without staring at the girls too directly, she can tell that their eyeliner isn't smudged, their hair is smooth and straightened, their concealer still effectively hiding any blemishes on their upper jawlines. She swallows and rubs the toilet paper against her nose even harder, letting out a cough for good measure.

"So what are your plans for today?" Tony says, reaching for an untied shoelace. Hours earlier, she mistook it for a long black worm drowning in a puddle as they stood smoking outside the club entrance.

She almost says, *Watch porn and masturbate,* but instead answers, "Just chilling, I guess." Was it a thick clump, clinging to her nostril hairs? A delicate crust around the rims? Did she look like the Dormouse, waking up with a start after falling asleep in the sugar bowl at the Mad Hatter's tea party?

"I might cook some steak, if I go to the store." His eyes are bloodshot, but his pale skin is clear.

"Cool," she says, furiously digging in her nose as deep as she can. One of the girls, the one with perfectly straight bangs, is staring at her, or maybe she's just looking vacantly at the subway map behind her head.

"Maybe some chili con carne. Chili with flesh." He laughs.

Carne means "meat," but she doesn't correct him. She's about to tell him that sounds good when something thin peels away from her nostril wall. It makes a faint crackling sound beneath her fingernail. She tries to stay calm as she yanks it out, ripping some nose hairs, cupping it in her palms as her eyes water. She can hear the girls' voices in her head, sees their mouths forming Os and eyes bulging as they stare and nudge each other: OMG, *look at her, she's totally Michael Jackson–ing!*

It's a dry leaf. Disintegrating in her hand, crumbling into thin brown flakes. She can suddenly feel the stem, shoved high up her nasal cavity, scratchy and tickling. She smashes her nose against her cardigan sleeve and blows hard.

"Whoa!" Tony says. The girl with the green backpack looks up, and one of her friends makes a noise that could either be a cough or a choked laugh.

She squeezes the leaf bits tightly in her fist and drops them onto the floor, wiping her hand off on her bare leg. For a second, she thinks she hears giggling, but when she looks up, the girls haven't moved. She makes eye contact with the backpack girl, who raises her eyebrows and pulls her lips inward, the classic American expression of feigning indifference.

As the subway car slowly whines to a stop she says, "This is me," at the same moment that Tony says, "So, I'll see you around?"

She's calling Paco the second she steps into her apartment. When his voicemail beeps, she's already speaking, her recording starting in midsentence: "—some nerve. I don't know what you're doing, but that's some serious bullshit, man. That shit is not okay. And I know that you know what I'm talking about, so please don't bother to pretend otherwise." She likes the way her voice sounds as she moves around the kitchen, picking up and putting down dirty glasses streaked with the grainy smears of ancient smoothies. She can hear New York in her voice, the years of arguing with Brooklyn dealers, the smirking college boys at Upper West Side house parties. Her head suddenly fills with an image of her grandmother, the way she'd lean against the kitchen doorframe back home, brow furrowed as she reprimanded Nellie with kind, expansive hand gestures: *I just don't understand, you see. What is so hard about following the menu that I specifically wrote up for you? Do you think you could maybe explain that to me?*

She hangs up and tosses her cellphone onto a puppy-shaped pillow on the floor. Paco is Guatemalan, so every once in a while when speaking to him she'll slyly throw in the odd Spanish word or two, a curse word or even a *dicho,* just to show that yeah, okay, she's lived in New York for what, fifteen years now, but she still knows how to conjugate verbs, knows which nouns are feminine versus masculine. She's not like those Bogotanos she keeps meeting at warehouse raves, those Barranquillan trust fund babies or Caleña sugarcane plantation heirs, who spent their whole lives in Houston or Miami and now try to pretend they're bicultural-bilingual when she knows the truth, that they're no better than any common gringo. (Something that she herself most definitely is not. No way. Not a chance. *Gringo* is a word she's always hated, fat and puffy and pastry-shaped in her mouth.) "I'm not the cow that shits the most," she'll say to Paco on the phone, keeping her voice as casual as possible, hands shaking with excitement, or "I'm not the kind of girl who gives away papaya, if you know what I mean." This one time, against her better judgment, she even told him her childhood nickname, dropping it in casually as though it was nothing, meaningless. "You can call me 'Flakis,' if you want," she said to him in

Spanish, laughing too hard, almost hysterically. " 'La Flaca' is a bit of a mouthful, I know!"

Paco still calls her by her full name, though—the one she's used since moving to New York. And he never responds to her in Spanish, only English. It makes her feel strange. Once while on the phone, she abruptly hung up on him, and when he called back she pretended she'd lost the signal.

She lets herself flop forward onto the bed. Her fashion history class isn't until two P.M. At this point, she usually takes a clonazepam and puts on a YouTube video of a girl showing off what's in her bag or applying concealer to hide her acne. Either that or power through—keep the party going, as Tony said earlier, eyes fixed on her purse as she rapidly zipped it open—take an Adderall and finish her reading, maybe even sketch out some dress designs, post on her blog. Instead she just lies there with her eyes closed, fingers tugging gently at her hair.

Paco. Most likely he'd have been in his overcrowded apartment in Queens, a dying potted plant in the middle of the table. There must have been a dead insect somewhere too, dangling from a dry leaf or something, Paco busy in front of his scales—pouring out, weighing, sorting, maybe even sniffing from time to time, his son crying in the bedroom. He must have knocked the plant with his elbow. Or maybe his kid snuck in while Paco was in the bathroom and started messing around, shaking the plant until its leaves fell off, giggling maniacally. Did that make sense? Is that how it could have happened? Did Paco have to measure it into baggies, or did they arrive as is, neatly lined up in suitcases? Did they come in bulky FedEx packages, bundled in brown packing tape and

bubble wrap? In beat-up cardboard boxes? In secret compartments of carry-on athletic bags?

She rolls over and opens the desk drawer. There they are.
Snuggling in the yellow envelope he handed to her in the
Whole Foods parking lot. What once were five now are three.
Lined up like stuffed animals, waiting for their turn to be
picked up and held. She can't help smiling as she remembers
the stuffed-animal sleeping schedule she made when she was
little. It took up at least two pages in her purple Barbie diary,
three weeks' worth of plush creatures, a different one every
night so that they could all get a turn. Her favorites were Per-
rito, his Labrador tail sticking out of his candy cane pants,
hand-sewn by Leticia; Chinchilla, with the purple silk ribbon
tied tightly around his neck; and Honey Bunny, gray-eared
and floppy, smelling faintly of mothballs.

She reaches into the envelope, pulls out a baggie, and automatically starts rubbing it between her thumb and middle finger, breaking up the chunks inside. Just like she learned to do
in boarding school upstate. She opens the baggie slowly, but
of course there's nothing there that's out of the ordinary. Of
course.

From where she's lying, if she slides her eyeballs as far to
the left as possible, she can see it: the orange suitcase, sitting
placidly on top of her armoire, under the extra sheets and
towels she never uses.

The smell hits her hard: the steam of chicken broth bubbling on the stove, warm and salty.

She abruptly shoves the baggie back into the envelope and
slams the desk drawer shut. Lies down on the bed, eyes closed

and palms pressing against her temples. The back of her
throat is still dripping.

She's in the elevator going up to her friend's apartment. The
doors close behind her as she unzips her purse with one hand,
reaching the other deep inside, her fingers nimbly detecting
the sparkly unicorn key chain. The keys rattle slightly as she
pulls them out. Her purse today is covered in yawning jaguars,
purple and orange and pink, their stitched bodies stretching
and leaping across the black cloth background.

As her hand plunges back inside for the baggie, she imagines raging-hot infrared vision blasting from her fingertips,
zooming in on the required materials with the expertise of
Luke Skywalker's computer detecting the Death Star. All
forces ready! Mission accomplished! There it is, hidden in the
tiny side pocket, next to her lipstick and lighter. Wrapped in a
thin square of toilet paper. She loves keeping it tucked away
like that, curled up in the darkness like an animal in a cave,
taking it with her everywhere she goes, without anybody having any idea that it's there. As she pulls it out, the fluttering in
her chest moves down to her stomach.

She's already poking the key inside the baggie when she
sees it. Half-buried in the powder, but unmistakable.

An insect wing. Brown and translucent. Oval-shaped. Faint
veins like the underside of a decayed leaf. Like the wings that
dangled from the orange flyswatters wielded by the maids
back home. What were their names again? Nellie and Rosa.
Pastora and Leticia. They'd shake the dead insects into the

tanks of tropical fish while she watched, pressing her nose against the glass. The fish would rush toward the surface, mouths plopping open and shut. It got to be so that whenever anybody picked up a flyswatter the fish would go crazy, eyes bulging as they clustered at the surface, frothing the water with their desperate hunger.

The elevator dings and her hand shoots forward, pressing hard on the CLOSE button. She pulls out the wing and throws it on the floor, jamming the baggie and keys back into her purse. Before letting the door open again and stepping outside, she looks down at the shiny elevator floor. All she sees is a blurry reflection of her high heels, the ones she likes to think of as her Beyoncé shoes. It looks as if she is swimming on the opposite side of a mirror, upside down, shoes barely skimming the surface, on the verge of breaking through to the air above.

At the party, whenever she introduces herself, she makes sure to pronounce her name with an American accent (her full name, of course—not her childhood nickname. She would never refer to herself as anything so silly as that). Two girls from the New School admire her purse, touching the jaguars' stripes. "It's so cute," the one with braided pigtails says. "Where did you get it?"

"I'm not sure," she says. "It was a gift."

She excuses herself to go to the bathroom.

She doesn't mention it to Paco. Not the wrinkled flower petal at the bottom of the third baggie, found as she was crouching behind a tree in Central Park, poking her spit-dampened pinkie finger in for the very last crumbs. Not the Communion wafer in the fourth, sticking out like a sundae decoration. (She remembers the visiting Jesuit priests, bringing tiny plastic bags filled with these bland white disks as gifts, how she would steal them to eat in her room with orange marmalade and feed them unblessed to her dolls, until her grandmother caught her and, with a shaming frown, put an end to the sacrament.) The fifth one she poured out onto a dinner plate so that she could use her eyebrow tweezers to pick out the crumbling fragments of moss and bark.

She doesn't bring it up—not a word as she sits in Paco's Honda, her back ramrod straight, squeezing the jaguar purse between her knees, resisting the urge to look for split ends in her hair that she can break off with her teeth. Paco's wife is driving them around the Whole Foods parking garage while he digs into his bag in the front seat. His son is sitting next to her, backpack tucked between his legs. His Spider-Man shirt has a white stain on the front that might be toothpaste, and his eyes are fixed on his Game Boy, mushrooms and turtles flying across the screen.

"So," she says to Paco's son. (Did he go by Paco too? Or was it Junior?) "Where do you want to go to college? Like, when you grow up?"

"What's that?" he says, eyes still on the Game Boy.

She doesn't ask him any more questions.

"Here you go, *mija*," Paco says, turning around and passing her the yellow envelope. She leans forward and shoves the fistful of bills into his hands. She had it all counted out fifteen minutes before they were supposed to meet, her H&M heels clicking against the concrete floor as she paced.

"I have some Adderall too, if you're out," he says. "Oxy-Contin. Molly." He lists the names like World Cup team members.

"That's okay." Now that she has the envelope, all she wants is to get out of the car as soon as possible. He hasn't brought up her voicemail yet, but if he does she has a plan: She'll just say, "Oh, ha-ha, the stuff just wasn't as strong as last time. No big deal, it happens." If only she could force the door open with her shoulder and roll across the parking garage floor like an action hero, chin tucked into her chest and arms wrapped around her torso, hugging the envelope close. She has to take a deep breath to stop herself from breaking into a wide grin at the thought. Beside her, Paco's son lets out a lusty yawn.

"It was good to hear from you," Paco says as his wife pulls into a parking spot that says CUSTOMERS ONLY. "It'd been a while—I was worried!" He laughs as his wife twists around, unlocking the back door.

She opens her mouth to answer him in Spanish, but the words don't come, her tongue thick and helpless, hesitating against her teeth. So she has to say it in English instead, slowly: "You don't ever have to worry about me."

When she gets out she doesn't shut the car door hard enough, so Paco's wife has to rap on the window and signal for her to do it again. She waits until they've turned the corner before ducking behind a concrete pillar. Her fingernails are too shredded, so she rips the envelope open with her teeth.

Checking one bag is enough. This time there's a tiny gray drumstick bone, smothered in powder, as if ready to be dropped into spitting-hot frying oil.

It's easy to identify the feeling as she seals the baggie and shoves it back into the envelope. It's an unmistakable sense of relief.

She crawls into bed that night with numb lips, her body shivering, dressed in her lime-green miniskirt and ballerina flats. The apartment has smelled like a smoky wood fire for two days now, with the faint undertone of stale powdered milk. She let number six flutter away on the subway tracks (the blast of air from the incoming train made it dance around like a transparent butterfly); number seven, half-full, hibernates for now in her purse, jaguars again.

"You got it from where?" one of her classmates said at the restaurant. "Wait, did you go there on vacation? You're so brave!"

"I went to Cartagena last year," another one said as the waiter brought a second bottle of wine to the table. "Everyone there was *so* friendly."

She reaches for her laptop, pulls it across the mattress until it bumps against her chin. Instead of watching a makeup tutorial, though, she starts surfing Google Earth. She can't remember the name of the street she grew up on, but she manages to find the international private school she attended from kindergarten to third grade. There are hardly any blue dots on the screen linking to Street View photographs, so the tiny orange Google man keeps refusing to be dragged onto the map, rushing stubbornly back to the compass again and again. She clicks on the school website link and scrolls through pages of photos of three-walled classrooms, the kiosks with palm-thatched roofs, gymnasium murals of floating peace signs and multicolored citizens holding hands. It makes her dizzy. It's the same feeling she gets when she passes Mexican families on the street, speaking rapid slang-filled Spanish, or when Puerto Rican construction workers catcall her with words she doesn't recognize, as if they are speaking to her from a parallel universe, one she should understand but just doesn't. The feeling gets stronger with every photograph she clicks through, the parallel reality brushing up against her, sleazily pressing its weight against her torso, breathing wetly in her ear.

She drags the cursor across the screen, clicking on whatever pitiful scattering of dots she can find. It makes her feel as though she is surveying an apocalyptic wasteland, searching for the tiniest signs of life. She finds the traffic light where the black man from the coast sold mango Popsicles and tiny bags of salt out of a Styrofoam plastic cooler, and when the school bus stopped, the kids would lean out the windows to hand him five-hundred-peso coins. She finds the metal gate of the Jewish country club, where her grandmother would take her on weekends for tennis games on red clay courts, swimming lessons, lunches of grilled cheese sandwiches brought by a scraggly-haired waitress she secretly called Mafalda, after the comic book character. She finds the nature park filled with lagoons and herons and cicada-covered trees, where she would walk her grandmother's poodle in circles, the bodyguard and chauffeur sweating under the acacia and ceiba trees at the entrance, eyes never leaving her.

And then she finds a photo of a gray stone wall with shards

of glass jutting along the top and an enormous automatic gate. The country house of one of her classmates. A giant ranch on the city's edge. She zooms in. She went there in kindergarten once for a birthday party—she and her classmates gathered at the airport to take the short helicopter ride. They stayed all day: swimming in an enormous blue-tiled pool, chasing one another around angel statues and marble fountains. There were colorful balloons tied to a swing set and charred-black hot dogs grilled over a barbecue pit. And then there were the animals: a wooden birdhouse full of macaws and peacocks, a parrot that could recite the names of all the players on the national soccer team, a spider monkey that could kick a football, and a lion that slept in its iron cage all afternoon, no matter how loudly they shouted at the gardener to let them pet it. And the rabbits, snuggling in their metal hutch with their nests of knotted white fur, noses nervously quivering. She and her friends pushed blades of grass in between the bars for them to nibble on, calling out, "Hey, little guy, sweet little thing," wiggling their fingers at the blinking pink eyes.

At one point, the birthday girl (Melissa? María?) came up to her. "If we stand under the drainpipe together," she whispered, "and sing a song to Candy Bird, he'll come visit us." So they stood by the jacaranda bushes, arms linked and faces turned upward, singing the same verse over and over: "Candy Bird, Candy Bird, come see me." And then, as if by magic, candy started raining down from the sky. It hit them on the forehead and cheekbones: coffee-flavored caramels and Milo malt balls, Jet chocolate bars and Bon Bon Bum lollipops, purple packets of Sparkies and dark green Bombón Supercocos. At the sight of the candy everyone started screaming and ran over, scrambling and diving in the grass, clods of dirt flying. It was like a piñata but better—you couldn't see where it was coming from. She hadn't hesitated to join in, elbowing others out of the way and scooping up, with grim-faced determination, as much candy as she could carry.

She knows now, of course, that it must have been one of the maids, or maybe the gardeners or chauffeurs, ordered to hide behind a curtain upstairs and throw candy out the window for the guests' amusement. How long had they waited? Standing there and watching the children scream and fight for sweets.

She reaches for her computer cord on the floor, the battery icon now a thin red line. By keeping her eyes fixed on the screen, she avoids the possibility of glimpsing the orange suitcase, still resting on top of the armoire.

No matter how many times she zooms in on Google Earth, though, the house remains a blur. All she can see are the fuzzy smears of the mango trees on the other side of the wall and the light glinting off the jagged glass.

She's been waiting for twenty minutes when Paco finally arrives. He's on foot this time, wearing a ragged orange shirt with a diamond-shape sweat stain on his chest, the faint shadow of a mustache on his upper lip. They've never stood this close to each other before. Under the fluorescent parking-lot lights, she sees for the first time how pockmarked his skin is, a mess of lines and cracks, as though someone had cut up his face with a pair of blunt scissors and glued it messily back together. She keeps her eyes lowered as she hands over the money.

"Actually," she says after he passes her the envelope, "just wondering. Any chance that you—"

As soon as he nods, she excuses herself to run to the ATM again. *Would you like to view your current account balance before proceeding?* the machine asks, and she jams her thumb against the NO button again and again until she gets to the withdrawal screen.

"Sorry I was late," he says, handing over a second envelope. "I had a football game."

"Don't you mean soccer?" Her voice echoes off the concrete parking lot ceiling. He raises his eyebrows as she sticks both envelopes in her purse.

"Have a good night, *mija*."

She's still struggling to get the zipper shut as he walks away. When she finally looks up, she catches a glimpse of herself in a nearby car window, mouth twisting as if tasting something bitter.

For number eleven, she uses a sieve to separate out the dry white cracker crumbs. Number twelve requires the tweezers again, to pick out the thin blades of grass. Somewhere in the apartment, her cellphone buzzes with an incoming text message, but she doesn't look up. Her two front teeth keep scraping nervously across her lower lip, peeling off the dead skin.

"Damn Communists," she says in her grandmother's voice, knocking her forehead against the laptop screen as she leans in too close. "Why forgive? Why forget?" Google's image search shows rows of eucalyptus trees, fields of sugarcane stretching like the sea (that rotten egg smell from the fertilizer!). Message boards describe visits tourists can take to coca laboratories hidden in the jungle; Wikipedia lists the departments where most of the cultivation takes place: Putumayo and Caquetá, Meta and Guaviare. YouTube has a documentary about how to set up your own lab. Key ingredients are gasoline and hydrochloric acid; helpful materials include yellow plastic gloves, metal buckets, and black garbage bags full of coca leaves, dark and light green like limes, not a single one brown or withered.

Hours later, she finally checks the phone: "How's it going? XO." The number isn't saved in her contacts. It takes her a second to remember the Charlie Brown sweater, yellow with a thick jagged black line wrapping around a stomach. She lets the phone fall with a loud clatter, and the protective pink case bounces along the floor.

Charred kernels of grilled corn, burnt black and stiff. Squishy papaya seeds, moist and fresh. The time she told her grandmother, "The fish are all assassinated," assuming it was synonymous with dead, thanks to the newspapers and TV. The cracked sidewalks. The men puckering their lips and making wet kissing sounds. The accordion music blasting from the maids' rooms at the back of the house. "Hurry up," she says to the servants setting the tables, bringing out the boiled eggs spread over toast for breakfast. "What's a paramilitary?" she asks on the playground, arms aching as she hangs from the swing set. "Don't say 'war,'" she lectures the orange suitcase, which eyes her nervously. "Say 'situation.' Say 'insecurity.' Don't say 'kidnapped'—say 'forcibly detained.'"

She keeps Googling, clicking, one news article after another. The statistic for forced disappearances is estimated at over fifty thousand—no, sixty thousand—some articles say over seventy thousand. The articles have titles like "A Nightmare with No End"; "Colombia's Unknown Tragedies"; "In Search of Justice." Environmental activists, labor unionists, indigenous leaders, young men. Even teenage girls, straight out of their own homes. It makes her think of fables the maids used to tell her: the *paisa* farmer who went to heaven, *la patasola* and *la llorona*. Ghosts who would come knocking on your door, ringing on your bell, long dead souls with scarred faces, wandering the country with no name and no past. If you unlocked the door for them, they would wrap their hands around your wrist and lead you away, make you vanish into thin air, disappear without a trace. If you were unlucky, no one would even remember your name: your real one, the one that everyone called you.

The seventeenth one she shoves into Tony's hand on the dance floor, not even bothering with the tiny square of toilet paper. She leans against the wall as she waits for him to come back, pulling strands of hair into her mouth as the DJ starts playing a remix of an English Shakira song. She fingers the clumps of rabbit fur in her purse, dragged out of the baggie in long white strands, thick and knotted as if they've been tangled in cage wire for days. She sucks on the tip of her ponytail, brushing it against her lips, a strangely familiar gesture—familiar of what? What does this remind her of; what is she trying to remember?

Just then a hand reaches out and yanks the hair out of her mouth. Saliva streaks across her cheek as though dabbed there by a sloppy paintbrush. Before she can cry out or even protest, Tony speaks close to her ear. "Don't do that," he says. "It's gross."

Her face freezes into what she hopes is a smile. "What?"

He places a hand on the small of her back. "It's really gross," he repeats, "when you do that."

She can't move, can't turn her head, the spit on her face growing cold. Tony has to guide her into the dancing crowd, pulling her by the wrist. Under the flashing strobe lights, his cheeks glow blue, as smooth as a skating rink.

"So," he shouts, loud enough to be sure she can hear him over the booming music, "did your family, like, know Pablo Escobar?"

She stuffs the last yellow envelope into the trash, cramming it down as deep as it will go, the paper crinkling like an accordion. Cradling the last few baggies in her arms, she heads to the bathroom. Leaning over the toilet bowl, she hesitates. Presses her forehead against the ceramic lid.

She heads back to her bedroom instead, where she grabs her purses off the floor. Her eyes flick to the top of the armoire.

She yanks the orange suitcase down with a clatter. Its plastic surface is dotted with holes made by a customs agent's drill at JFK, fifteen years ago. She was too young for the strip search, but old enough to be taken aside into the interrogation room. ("So, do your parents like to party?" the agents asked. "Ever help them out?") The first latch is a little creaky, but the second flips open with no problem. She knows that the can of ChocoListo cocoa powder won't be there (they poured it out on the table, combing through it with their rubber gloves), nor the pair of Nike soccer cleats (they cut off the rubber tops, searching for hidden compartments).

Everything else, though—it's still there. The wallet made out of a milk carton, a gift from her bodyguard, thrust into her hands before she climbed into the car to be driven away to the airport, clutching her grandmother's purses in her lap. The wooden toucan that used to sit in the middle of the dining room table, covered in long white scratches. She pulls out the pink striped alpaca poncho, the folder of papers the lawyers gave her, full of instructions on how to access her trust fund. American books, foreign books, stories about anywhere else: *Anne Frank: The Diary of a Young Girl, A Day in the Life of the Siberian Tiger.* Pink and purple envelopes, pen pal letters covered in glittery Lisa Frank stickers: *Dear Flaca: I miss you already! How's the big city? Did you know Betsy is moving to Washington, D.C.? When are you coming back to visit?*

When there's only one item left, she pauses. There's no sign of them—no candy cane pants, no purple silk ribbon, no droopy ears smelling of mothballs. Her hand trembling, she reaches for the battered brown square cardboard box sitting in the middle of the suitcase's gaping orange mouth. Third-grade geography class. When she holds it close to her ear and shakes it, she can hear the pieces rattling around inside.

She pours them out onto the floor and gets to work. They are so flattened that there's no satisfying "click" when they connect. The wrinkled cardboard reminds her of her grandmother's hands, the way they squeezed her shoulders before gently pushing her toward the departure gate. She builds the central mountain ranges first, then the bordering coast, the northern desert, the southern jungle, the eastern plains. Slowly but surely, the shape becomes clear. The snout of Guajira, sniffing the Caribbean; the square tail of Amazonas, poking into Brazil. Cities make up the organs: the Bogotá heart, the lungs of Medellín and Bucaramanga, the kidneys of Cali and Popayán. Andean mountains ripple like fur, rivers and highways run like veins.

In the end, though, one of the biggest pieces is missing— the department of Meta. The creature is left with a hole at the center of its body, an open wound exposing the floor tiles beneath. She settles back on her heels and looks down.

She'd completely forgotten that more than half of Colombia was jungle.

"Come here, you," she says. "Sweet little things. I won't hurt you—I promise!"

They nuzzle close, warm and soft in her hands as she brings them toward her face. The plastic crinkles when she squeezes them too tightly, so instead she holds them carefully, delicately. She lies down, cradling them against her cheek, smelling their sweet familiar scent, as recognizable and comforting as mothballs. Never mind how much her eyes burn, or her nose itches, or the back of her throat goes numb. She curls up into a fetal position, the wooden toucan poking into her thigh, the puzzle pieces pressing against her arm, the purses softly bunched up under her head. The unfinished country is underneath her as she pulls them close, holding them tenderly, whispering sweet nothings. She starts with English—sweetie pie, candy bird, honey bunny—before moving on to half-remembered Spanish: *corazón, querida, mija.*

She closes her eyes.

It's not the world's most comfortable nest.

But it's a start.

The Tourists

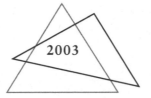

2003

CAUCA

Who's coming to the Montoyas' party? A lot of people; it's going to be a big success: the Mendozas and the Vasquezes, the Lorenzos and the Smiths. The maids drag the white plastic chairs into the yard, forming half circles beneath the mango tree and around the barbecue pit. The gardeners carry out the big wooden table, a security guard following closely behind with a ruler to scrape off the white globs of dried candle wax, accumulated in thick layers from weeks of blackouts. The dogs yip excitedly, nipping at people's ankles, and behind the safety of their chicken wire cage the rabbits shuffle anxiously, scandalized by the noise. Inside the kitchen, staring out the window, one of the cooks says, "We really need to lock them up. Can you imagine Lola rolling in her poo and then licking Mrs. Smith's hand?"

The caterers have arrived; they're setting up. They're carrying wide metal trays filled with whitefish soaked in lemon juice, red peppers for the grill, raw bloody steaks and chicken breasts stabbed by forks. Nothing is extravagant, nothing is over-the-top, except for maybe the lobster claws on ice, the tins of caviar, and the oysters that the cooks are busily prying open with their special metal knives. Extravagance is not his style.

Here he comes. Folding the cuffs of his black shirt above his wrists so that a strip of pale skin shows, like a patch of exposed land on a jungle hillside. The skin on his face is smooth, not a trace of the plastic surgeon's knife. People rarely notice, but the three middle fingers of his right hand are little more than pink stumps, neatly aligned with the humble pinkie. "Looking good," he says to the blinking white Christmas lights hanging from the branches of the grapefruit tree. "Excellent," he says while strolling past the arts and crafts supplies set out for the children by the pool: crayons and candles and paper plates. "Go along now," he says to one of the many cats sitting on the drainpipe above the jacaranda bush, a distasteful expression behind its droopy whiskers. Who knows how many pets they have at this point? Just the other week he saw a turtle lumbering under the sofa in the living room, but when he got down on his knees to check there was nothing there, not even dust balls or coffee-flavored candy wrappers.

He wanders inside the house through the swinging patio

door, scratching the back of his neck. The maids have done a good job. The bookshelves have been dusted, the broken electric piano cleared away (a lizard got electrocuted deep inside its mechanical guts years ago and ever since it's refused to make a sound, not even when the cats frantically chase one another across the black and white keys). Considering that they only come out to this country ranch every few months, for Easter or holiday weekends, the house still feels fairly lived in: the living room fresh-smelling with the sharp scent of laundry powder, the lampshades shiny without a single dead moth smear, no cobwebs around the chandelier or shelves of VHS tapes.

"How's it going?" he says, knocking on the door to his daughter's room at the same time that he pushes it open. The room is deserted—the only sign of her presence is a stack of CD cases spilled all over the bed, next to some shredded packets of plantain chips. It's hard to restrain himself, this rare opportunity to intrude into her bedroom—normally the door is firmly locked, American bands screaming their angst-filled rage from her stereo on the other side. So he now finds his eyes flickering greedily, taking in one new poster after another hanging on the walls. The one of a mournful-eyed American singer with shaggy blond hair holding an acoustic guitar, that's definitely new; Snoopy dancing with a balloon, that's been up since she was in kindergarten and received it as a present at one of the epic birthday parties she hosted here for all her classmates. The closet doors are half-open; he can glimpse the shelves lined with stuffed animals that couldn't fit into the storage trunk in the hallway, Care Bears and shabby dogs and other beasts that were never loved enough to be guaranteed a spot at their main house in Cali. There are rows of plastic toys based on countless American cartoon shows, *Transformers* and *ThunderCats* and *The Real Ghostbusters*, stiff plastic bodies randomly positioned in a messy parade, silently poised with their daggers and ray guns, ready to leap into battle with invisible enemies at a moment's notice. Everything slowly gathering dust.

From where he's standing he can clearly see that the empty packets of plantain chips have been licked clean. Shaking his head, he picks them up between two fingers and drops them from the bed onto the floor where it'll be easier for a maid to sweep them up. That's when he sees it—the small ziplock baggie lying on a pillow, half-filled with bright red Jell-O powder—the kind of treat you can purchase from street children at traffic lights. He picks it up and shakes it, the powder accumulating at the bottom, except for the wet clumps clinging near the baggie's thin lips. He can already picture the garish stains across her front teeth and mouth, the demon-red color of her tongue flashing at the guests as she utters a sullen *hello*, the sticky finger smears on her shirt, running up and down the fabric as though a tiny animal with miniature bloody paws had danced all over her body. *Ave Maria*, the maids will say when they see her, closing their eyes in supplication. *Mariela, what were you thinking? What will your father say when you show up looking like that for his party?*

The automatic gate rumbles at the same time that he hears car wheels crunching on the gravel driveway. He puts the Jell-O baggie in his back pocket, tucked neatly beside his cellphone. After closing the door behind him, he pulls his right shirtsleeve down as far as it'll go, almost completely covering the wispy white scars snaking over the backs of his hands.

Here they come. Black and blue high heels clicking, jackets draped over arms, strands of thinning hair combed neatly back. The chauffeurs park the mud-splattered jeeps with Bogotá license plates under the fig trees; the bodyguards climb out and immediately cross their arms, already hovering in the background. He waits under the mango tree in the backyard. Smoke rises from the barbecue pit. The chefs grimly rotate sausages slashed with deep knife cuts over the fire, red peppers and onions impaled and sweating on wooden sticks.

"Hello, hello," he says in greeting. His right hand is hidden behind his back in a clenched fist, his left hand extended and welcoming, fingers spread wide.

Everyone arrives safely, happily. Nobody's been chased by the crazed spider monkey, the one the maids have nicknamed "Baloo" for the size of his black testicles, so impressively heavy that the housecleaners whisper among each other, *Now that's a real man, Linda, just what you need, someone to keep you satisfied,* before exploding into giggles. At the last big party (Two years ago? Three? Was it celebrating the successful Congress run, or hosting the visiting HSBC managers?), Baloo ran back and forth over the stone wall for hours, staring hungrily at the food, the tables, and the guests most of all (this was before the shards of glass were installed, before Uribe's successful presidential campaign based on vows to "restore national peace and security," before he started hearing the clicking sounds of recording instruments every time he lifted the phone). At one point, Baloo jumped down and stuck his head up Mrs. Smith's skirt, and her banshee screams caused the maids in the kitchen to raise their eyebrows at one another.

Thankfully there's been no sign of Baloo for months now—the fact that the security guard has been tossing his slimy orange and banana peels inside the forest, well away from the main house, has possibly helped. As a result, the party is going well, the conversation gliding along smoothly. The oil company executives and the mining company investors mingle easily with the expats from Belgium and members of the school board. No bottles of aguardiente or rum yet, it's still early, the sun casting hazy yellow light over the freshly mowed grass, the mosquitoes blessedly absent. Instead it's green glass bottles of chilled beer for the gentlemen, tall slender glasses of champagne for the ladies. The hired waitstaff stalk silently back and forth across the patio, black-and-white uniforms still free from wine splatters and crumbs. Everything is under control; everything is fine.

He doesn't see us, but we're watching.

We've been doing so for a while now. We didn't get any greetings, no gentle air kiss near the cheek, no firm pumping handshake, but that's okay, we don't take it personally, we don't mind. Instead we take our time, take things slow: There's no reason to rush, no reason to make things happen before they need to. We walk in slow circles around the barbecue pit, deeply inhaling the smell of the charcoal fire and the crackling chicken skin. We reach our hands tentatively into the glass bowls of peanuts; what a nice rattling sound they make when we stir our fingers. We take turns gently touching the beer bottles, admiring the streams of condensation running down their smooth glass bodies. No one makes eye contact; nobody pats us on the back or slings an arm around our shoulders. But we're not bothered. For now we're happy, watching the hummingbirds dart nervously among the orange flowerpots. Everything is so tasteful, nothing over-the-top—no helicopters landing in the football field, no spray-tanned models greased up and wrestling each other while the guests cheer them on. No one's slinging their arms around each other, singing classic Mexican corridos at the top of their lungs; no one's pulled a gun from their holster and started shooting wildly at the darkening sky. Nothing like that. The food is delicious, and everyone is having a wonderful time.

He loves it when parties are at this stage—the post-beginning and pre-middle, when no one has gotten too drunk or noticed who's been pointedly ignoring them. It means he can sneak away to the bathroom in his private bedroom, lock himself inside for up to fifteen minutes at a time, sometimes twenty. He sits on the bowl, chin resting in his hands, trousers sagging around his ankles. It's moments like these when it's impossible to ignore: how all over his body there are patches of skin now drooping where they used to be firm and taut. There are brown and purple spots all over his arms that definitely weren't there twenty years ago, and red moles on his upper shoulders he keeps mistaking for insect bites. This year too he suddenly found himself mentally adding secret descriptions to his friends' names: prostate-cancer Andrés, emphysema-cough Pablo, beet-juice-diet Mauricio. More and more lately, it seems as though everyone he knows is talking to doctors instead of priests, men with stethoscopes around their necks instead of crucifixes. He can't pinpoint the exact moment when

it changed, but there's a new fear now lurking beneath everyone's low-volume conversations. It's not just extradition to
Miami prisons or undercover DEA agents or stash house security guards secretly wearing wires beneath their collared shirts.
It's also cancer cell counts, will drafting, uneasy conversations
with mistresses, even more uneasy conversations with wives.
He's started biting his nails again too—they haven't been this
short since he was seventeen, doing deliveries in the hillside
neighborhoods for local bosses. His first job. He would sit in
the front seat for hours, waiting for his partner's signal, and
tear off every last possible shred of nail, until the cuticles were
nonexistent. (The fingers of his right hand were long back
then too.)

But now's not the time to dwell on it. Not tonight. He pulls
his trousers up briskly and rebuckles his belt. As usual, he
flushes but doesn't wash his hands. He wanders past the bookshelves, back out to the porch. Under the drainpipe, Mauricio
is telling the Mendozas about his recent senatorial trip to
Uruguay, how uncomfortable it made him to see all the small
children at his official reception, the way they honored his
presence by saluting and marching across the basketball court,
military-dictatorship style.

"At least we've never had that issue here," he says, beer
bottle coming dangerously close to clinking against his coffee-
stained teeth. "Long live democracy."

"Down with Communism," Mr. Mendoza says, sounding
like he's joking, but Mrs. Mendoza raises her champagne glass
in a toast. "Thank God for the paramilitaries," she says, clinking her glass against Mauricio's beer bottle. "At least they're
actually doing something."

By the mango tree Restrepo's wife is already drunk; he can tell by how closely she leans toward Alonso as he speaks, summarizing a TV series about medieval knights in Spain that he's just finished watching. Alonso is half-Mexican, which may explain why he uses so many hand gestures while talking; the way he darts forward, parries, blocks, defends, you'd swear you could see a sword glowing a luminescent silver in his hand. Restrepo's wife keeps laughing and reaching out, trying to brush her maroon-colored nails against his chest.

The Rossi brothers are sitting in the white plastic chairs by the barbecue pit, smoking red-boxed Marlboros. When they make eye contact with him they both raise their hands at the same time like choreographed puppets, crooking their fingers in a *come here* gesture. He shakes his head; he's not in the mood to discuss business. Not at the party; not here.

He turns around and nearly collides head-on with Mrs. Lansky, who immediately begins apologizing for the lack of Stephanie's presence, drumming her nails against the champagne glass—you know how daughters are at this age, unpredictable, claiming out of nowhere that she now gets carsick, would rather stay at home all weekend with the maid, imagine that. "Yes, yes," he says, taking a step back from her pale green blouse. "Of course. No worries, no offense taken." He keeps walking backward until her face looms at a respectable distance, the space between them too awkward now to breach with conversation, and he merges with relief into the group of sullen-faced teenagers huddled by the swimming pool. They fall awkwardly silent as he stands among them, the girls playing with their earrings and shiny gold bracelets, the boys' hair slick with gel.

It only takes a quick scan to see that his own daughter's not among them: no long black braid hanging down her back, no baggy blue T-shirt with holes in the collar from her anxious chewing. His fingers brush briefly against the slight bulge in his back pocket from the Jell-O baggie. The younger children are all busy, hunched with intense focus over the paper plates. They're dripping crayon wax into the center of the plates, creating a base that will harden and keep their candles propped up. The plates are then set adrift into the swimming pool, transformed into tiny, fragile boats, the orange flames casting faint reflections in the dark water below.

"Oh!" he shouts when one candle topples over and extinguishes with a mournful hiss. Some of the kids jump, startled by his cry; most simply turn slowly and stare. He tries to smile, even though he knows this never looks comforting, not with a face like his: the scar splitting his upper lip so that his tooth pokes out, the pink hairless arch over his left eyebrow.

"It's fine," one of the older girls says to a little boy she's been helping, whose eyes are getting bigger and more watery-looking by the second. "Just make another one. What color crayon do you want?" She shoves some crayons into his fist.

He turns away, shoes crunching on the gritty patio tiles. He does this all the time: He'll bang his knee against the dining room table, or drop a tangerine onto the floor immediately after peeling it, or accidentally fumble a fork, and then let out an explosive bellow of *Oh!* It makes the maids come running, the bodyguards look up sharply. *Everyone keeps thinking you're having a heart attack,* his daughter once told him, *but then it turns out you just spilled some milk.*

By now he's wandered over to the mango tree, where

Alonso is still breathlessly summarizing his beloved TV series to a growing circle of people. Alonso has the unfortunate type of skin that turns as pink as strawberry juice no matter the humidity level or how slowly he's been drinking.

"So they bring in the red-beard guy, begging and screaming," Alonso is saying. "But when the blade comes down, he doesn't cry out for his mother or wife or daughters. Instead he starts sobbing for his country, his army. *I did you wrong, I did you wrong*, he's shouting, and the crowd starts cheering."

"Like the Romans," says Restrepo's wife, lightly touching a small mark by her lower lip that she hopes nobody else has noticed—a pimple? A mole? "The Christians and the lions."

At the border of the group, Mrs. Smith has just finished her story about Baloo, how he chased her around the yard, tugging on her skirt and smacking his thick black lips. "Thank God they got rid of him," she says, gesturing toward her feet. "There's no way I could run in these heels." Tom Harris and Robert Smith nod in unison, even though they're in separate departments at the fruit company (agronomy and marketing, respectively) and don't really know each other that well. They're both secretly glad that Mrs. Smith's incessant chatter is filling in the silence between them. When she finally heads back to the patio to refill her drink, Tom asks Robert if he has a lighter. Smoking together, looking at the pool and the squat orange flowerpots, the Christmas lights dangling like fireflies stuck in the mango tree, Robert will tell Tom that Amanda Fernandez's husband has just joined a strange new American religion that doesn't allow you to cut your hair.

"What will he do once it's summer?" Tom asks, who's only

been here for six months and still sleeps with the fan next to his bed, blowing air in his face, even when it rains.

"He'll be hot," says Robert, taking another drag.

He blows the smoke right into our faces, but we don't blink, we don't move an inch. We've been listening carefully, behaving ourselves, lingering on the edges. Sometimes we lean in close, inhale the faint scents of cologne and perfume, study the sweat on the men's upper lips, the base of women's collarbones. An enormous black cicada buzzes past and hits the drainpipe with a clatter.

We're still watching *him,* too—the way he's rocking on his heels, rubbing his shirtsleeves as though chilled. "Excuse me," he says abruptly to one of the passing servers, a young woman holding a bowl scraped clean of lavender-flavored goat cheese. She immediately freezes in her tracks. "My daughter—have you seen her?" He pauses, trying to find the right words for a description: the tip of her black braid, permanently wet from her nervous sucking. The damp patches in her armpits, regardless of the temperature. The scowling, baby-fat cheeks, the sour curdling of her mouth that one time he hesitantly said, *You know, you could invite people over to spend the weekend—have a party, if you'd like.* The iciness oozing from her shoulder blades as she contemptuously turned away from him.

But the young woman is nodding, backing away, holding the bowl close to her chest like a shield. Right before she turns around, she says in a fast voice, "By the palm tree, sir—Ramón was bringing her shrimp." And just like that she flees across the patio, almost bumping into a flowerpot. As she disappears through the door, he thinks, *Ramón?* He struggles to come up with a face for the name: faint mustache? Stubble-covered chin?

He turns and starts walking deeper into the garden. He swings his arms purposefully, wrinkles his forehead in the expression of a man on a mission, so that anyone contemplating stopping him with a *Why, so nice to see you, it's been ages!* will think again. He pauses by the palm tree, rests his hand on the scars hacked into the trunk. They're ancient relics from his daughter's kindergarten birthday parties, epic affairs in which the garden filled with screaming children waving plastic toy swords, their lips smeared with bright blue frosting, the swimming pool transformed into a froth from their kicking legs and cannonball dives.

But wait, he said as she turned away. Struggling to find the right words, to speak to her as a seventeen-year-old as opposed to a child: *It doesn't have to be a party. How about that friend of yours? You used to invite him over here all the time. I don't think I've seen him in years. You know, the blond one?*

Dad, she said. *Why don't you shut the fuck up?*

On the ground is a solitary flip-flop, the pale ghost of her foot imprinted on the thin rubber. Nearby is a wooden stick smeared black from the grill, gnawed with teeth marks from where she scraped off every last piece of shrimp. He looks around, but the only eyes he meets are those of the rabbits, their trembling noses pushed up against the chicken wire, expressions the same as that of the young waitress moments before.

He walks ahead, leaving the flip-flop behind. He moves past the papaya trees, which have been afflicted by a mysterious disease for weeks now, the fruit stinking of rotten fish and the trunks covered in oozing sores. He passes the compost heap, filled with dry branches slashed from trees by the gardeners' sharp machetes, and kitchen scraps that the maids routinely carry out in orange plastic buckets. He walks by the abandoned birdhouse, vines hanging down the rotting wood, the lion cage with its rusty bars and leaf-covered roof. Carlitos the lion has been gone for half a decade now, the peacock a few years less than that. Carlitos died convulsing, mouth filled with a thick yellow foam that the keeper nonchalantly said had come from eating "something bad," while the peacock— what happened to the peacock? Its throat ripped open by a possum? An unexplained disappearance into thin air, leaving only glimmering blue-green feathers behind? Even five years ago he felt too exhausted to replace them, and it feels even less worth it now—it's just not the time and place for those sorts of extravagances anymore, for that kind of exhibitionism. The days of hidden bombs on Miami-bound Avianca airplanes are long gone, an appropriate gesture ten years ago but not now. Not anymore. He walks on, the house getting smaller in the distance, the sounds of the party becoming fainter. He ignores the dampness seeping into the hems of his trousers, the midge bites forming on his arms. If he keeps going, soon enough he'll reach the garage.

We follow him as best we can. We tread carefully over the squashed mangoes and dark green chicken turds curled up like undiscovered Easter candy in the grass. We follow him past the fenced field, the one with the steer who always looks so sad and never bothers to flick the flies away from its thick eyelashes. We pass the outhouse with the backup electricity generator, the acacia tree where the buzzards roost. The ranch is over a thousand hectares long, but he won't be going much farther.

We're just about to begin when it happens. At first there's hardly any sound, the canopy barely rustling, trees shaking. We freeze in our tracks as he spins around, staring deep into the darkness around him. "Sweetie?" he says. "Is that you?"

The sound grows louder, leaves and twigs crashing down.

"Who's there?" His hand moves to his hip, toward the hidden holster. Fingers tensed and ready.

The monkey takes its last swing out of the tree, landing heavily on the ground. It straightens up, wet black eyes blinking. His fingers relax around the holster but don't move away.

"Well," he says. "Hello there, old friend."

Baloo doesn't even give him a glance. Instead he stares right at us.

We stare back.

"Sorry, I don't have anything for you," he says. "Any, ah, goodies." He's touching his waist and back pockets, instinctively feeling for something, wishing he'd brought the flip-flop, or even the gnawed stick. His fingers suddenly detect the plastic baggie of Jell-O powder, which he immediately pulls out and throws in Baloo's direction. It flutters weakly through the air, drifting down by the monkey's foot. Baloo doesn't even flinch, his eyes still fixed unblinkingly on us. We shift around uncomfortably, glancing at one another, nervously crossing and uncrossing our arms. Some of us tentatively touch our cheeks and foreheads, tracing the skin with our fingertips, from the bottom of our eyes to the top of our lips.

It's almost like he's saying: *What happened to your faces?*

Or even: *What did they do to you?*

"Good monkey," he says, backing away, one slow but steady footstep at a time. "Nice little Baloo." In response Baloo releases a long lazy yawn, flashing a row of solid yellow teeth. His breath is warm and stinks of overripe fruit.

The cellphone rings, its high-pitched trill breaking the silence, and we can't help but jump as Baloo swiftly turns and flees into the undergrowth, bushes rattling like chattering teeth. He fumbles with the cellphone as he pulls it out, fingers clumsy, answers just before it goes to voicemail. At first he thinks it's Nicolás from the processing laboratory, speaking rapidly in muffled tones, but finally he recognizes prostate-cancer Andrés—he's agitated, calling long-distance from Medellín, asking repeatedly if it's safe to speak right now. He listens calmly to the update, strolling back toward the house. He interrupts with a stifled snort of laughter, after Andrés says, *My advice would be for you to take a trip abroad for a while—with your daughter, especially. Why risk it? Go to Europe; take her someplace nice. Just until things blow over with these guys. Until the situation is safe again.*

"We're not going anywhere," he says, cutting Andrés off. "I don't care what you have to do. Just take care of it."

The walk back to the house feels strangely short. Right as he passes the flip-flop he pauses, as if about to bend over and scoop it up, but at the last second he turns quickly away, leaving it behind in the grass. The party's now reached the point where it's either going to turn into anarchy or collapse into exhausted decay. Somebody's thrown up on the grass, leaving a sour orange puddle. The dancers and drinkers on the patio are still mingling, eyes glassy, cheeks stiff from smiling. Somebody's turned the music up so loud that the bass hurts his eardrums.

He's heading toward the patio door when he's spotted. *Hey, there you are! Where have you been hiding?* He's reluctantly tugged away, pulled into the crowd. His shoulders are slapped, his arms are squeezed, he receives winks and smiles, shouts and whoops. A shot of aguardiente, miraculously still cold, is pushed into his hand, followed by delicate kisses on his cheek. *Terrific party! Amazing! Best time I've had since Carnival!*

Everybody's happy to see him; they're thrilled that he's here. Somebody's brought out a mirror to set upon the table; any moment now, the lines of powder will follow. He briefly scans the crowd one last time, but there are no children to be seen at this point, not even the teenagers—no small bowed heads, no hands stained with hardened candle wax, no hair slicked back with gel, no wet chewed braid. The phone sits in his back pocket, still warm from the call.

From the quietest corner of the patio, under the grapefruit tree by the swimming pool, he checks his messages one more time. There are no new voicemails. Not even a text.

He's walking past the swimming pool when he sees it: the last paper plate, bobbing up and down, half-submerged. Its candle is long gone, sunk to the bottom. The pool is now completely dark. He stops and stares at it.

There are more packages of paper plates deep inside the pantry somewhere—that might encourage the children to come back. He could go ask a maid to bring more out. Or even better, he could get them himself. Select a key from the chain, unlock the door, head inside. If he wanted to, he could spend some time slumped on the floor, leaning against the wall, eyes closed, hands resting calmly in his lap. It's the kind of place where he could stay forever. Stay secret. Stay safe. A place where he could lock himself away and never, ever be found.

We'll be watching, though. We don't mind. We're not in a hurry.

We're not going anywhere.

Junkie Rabbit

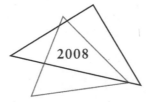

2008

It comes out of nowhere, a low voice spoken in the dark: *You guys feeling it yet?* Everyone immediately straightens up, ears jerking, blinking and twitching in the voice's direction, but I don't bother. It's one of the younger rabbits, I guarantee it, some kid with hardly any scabs or gunk in his ears, shiny white fur still clean and unknotted, bright pink eyes nervously scanning everyone's faces. *I'm not feeling anything yet. Do you think I ate enough? Do you think I need to eat more? Maybe I should eat more. Should I eat more? Are there any leaves left? Do you think we're going to run out? Maybe someone should go get some more. Do you think someone should go get some more, in case we run out?*

That's when everybody looks at me. As if I somehow know.

Like I have a clue. For what it's worth, I don't mind stepping up. What can I say—it's just the kind of rabbit I am, the kind I've always been. Take one for the team and all that. What else am I supposed to do? Like right now, when they're all looking at me with wet, worried eyes and quivering noses.

Don't worry, I say. *I've got this.* And then, even though no one stirs or says anything, it's suddenly like the air in the burrow just got ten times lighter.

I've got this, I repeat. *I'll go take care of it. I'll be right back. Can you guys just hang here for a while? Is that okay? Does that work for everybody?*

All through the burrow there's a line of nodding heads, ears bobbing. I shove another wad of leaves into my cheek and take off.

A good supply of leaves will last a single rabbit for seven days, ten if it's a big pile. When we start running low—when there's nothing in the burrow but dirt and squashed insects, with no leaves within reach, no matter how far we stretch out our tongues or flop our heads around—that's when it has to happen. Someone has to go see the Pastor. And when it has to be done, I'm usually the rabbit to do it. I guess that's just how it works: You're born a certain way, grow up to play a certain role, and that's it, you're you, unchangeable. It's like what my father used to say, those times when I didn't feel like helping out with digging and he'd cuff me across the head before turning away with an irritated frown: *You grow up to do the things you were born to do. What else would you expect from life?*

The long run I'm heading down branches off into dozens of passageways, some leading to old leaf storerooms, others to long-forgotten shafts and drops. I've chewed long enough now for the spit to dribble down my chest and stain my fur. My heart's not beating that rapidly yet, but I'm definitely getting the lip-tingling feeling, tongue going numb. That familiar jaunty sensation: Here it comes. When I pass a tunnel that leads aboveground, it's nice to pause for a second to enjoy the cool air, blowing down from above. If I wanted to, I could pretend to still hear the snuffling of someone plowing through a leaf pile, jaws clicking and grinding as they chew away, burrowing frantically forward as they rustle through the bags in search of one last leaf, just one more.

But I know I'm imagining it. These storerooms have been empty for a long time.

The run slopes downward as I crawl into the Great Hall. As usual, it's filled with everyone who's not chewing, a sea of furry white bodies sleeping, scratching, staring vacantly into space, mechanically cleaning themselves. It's a relief to raise my ears as high as I want, no need to worry about them rubbing against the cement ceiling. As I crawl forward I have to grit my teeth to prevent myself from crying out in disgust as I'm stepped on, crawled over, poked at, and kicked, like I'm swimming in a river of writhing white bodies. I push my way forward violently, *Coming through, out of my way, watch it,* jostling rabbits who turn angrily and glare at me. At one point I can't push my way between two heavy males, so instead I have to crawl over a giant pile of shit left behind by rabbits who can't even be bothered to go outside anymore. I close my eyes and plunge ahead, holding my breath, but it's not so bad; most of it's dry and crumbly from sitting here for so long. No fresh warm smears—those are the worst.

As I move forward, there's no avoiding it. At first I keep my eyes lowered, fixed on the sandy earth, but eventually I raise my head, as if to say *That's right, bring it on, do your worst.* There it is. The Platform. The raised shelf of dirt where my father used to sit, eyes closed and head drooping so far forward his whiskers nearly touched the ground. Whenever he spoke, though, his voice sounded loud and clear. My father. The General.

It used to happen here. When I was young, we'd gather together, all of us, to hear his stories—females, children, old folks, everyone, bodies pressed against one another, breathing in sync as we listened. He told us everything: about the metal hutch where he and the Pastor and the others lived, back when the Men used to be here. He talked about the Daughter, her long black hair hanging down her back like a skinny tail, who'd bring them vegetable peelings in an orange plastic bucket (my father's favorite were the potato skins). There were the Children, who would stick their fat pink hands into the hutch and say things like *Come here little bunnies, little darlings, little sweet things,* waving around blades of grass and wiggling their fingers at us. I loved hearing about the Man the most, who'd come and squash his face against the wire, black hair bristling out of his nostrils, and my father and the others would huddle against the hutch wall as far away from him as possible (during this part we'd always huddle closer together too, shivering from something that was either delight or fear, I was never sure).

My father's stories always mentioned the Party: the day that the Other Men came, carrying long black sticks. There were fires and explosions, and holes appeared in the walls, and the water in the swimming pool turned red from blood (we bowed our heads and trembled during this part, our ears hurting from the explosions, our eyes burning from the smoke). The Daughter never came back after that to push her fingers through the wire. And then came the ending, everybody's favorite part, in which my father, the General, led the way and got everyone out. He figured a way to break out of the hutch and escape, bringing us here to found the warren under the swimming pool. And here's where we've been ever since.

My father would usually stop at that point, but not always. Sometimes he would go on to talk about how it had been his idea to get us the leaves out of the garage. The garage was a long walk away from the main house, where the Men would drag the black plastic bags and shake the leaves out on tarps spread out over the earth, mashing them with their feet into a thick brown paste. It was my father who figured out that the leaves would make us each bigger and stronger than any rabbit had ever been, capable of digging longer and harder than any rabbit had ever dug. As soon as he said this, though, he would fall silent, staring wordlessly at the ground. When the silence went on long enough we'd pull apart from one another, shuffling away uneasily.

Nobody has spoken on the Platform in a long time.

I'm just about to head down the Pastor's tunnel when this really fucked-up-looking rabbit pops up out of nowhere, shoving his face against mine. *Watch it,* I say, pushing him away, wincing at his musty smell. *Get a grip, friend.* His face is a mess of pus-encrusted cuts, so thick his eyes are thin little slits, and his chest is covered in sticky foam. He whirls his head around in half circles, staring blindly at nothing, before finally flopping over sideways.

The children, he says in a garbled voice, slimy green liquid spilling from his mouth. *The children!*

When I get to the Pastor, he's busy, as usual. I keep my distance, hovering at the burrow entrance, picking at the dried-up leaf juice on my chest fur. He's speaking to a young female, the kind who've been born lately with their ears drooping low over their faces. I almost never see females these days, what with them keeping to themselves all the time, clustered in the deepest, most tucked-away burrows. I can't help but sneak glances at this one. Instead of eyes all I see is a thick yellow crust, and suddenly there's nothing I want to do more than reach out and scrape it away.

By turning my head sideways it's easier to make out the Pastor's words. *It's very hard, you know,* he's saying right now, *for life to turn out the way you want it to. That's just the nature of things, especially around here lately. But there are different ways for you to deal with it. There are always different choices you can make.*

At this point my skin feels tight; it's like there are two different pairs of teeth sinking into me, pulling the skin in opposite directions. So I go ahead and saunter in, give the Pastor my very best grin, the same storyteller smile my father used to flash when he'd finish a real crowd-pleaser.

Pastor, I say. *Long time no see.*

He looks me up and down, blinking slowly with those wet

black eyes that always remind me of the moldy leaves rotting under the mango trees (trees I haven't seen for myself in years—when was the last time I went aboveground? When did it last seem worthwhile?). Eyes that linger on my ears, staring long and hard before looking away.

How are you, the Pastor says flatly. *General Junior. Scratching yourself again, I see?*

Don't call me that.

From the way his eyes move I can tell that he's looking at the crumbs of shit on my chest, the clumps of half-chewed leaves. But I don't even care at this point. Why should I? It's all I can do to keep myself from wiggling in anxious anticipation, almost bouncing with the knowledge that every word with the Pastor is taking me one step closer to the leaves, like I'm skipping on a trail of stones laid out over a river.

Well, I say, keeping my eyes politely averted from the female, who's hunched over by the Pastor, shivering and wordless. *You know what I've come here for. Old buddy. Old pal. Amigo, compadre, partner in arms, a friend in need . . .*

Yeah yeah yeah. He scratches a spot by his ear.

You know, he says, *there are too many damn rabbits in this burrow. It's really starting to drive me crazy. Nobody's mating anymore—did you know that? Nobody's fucking, and by nobody I don't just mean my ugly ass. It's all falling apart—a real mess. Have you noticed that? Never mind, that's a stupid question. You and that little crew of yours don't notice anything.*

Hey, I say, *I notice plenty. I saw this one rabbit on the way over here. His face was all cut up.*

Really. Bite marks?

I can't help but laugh. *What are you saying?*

He sits up and begins cleaning his face.

I start shaking my head. *Come on, Pastor. Rabbits don't eat other rabbits. That's not something we do.*

No, the Pastor says, his eyes flickering briefly to the female, as if only just remembering that she's there. *That's right. It's not.*

He takes a deep wet breath.

Well, you're going to be disappointed. The warren's all out.

I don't say anything.

That's right. You heard me. You remember the black garbage bags? Of course you do. Even if you didn't drag them here yourself you must remember seeing us when you were just a kid, the way we dragged them across the yard, pulling them with our teeth. We don't usually carry things, you know—some would murmur that it wasn't normal, that it was unnatural. But your father said we would learn, and that it would be useful to have a store. And you know what, he was right.

He coughs and a thick clear liquid drips down his chin.

But it's gone now. The storerooms are empty. Search all the runs and burrows if you like—it'd take you months, if not a year, but believe me, I know what I'm talking about.

I still haven't spoken. There's a fluttering in my chest, as though I've swallowed a winged insect that's beating weakly at first against my rib cage, then harder and harder, and it's making me feel like if I don't find something to shove into my mouth to start chewing, then I'm going to sink my claws into myself and tear the layers of fur off, scratching as deep as I can.

I don't even realize that I've been backing out until the walls of the burrow exit scrape against my shoulders and the Pastor calls out, *Wait—mijo.* The human word for "son."

I stop in my tracks.

If you really wanted to, he says, *you could get more.* He hesitates for a second, lip trembling.

There's a way. But you'd have to go to the garage.

He's breathing heavily, those huge nostrils of his flaring like the flapping wings of a beetle. The female stirs, moving her mouth as if she's trying to speak, something thick and pink slowly poking out between her lips.

Nobody's done it, the Pastor says. *Not in your lifetime. And why would they? What would be the point?* His voice sounds angry, as though the thought of it is a terrible insult.

Well, okay then, I say. *That's fine. That's great. That's wonderful. I don't even know why you're making it sound like a problem. Why would going over to the garage be a problem? I don't see why it would be a problem. You're making it sound like there's going to be some kind of problem when there is no problem.*

Junior, the Pastor says, his eyes still big wet pools. *You have no idea. You talk too damn much. You're just like your father—*

Yeah, except he actually had something to say, right?

The female jumps at how loud my voice is, crouches down and closes her eyes, digging her claws into the dirt. The Pastor doesn't move. He just sits there blinking until I finally start backing out of the tunnel, as fast as my shaking legs will allow.

That's right, he says, turning away so that I glimpse the

burns on the other side of his body. *You better get going. Before it's too late.*

Too late for what?

He doesn't answer. My eyes slide over to the female one last time. Her tongue is sticking out, so big and pink and thick that for a second I'm confused: How could a rabbit have a tongue that thick and big? As it keeps sliding out of her mouth, I can see the tiny whiskers, the perfectly formed front feet, the miniature ears, and that's when I realize the dark hole is really one of the baby rabbit's eyes. Everything that comes out of her mouth after that is so bloody and chewed up and mangled that I start backing out through the tunnel as fast as I can, my forehead pulsing so hard I can feel my ears jerking up like an insect's antennas. I can hear my jaw clicking, grinding away, searching for leaf pieces that aren't there anymore but it's okay, it doesn't matter, because inside me there's this tiny glowing light, a faraway exit glimpsed at the end of a long tunnel, and the beating heart in my chest echoes like a voice in my head, and what it's saying in rhythm to the throbbing blood is *more, more, more, soon, soon, soon.*

One last long uphill tunnel. Crumbling soft dirt in my face. And then I've done it, I'm outside, blinking in the sunlight at the edge of the swimming pool, bushes with thick pink flowers hanging heavy over my head.

I don't waste time; I head straight for the barbecue pit under the mango tree, just like my father described in his stories. The air is quiet and hot, filled with buzzing insects that circle curiously around my face. Part of me wants to freeze in the long grass, keep my head bowed low, the position my father taught us to keep us safe from enemies. (*Not that you'll ever meet any,* he said, his clawed foot pushing my face even deeper into the dirt, crushing my whiskers. *Our enemies are gone. Vanquished. There's no one left now but us.*) The thought of his claws against my face makes my heart pound even harder. It sounds like it's saying *go, go, go,* so I keep moving, keep dragging myself forward. I go past it all, everything he described to us, every step of his journey: the empty concrete hole that was the swimming pool, the moss-covered fountains and angel statues. The swing set dotted with yellow butterfly eggs and misty with spiderwebs, the rotting wooden birdhouse and enormous rusting lion cage that still stinks faintly of rotten meat. I drag myself through the grass, past the dried-up pits of long-decayed mangoes, the field surrounded by a half-collapsed fence. It's just like my father's stories, the ones he told us in the dark, the only light coming from his trembling eyes. The outhouse with the collapsed door, the acacia tree covered in fungus. And soon enough it's waiting up ahead. The garage.

The doors are still open, leaning against the wall, dotted with dozens of holes as though they've been pecked by a thousand birds. I take a deep breath as I duck inside. Even after all this time—it's still here. Just like he described it. The crusty barrels and stained metal buckets. The black plastic tarps spread over the floor, where the men would spread the leaves. The swirling stains on the cement floor, left behind by the chemicals. Even their sickly smell is still heavy in the air, making my eyes water. It feels strange to walk around, ducking under the metal tables and navigating among the crumpled yellow gloves, like I'm moving through a picture that's come to life, an image that previously existed only in my head.

Everything he talked about is here. Except for one thing. No leaves. Not a trace. Not even empty black bags, crumpled like shed skin. I hop around and sniff everywhere as hard as I can, but my nose has gone numb; the only smell is the chemicals, thick and burning. The fluttering in my chest has come back. My rib cage is vibrating, and all of a sudden I can't help myself anymore, I can't hold it back, I start jerking, and it takes all my strength not to start scratching away furiously, tearing each and every single hair out of my skull until I'm left clean and empty and smooth.

General. What happened to your ears?

It comes out of nowhere. A dry whisper, cracking like leaves. I turn around sharply, but all I see is trash, a metal hutch in the corner, dirty yellow gloves, piles of crumpled paper. Then the paper twitches, and that's when I see the rabbit. He's slumped on the floor, head leaning against a glass tube. His fur is white like mine, his eyes the same color as the Pastor's, but instead of pools they're more like holes in his sockets, as though his eyeballs were scraped out. As I crawl closer he begins bobbing his head from side to side in peculiarly slow circles, as though searching for something I can't see. Over and over again, never stopping. It makes my stomach feel queasy just watching him, like I'm the one who's getting dizzy instead of him.

His eyes widen when I sit next to him, and his head slows to a stop.

General, he says again, voice cracking. *What did they do to you—*

No, I say. *I'm his son.*

He stares at me, then presses his mouth against the end of the glass tube and inhales deeply. The end of the tube is filled with pea-colored rocks, some the size of tiny pebbles, others big solid chunks.

I came here, I manage to say, *because I was looking for leaves.*

They're all gone. They've been gone for ages. All that's left are the rocks.

He nods in the direction of the glass tube. He's still bobbing his head from side to side, eyeballs jittering in their sockets, as though frenetically scanning the floor, searching every inch of it.

I think there might be some tiny rocks under your feet, he says, *where you're standing. Would you mind bringing them here?*

He wraps his lips around the glass tube and presses a paw down on a black stick on the tube's side. There's a clicking sound, and then he begins to inhale steadily. The inside of the glass becomes smoky and unclear, like it's filling with the vapor that used to rise from the swimming pool on hot days.

Here, General, he says when he's done, his voice tight from the breath he's holding. *You can go next. Just like we used to.*

Despite the tightness in my stomach I take a step closer. It would be so easy. I can see myself already, slumped beside him, our mouths taking turns on the tube.

Come on, he says. *You remember, don't you? The Men would bring in the Women, make them put their mouths on the dogs, and we would sit here and watch. They brought us the leaves and that was good, but then they brought us the pipe and rocks, and that was better. They'd watch us and laugh the same way they laughed at the Women and the dogs, but it didn't matter. We didn't care. We didn't eat. We didn't sleep. We didn't need to. We didn't need to do anything.*

His tongue darts out, like he's trying to lick the smoke as it drifts away.

But then you took us to the warren. I wanted nothing to do with it. Dragging bags? Like we were dogs with sticks? Unnatural. Sick. Just not something we do. So I came back here. I've been here ever since. But you—you were so scared—

The words fly out of me with spit: *My father wasn't scared. Come here. Say that again, and I'll fight you.*

Don't be ridiculous. We're not young anymore.

He exhales steadily, a thick cloud of smoke circling his head as though something inside the cage has caught fire. A sweet and musty smell fills the air. That's when I see it, a creamy white liquid leaking between his legs. I'm about to open my mouth and ask if he's all right when I realize that he's ejaculated.

Maybe you can come back, I finally say, only because I can't think of anything else. *Maybe we can help you.*

And your children, General? Who's going to help them?

I don't speak. Instead I take a step back, then another. He doesn't say anything either, doesn't even turn to look at me. The last I see of him is his head turning toward the glass pipe again, his lips wrapping around the end of it, and as I turn away I hear the clicking sound of the igniting flame. It sounds like a voice in my ears, and the question that it's asking sounds like *When?* When did it get too late? At what point was there no going back?

When I exit the garage doors I have to stop and rest. I'm shaking hard. I can't control where my eyes are going anymore. Following every glint of sunlight that shines off the jagged glass running along the walls, every brown leaf fluttering down into the empty pool. I curl up into a tight ball, paws folded over my ears, pressing them against my face. If I'm careful, my claws won't get snagged in the jagged holes, won't touch the patches of raw muscle, brush against exposed bone where I've scratched away the skin. When I close my eyes, it's like I'm sprawled at my father's feet all over again. Resting before the Platform, everyone's bodies warm and snuggled against me. The images flicker through my head, crowding into my skull, squeezing in behind my eyes. Everything's clear, a coherent story I can understand, like something I once heard in my childhood that made perfect sense. In my mind's eye, we're in the burrow together. All of us, nothing but rabbits as far as the eye can see, jammed in shoulder to shoulder. Even though I can't turn my head to look, I know that the exits behind us are blocked, filled with layers of crumbling black earth, dirt-encrusted roots, tiny pebbles, glittering rocks. I somehow know that even if I were to scratch and dig until my claws fell off and my mouth filled with dirt, there would be no other way. The only way out is forward, and together that's what we're all doing, slowly but surely: squeezing ahead, moving steadily toward something in the distance that we can't see but that we're eventually going to reach, whether we want to or not.

I can feel my heart beating in my chest, that insistent pounding. When I open my eyes, they'll be there: the Children, faces crinkling as they smile, small hands reaching toward us, fingers wiggling. "Hey, little guy," they'll say. "How are you doing? You sweet little animal, darling little thing. Sweet little bunny."

The Bird Thing

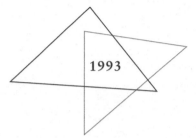

1993

VALLE DEL CAUCA

You are worried about the bird thing but you don't want to think about that right now, smoking the first of your secret birthday cigarettes. You're outside the house by the giant concrete sink, laundry covering the surface—today it's the daughter's underwear, the wife's scratchy lace bras, the husband's tennis shirts with holes in the underarms. Delicate things, white things, things that deserve to be washed carefully by hand as opposed to being thrown into the American-imported washing machine, which will ruthlessly transform anything into a wilted gray smock if you're not careful about sorting through every single item and removing the ones with even a hint of darkness. The sun's only just coming up; everyone in the house is still asleep, though the husband's alarm will be going off soon so that he can escape the Monday-morning traffic jam. He never needs breakfast prepared though; he'll have a ham-and-cheese sandwich in the office, but as soon as you finish this cigarette you'll have to head to the kitchen to begin making the coffee. Not yet, though. You still have some time.

You hold the cigarette between your thumb and index finger, like the men sitting on stools you used to see during your childhood. You inhale deeply, enjoy the brief sight of the flame glowing at the tip before tucking the stub under a triangle-shaped rock, where the stiff orange corpses of previous cigarettes are neatly lined up, buried away, hidden. You wash your hands with the thin sliver of blue soap that always leaves your skin terribly dry, the areas between your fingers red and cracking, but there's nothing quite like it for getting rid of the nicotine stink from your fingertips. This way, you can be sure that nobody will notice.

The last thing you need to do before heading inside is to check on the bird thing, which should take less than two minutes, assuming there aren't any problems (which there very rarely are). Five quick strides toward the lime tree is all it takes. The banana you nailed to the trunk is still there, black and slimy and already attracting shiny green flies. The peel has been tugged down near the top and a large chunk of the banana is missing. You crane your neck back but all you can see are the rowboat-shaped leaves and limes swaying like tiny green suns. You exhale slowly and take the single slice of orange out of your apron pocket (the rest of the orange sits in the bowl of fruit salad in the fridge, waiting patiently for the wife's yogurt and granola). You leave it resting on top of the

banana, so it now looks like the banana is wearing a tiny fes-
tive hat.

That should be enough for now—enough to keep it happy.

Men sitting on stools. Hairy men, dark men, men in sleeveless
white shirts, legs sprawled lazily as they watched you run past
in your bare feet toward the river. Nobody ever wore shoes;
the roads in town were only ever made of sand or mud; you
never got blisters and never got sick and never stayed out past
eight o'clock because that's when they would ride by on their
motorcycles and your mother would tell you in a sharp voice
to come inside, stop wandering around the yard like a lost
chicken just asking to get its head chopped off and turned into
soup. Your father is going to buy you a pair of red running
shoes for Christmas, assuming the crop of yucca is good.

You're placing the glass of freshly squeezed orange juice on
top of the daughter's Little Mermaid placemat when you hear
a clattering sound in the kitchen. *Make sure you swallow all
the pulp, love,* you say, hurrying back as fast as you can, not
waiting to make sure she takes her multivitamin.

The bird thing has just left. You can tell even before you
open the door. The pot has boiled over; the stovetop is covered
with a strange white crust, the egg cracked open and cooked
away into a frothy gray mist. You deal with that first, pouring
the water into the sink and tossing what remains of the egg-
shell into the trash. You quickly clean the stovetop with a
damp rag. Put on a new pot to boil; place a fresh egg on the

counter. You take the bread out of the fridge along with the parsley leaves you've let wilt and go sad (you'll have to hide them in a soup instead of using them for the salad like the wife requested for this week's menu). You've long since removed the daughter's lunch box; it now sits in the hallway beside her backpack and thermos—you'll put in the tiny cup of Alpinito yogurt at the very last second, right before the bus arrives, to make sure it stays chilled long enough for her mid-morning snack.

After closing the fridge, you lean against the door for a moment and take a deep breath. The handles press into your stomach in a way that makes you feel slightly sick, but there's no sign of a headache yet, your mind is still clear, vision unblurry. And there's no bird thing smell in the air either. No traces of sulfur. Just faint whiffs of orange peel and of scraps in the garbage from the wife's fruit salad, bananas and apples and grapes.

When you finally bring out the toast and egg (soft-boiled but not watery), the daughter is slumped forward, her cheek resting on top of Sebastian the crab. The glass of orange juice is empty but the vitamin tablet is still there. *I'm starving,* she says as you place the plate beside her forehead. *I've been sitting here forever.*

You wipe your hands off on your apron, a few breadcrumbs falling to the floor that you instantly know will be difficult to sweep up later; you'll have to use the tiny handheld broom instead of the big one. *Well,* you say, *why didn't you come to the kitchen and get it yourself?*

She stares at you like you've said something incomprehensible—like you're suddenly speaking a foreign language.

And now it's the nuns in primary school all over again, shortly after you muttered under your breath a Chocoan expression you learned from your grandfather, and the nun who always smelled like dead flowers took the lobe of your ear between two icy-cold fingers, twisted it sharply, and said, *Only Spanish here.*

(Somewhere deep within the garden—you can hear it—the bird thing is raising its scabby head and croaking out its bird-thing song.)

You pick up the daughter's glass and study the streaky trail left behind by the pulp, a single seed on the bottom.

Good job, you say. *I'll strain it better next time.*

The school bus honks and the daughter's eyes widen.

Eat what you can, you say, rushing to the kitchen. When you return with the front door keys the daughter is gone, the toast missing a single bite, orange yolk hardening on the fork. You find her in the bedroom, tearing through the bookshelves, throwing stray papers and plastic ponies over her shoulder. *My library book, I can't find it, it's due back today!* You bring her the backpack so that she can check what you placed inside. *No, not those, this one's different, it has four children on the cover. Now I'm going to have to pay a fine.* Sighing heavily, she follows you to the door.

You spot it before she does: a pile of stiff twigs scattered over the tiles. Dusty, thin twigs, the bark peeling away to reveal the pale flesh underneath, the kind of twigs dragged inside by something planning to build its nest—or already starting to. Darting forward, you throw yourself toward the door, dragging the daughter forward. *Have a good day,* you say, turning the key at the same time that you shove the twigs roughly out of the way with the side of your foot. She looks at you suspiciously, rubbing her arm, but then the school bus honks again. *Thank you for breakfast,* she says, rising onto her tiptoes and turning her cheek toward you for the usual kiss. It is only when she is clambering up the black rubber steps, the bus doors on the verge of wheezing shut, that you realize you have forgotten the yogurt.

That nun always smelled like dead flowers; the other one had terrible breath and never let you wear your tiger-tooth brace-let. But you could wear it on Saturdays, when you got to run to the riverside, slide down the bank, and go swimming or throw stones or try to catch tiny silver fish with your bare hands, then feed them leftovers from lunch. Except when the bodies were floating in the water. Rumor was that men always floated faceup, women facedown. Sometimes there were vul-tures sitting on them and sometimes not. But if there were bodies, you would just go to the little stream instead and that was better. There the fish would eat rice straight from your hand, grains floating through the water like confetti thrown at a wedding.

The wife turns back and forth in front of the hallway mirror, yanking the black cardigan down over her belly (four months now and just starting to show) before slowly unbuttoning it. Leaning against the wall, the other sweaters draped over your arm, you ask about tonight's dinner, if she wants you to in-clude lentils or eggplant in the vegetarian lasagna. The wife smiles and touches your forearm with her hand, a kind touch, a light touch, her hand always so soft and white you can't help but be reminded of the puffy bread rolls the husband sometimes brings home from the French bakery. *Cook it like last time,* she says. *It was delicious.* Her words produce a swelling inside your chest, a kind of rising heat, and you can't help but smile and nod vigorously as she tells you she won't be home for lunch today, she'll be visiting cousins all morning— Roberto will be driving her, you remember him, the one with the overbite, just so you know he was asking about you the other day. You roll your eyes and run a finger across your throat, and she giggles like the daughter does when you find her during hide-and-seek. And then she has meetings with students all afternoon, but if you could have the table set for dinner by six, that would be lovely.

As she hands over the unbuttoned cardigan she pauses in a way that makes you instantly want another cigarette, a craving so fierce you press your fingers into your palms, as if to prevent your hand from automatically reaching toward your mouth. *Do you need,* the wife says, *some more headache medicine?*

No, you say, folding the cardigan so that it won't get wrinkled, the arms neatly aligned, then draping it smoothly over your arm. *That won't be necessary. Thank you, though.*

It wouldn't be a bother. I can ask Roberto to stop by the pharmacy.

That would be a waste of time. But thank you.

She falls silent, smoothing the bottom edge of her shirt as if to get rid of wrinkles, and you immediately find yourself tensing up: Did you forget to do the ironing last week? Was that even possible? Could you honestly have taken the clothes off the laundry line, folded them up in the wicker basket, then retreated to the bedroom to rehang them in the closets, put them away in drawers, all without remembering to head to the ironing board first? If you actually did that, what on earth are you capable of doing next?

    . . . *next weekend,* she's saying, and you have to blink and point at your ear, smiling apologetically, saying, *I didn't catch that, sorry.*

    Your time off, she repeats. *Would you like to do it sooner?*

    You look past her shoulders to the door. The driveway outside can only be seen through the crisscrossing bars, tiny diamond-shaped slices of the hedge and sky.

    Yes, you say. *Next weekend would be fine.*

    She smiles but her eyes still look slightly wide, as if startled. But then it's okay, she's reaching into her purse, she's handing you money in case the water man comes early, she's reminding you to make sure the daughter doesn't have any treats until she finishes her homework, and is there any chance you might have seen her blue-green scarf? *It's in here,* you say, turning to the hallway closet.

It's time to make the beds. The sheets and pillowcases are stripped on Saturdays; for now it's enough to tuck the blankets into the corners, pulling them into a taut embrace with the mattress. You dust the fan with a single wet rag, punch the pillows and stuffed animals as hard as possible in order to fluff them up. Toy ponies are put in the blue plastic container, rubber dinosaurs are lined up on the bedside table, books are returned to the shelves where they lean wearily against one another. Everything is put back into its proper place, everything has an order. You place a book that might be the missing library one on top of the daughter's pillow, where she is sure to see it.

Lunch is simple: dried beef left over from dinner, chewy white rice, arepa, a fried egg. You eat at the white plastic table at the back of the house, among the orange barrels where the bags of lentils and pinto beans are stored, next to the peeling green cabinets filled with mosquito repellent and garden fertilizer. You listen to your favorite soap opera on the radio and use your fingers to push a little bit of everything onto your fork at once. You like it when the plate has plenty of options, lots of different bites you can choose from. The afternoon is for watering the plants in the garden with the long green hose, for taking a cup of coffee out to the bodyguard. You bring a cigarette with you and share it with him, passing it back and forth, and when he brazenly asks what you're doing this weekend, if you have any plans, you tilt your head to the side so that your hair falls across your face and say, *Going to church, of course,* smiling broadly as you flick away the ash. Then it's time for Clorox bleach in the bathtub, for swiping cobwebs away from the crucifixes. The toilet bowls need a generous squirt of bleach and a hearty scrubbing to get rid of the shit smears. The cockroaches in the shower are killed with a broom, the horseflies on the windowsill with a quick slap.

The afternoon is not, however, for finding half-eaten earthworms or cracked black beetle shells scattered across the floor in the husband's study. It is not for finding long white scratches on the table left behind by dry talons or crooked claws. It is not for finding a single black feather resting on the middle of the carpet, as light and silky as dandelion seeds. The afternoon is for none of these things.

Everybody knew about the river, but nobody wanted to know. The time your mother took you to the cemetery, hundreds of tombs stacked on top of each other like empty cupboards waiting to be filled. She took you to the section of the anonymous and unnamed, half-peeled bananas and orange segments resting on the tomb entrances. She made the sign of the cross on your forehead and told you to always make time in your prayers for the people suffering and in need. *Not everybody has what we have. We're very fortunate.* All things considered, things were much safer now: Crucifixions and hangings were rare, the bayoneting of infants too. The time she slapped you on the mouth when you asked her about the group of young men on motorcycles, huddled together in the plaza: Why did they have such short haircuts, why did they have red bandannas covering half their faces, who were they and what did they want? She slapped you in a way that cut open your lip with her nail. You wanted to ask her about the oil company executives, the mining company investors, with their blond hair and European cars. Even the way they whistled at you was different, their gazes at your legs long and slow, but instead of telling your mother about them you bit your lip and didn't say a word. The time your father took you down to the river when there was no one in it and you helped him catch turtles. You put a stick in the turtle's mouth so that it wouldn't bite your fingers and your father cut the feet off first, pulling off all the meat while it was still alive, saving the head for last. Without its shell the turtle reminded you of a newborn baby bird, wrinkled and sad. Turtle was always best in your mother's stew when it was all mixed up with everything else, an indistinguishable mush, impossible to tell which body part was which.

The daughter arrives home with one of her school friends, who raises her arms when she sees you for a hug. *Penelope,* you say, *so lovely to see you,* and you turn your cheek to receive her kiss. The daughter gives you a drawing she made in class today: two people sitting at a table together. One wears an apron, hair black and frizzy, while the smaller figure's hair is brown, a faint scribbling of yellow crayon on top. A tray full of food is set up before them: a steaming fried egg, a tall glass of orange juice, a brown scribble that you guess must be toast.

That's you, she says, *and that's me. I wrote you a note too.*

She taps the bottom of the page but you don't bother trying to sound your way through the squat row of handwriting. Instead you look at the two figures, sitting down together, food to share before them.

Thank you, you say as she presses it into your hands. *It's beautiful.* You'll put it in your room later, in the pile with the others.

The daughter hasn't had friends over that often since the wife's pregnancy. (*Just a phase,* the wife said that one time you mentioned it to her. *She'll get over it. Remember her long sulk about Easter?*) It feels like a good decision to bring them both treats, despite the wife's instructions. You take Coca-Cola bottles out of the crate in the garage and pull Tocíneta chips out of the plastic bag kept under your bed, where all the rest of the junk food is hidden. After a moment's consideration you take out a few packets of Festival cookies too—vanilla sandwich ones, her favorite. You use the Winnie the Pooh plate for the cookies, the one you bought her as a present for her fifth birthday three years ago.

You carry the tray out to the swimming pool, where the daughter is splashing and playing Little Mermaid: *Look, see how deep I can dive, I'm being chased by a shark, come save me!* Penelope is doing—you are not sure what. Some sort of float, her knees pulled into her chest, the bones in her spine sticking out. She bobs in the water facedown. Hair drifting, not moving.

Very nice, you say. *What wonderful swimming.* The scent of rotten eggs—thick, sulfurous—is flooding your nostrils, a wave so powerful you can't keep yourself from gagging, covering your mouth with your hands. The daughter screams. You turn toward her quickly, your mouth already starting to form the words, but before you can get them out something hard smacks against your foot. You look down; there are ice cubes scattered across the gritty patio tiles, pieces of dirt stuck all over them. The Winnie the Pooh plate is cracked neatly across the bear's face; the cookies are rolling like wheels until they hit the flowerpots and tumble over.

Penelope pulls her face out of the water with a deep gasp, water streaming down her face, blinking furiously. She and the daughter float there, staring at you, but you keep looking down at the plate as though searching for something important.

———

They said that without a body, the memories of the dead stay alive. They're countless, nameless—hovering around the living like horseflies on cattle, flitting at people's hair like birds. They said the bodies in the river were put there so they wouldn't be recognized and that some had been cut open so that they wouldn't float. They said that they were workers from the mines. They said it was the boy who sold lottery tickets and the woman who sold empanadas. A young man was found dead in the middle of town with pieces of his fingers and tongue cut off, like your father used to do with the turtles. They put his body in the truck, throwing it in toward the very back.

You can run from them, your mother said, *but you can't hide.* Your fingers stung from the orange you had just peeled; the tall grass of the cemetery scratched your legs as you walked beside her. *You'll think that you've gotten away,* she said, *but they'll always come back.* The memories you think you've forgotten: If you're not careful, they'll track you down, swarm over you until you don't know who you are anymore, where you end and they begin. That's what a memory you try not to have can do to you—swallow you up until there's nothing left, until it's like you've vanished into thin air, gone, disappeared. *You'll be lucky,* your mother said, *to even keep your shoes.*

Years later, she said, *if you're not careful, they'll come for you. Knocking on your door, ringing at the bell.* "I'm here for you," they'll say. "Are you ready to run?"

———

The daughter and her friend want to help you put the cookies into the trash bag but you tell them to stand back, watch out for the glass shards. You set fractured pieces of Winnie the Pooh aside—you'll piece it back together later, pay for repair glue with your own money the next time you go grocery shopping. You bring out fresh packets of cookies and chips, and the daughter and her friend eat them while sitting at the pool's edge, swirling their feet around in the water.

Wait at least fifteen minutes before you swim again, you say as you head to the door, the garbage bag slung over your shoulder. *Or else you'll get cramps.*

The daughter smiles at you with a mouthful of mushed-up cookies.

You follow the rotten egg scent through the house. You scan the living room, the dining area. The chairs are still upright, no candles have been knocked over. There's no trail of dirt on the rug or stray bits of leaves on the bookshelves.

You leave the garbage bag in the kitchen for now, take a cigarette out to the lime tree. Inhaling and exhaling, hand trembling as your raise it toward your mouth. The daughter could see you at any second, wandering over in her towel. (*Could we have some more chips, please? Come play Penguin with us!*) The husband could arrive home early with the tennis rackets in the back of the car, stare at you in brow-furrowed confusion. But you keep smoking anyway, keep your eyes focused on the small light hovering before your face as though the rest of world around you is pitch-black and that's the only thing you can see. You lean against the lime tree, the bark scratchy through your dress fabric. The piece of orange is gone; the banana is still untouched. You crane your head back, staring up at the branches, but as usual there's nothing to be seen.

It's when you shove the cigarette stub under the rock that it hits you. Staring at the neat row of cigarettes, tucked away in their secret hiding place—it occurs to you that there are many ways that something can come to be buried.

You now know exactly where to look.

Through the kitchen. Past your bedroom door. To the very back of the pantry. There are stacks of red brick from the men who redid the roof, the lamp that no longer works, the gardener's tools (lawnmower, rake, hoe). By the back wall is the big trash barrel.

You walk right up to it. You pull the lid off and push back the top layer of molding newspapers, wrinkled plastic bags, and dried-up orange peels. Spiders drop to the cement floor and scamper over your toes and up your legs; you kill them with a few brusque slaps.

The bird thing is hiding at the very bottom. It's trembling. It smells absolutely terrible. It's surrounded by leftovers from its meals. Pieces it didn't have any use for. Bits it discarded.

You lean over the barrel edge. And just for a second, you can see everything.

You use the gardener's rake to push it down. It makes a crackly sound like the dried cicada shells clinging to tree trunks, the ones the daughter likes to crush in her bare hands, toss into the air like confetti. Like the snake skins you used to find discarded by the trees at the riverbank, crumbling under your bare feet. Brittle remains, discarded remains, vomited up and spat out and now bundled at the bottom of the trash. You push down its undigested leftovers. Grains of mushy rice get stuck to the rake and your mother's turtle stew stains the side of the barrel, where it will gradually harden. You poke down the white dress with pink blossoms that you rented for your first communion, the copper smell of blood so similar to money. The words you used to know—*sapos*, snitches; *vacuna*, extortion tax. The motorcycles without registration plates, the red bandannas. The lined-up rows of the massacred, nameless dead: their shapeless brown robes and hairless thin legs; the jagged machete cut running from eye to lip. The way the plastic gearshift of the European car pressed stickily against your knee, the executive's wet fingers on your legs trembling: *I'm sorry, so sorry, I didn't mean to hurt you.*

And then there's the nurse who took care of you in the hospital. She offered to buy your baby for a couple in France who wanted one. A baby like yours, with hair like that? Who wouldn't want it? You had to say no at the last minute when your mother said that she wouldn't let you—couldn't let you. Leave the baby with her instead. She'd take care of him while you moved to Cali and got a job, washing clothes and selling arepas in the street, maybe even working for a family if you were lucky. You could save up money that way, send it home to her, give him a good life. It's a wonder, your mother said, you couldn't get the father to help—with a baby so blond like this one (a dirty blond, true, but still blond), the father would have to be someone important. Someone high up, a foreigner, even. God knows how or where you were even meeting somebody like that.

You just pressed your lips together and turned away, not answering.

There are some things that not even the bird thing gets to have. Some things don't ever deserve to be told.

You make the lasagna with eggplant after all. You bring the husband's and wife's plates out first, then the daughter's, setting them down as the phone rings. You hurry to answer it as fast as you can, sandals slapping against tiles. *Hello,* you hiss through the tiny holes in the receiver. *Yes, fine. Very busy. Did you get the money?*

He's doing well, your mother is saying. He got to raise the flag up the pole at school last Tuesday. He misses you, of course. Wants to know when your next visit is. It's been so long. Only holiday weekends; that's barely enough, and you end up spending all your time in church anyway. Never a phone call, not even a photograph in the mail.

You twist the phone cord around your finger until the skin turns dark red, almost purple.

He should come join you in Cali when he's old enough. Live with his aunt, his cousins. It'll be so much easier for you to see him that way—

No, you say, cutting her off with an abruptness that startles even you. *That's not a good idea.*

But he's so clever, your mother says. *You should see him. He could get a scholarship when he's old enough—*

Back in the dining room, the tiny silver bell is ringing.

I can't talk anymore, you say. *I'm with the family.*

You rush back as fast as you can. When you push open the swinging green door you're greeted by the daughter pulling at your apron, wrapping her sticky arms around your neck, shouting, *Happy birthday!* There's a cake on the table covered in candles; there's a package beside it wrapped up in shiny red wrapping paper. It takes you a second to realize what's going on—to remember. The wife is smiling and the husband has his elbows on the table, his hands folded in front of his mouth. Your heart is pounding the way it does when you've finished smoking an entire cigarette. *Thank you,* you say, picking up the daughter's empty plate, only a scrap of eggplant remaining. *Leave it,* the wife says, reaching out and touching your arm.

Photo, photo, the daughter says in a singsongy voice. *I want to be in the photo!* You stand behind the cake, not smiling while the daughter wraps her arms around your waist, as the wife presses the button on the camera. You open the packet (not tearing the paper, folding it carefully so that you can reuse it later), hold the black cardigan against your chest. *If it doesn't fit,* the wife says, *I can exchange it.* You cut the cake evenly, your hand not trembling: The knife forms lines so straight it'd be as easy as anything to put the pieces back together again, making it whole. You pass them each a slice. You take your own back to the kitchen, the door swinging behind you.

When they've finished eating, the wife comes in to help you with the dishes. *It's your birthday; go sit down!* You shake your head—you wash, she dries. As soon as she leaves, you take all the dishes she put away and return them to their correct places in the proper cabinets. You set the table for breakfast: bowls, spoons, juice glasses. You sweep the floor. You tuck the daughter into bed, recite the prayers with her, including the one you taught her about guardian angels, making

sure to mention the people suffering and in need. You make
the sign of the cross on her forehead and she says, *Butterfly
kiss.* You lean in close so that you can blink rapidly against her
cheek, eyelashes fluttering on her skin.

As you pass the suede armchair, where the wife is sitting
and watching the news, you stop and tell her that you made a
mistake. Actually, you don't need next weekend off after all.

Are you sure? Her eyes flicker from the screen to you.
Things will be getting much busier soon. She touches her belly
lightly, the bump more of a bulge now in her saggy white
nightdress.

Yes, you say. *God willing.*

The wife tucks a strand of hair behind her ears—brown
like the daughter's, no gray at the roots. *Whatever you prefer.
But remember that we need you here for the summer.*

That's fine, you say. *I'm not going anywhere.*

Her eyes are shifting back to the screen when you ask if it
would be possible for you to have a copy of the photograph
taken tonight. *Of course,* she says, still smiling, though her
eyes are fixed resolutely on the screen now. *I'll have Roberto
take them in by the end of the week.*

You nod, say good night. You take the beef out of the
freezer and put it in the fridge so that it can defrost. Tomorrow's dinner will be goulash; Wednesday's dinner, soufflé—
one of the most difficult dishes to prepare; you already know
the daughter will refuse to eat it and you'll have to make an
extra side dish of soup or beans for her instead. Thursday,
chicken curry—easy. Anything with chicken is easy. You wipe
down the counters.

Last of all is locking up the front door—it feels strangely

satisfying, the act of turning the key in the lock, like you're scratching an itch that you've had for a long time. As you pull the key out, you find yourself thinking about it—how a photograph is a good idea. The boy will be happy to receive it. A photograph can be kept in a frame, on a bedside table. A photograph can be taken with him wherever he goes. Something better than abrupt phone calls or brief visits on holiday weekends, better than glimpses of a life he shouldn't know you have. With enough time, and a little bit of luck, it might just work out—sometimes it's for the best if certain things never end up knocking on the door.

You fold up the damp dish towels. Back in your room, you slip off your sandals and turn them upside down so no roaches will sleep in them. You hang your dress in the closet. Before crawling into bed, you pick up the battery-powered alarm clock and make sure the switch is set to the correct position. Tomorrow, the apron will have to be washed. Tuesday is ironing day, always.

Julisa

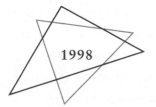

1998

ANTIOQUIA

Once again, she is not following instructions. Instead she's lying on her back on the orange-dirt basketball court, rocking her legs from side to side like windshield wipers, hands clamped in a prayer-fist on her dark blue shirt. Her mud-smeared socks are pulled up to her knees.

Eduardo stands nearby, biting his lip. It's nine A.M. and everything else is going exactly as it should. The children are filing into the building in vaguely straight lines: girls in pleated skirts, boys in trousers with white stripes running up the sides, chatter fading as they follow their teachers down the hallway. He hears the clucking of chickens from a nearby compound, the anxious whimpering of a three-legged dog crouched by a gap in the wire fence. Another Tuesday afternoon and everything is as it should be, except for her sprawled body on the ground, knees dipping back and forth.

Eduardo runs his hands through his hair. He has not worked here at the school that long. He is definitely still "one of the new ones," his education degree at the university a work in progress. Floating from classroom to classroom, standing watch during recess, helping out as needed. He has only just mastered the basics: reciting *Please keep your hands to yourself* repeatedly without sounding robotic, turning his body sideways at the last minute when the youngest ones fling themselves at him for a hug, breaking up fights by the garbage bins without getting or causing injuries. Instead of the calm military precision possessed by those who have worked here for years, he comes off as alarmingly manic, with a nervous energy that makes him particularly popular with the ten-year-old boys on the football field: eyes bulging, Adam's apple throbbing like a frog's throat, dark hair tousled wildly like that of a mad scientist who's just been electrocuted.

Even now he can barely stay still: He's drumming his fingers on his collarbones, tapping his foot, glancing anxiously at the director for support. But the director is stone-faced, standing watch as the last of the children enter. Before closing the scratched-up metal door behind him, the director sends him a glance that he is more than capable of reading by now, even with only two years of university and one semester of student teaching.

"Deal with this," the glance says. "Now."

Eduardo squats down.

"Juliana-Melissa," he says, using her full name. "It is very important that you listen and be respectful. If you don't stand up and go inside for class, then you won't be able to participate in recess today. Again."

Julisa closes her eyes. She shuffles her feet and begins to scoot along the ground sideways like a crab. He watches as she drags her torso along the dirt.

"Don't you want to go to class today? See all your friends? Learn interesting things?"

The words sound hollow, even to him. *No,* he imagines her replying curtly, pointing her sharp chin at him like a sword. *No, I fucking don't.* Can he really blame her? It's not like he was ever that good of a student either. Fuck school! Good for Juliana-Melissa, taking a stand, showing some spirit! That'll show them! Long live the rebellion against the Galactic Empire!

He sighs and clamps his fingers behind his head. Julisa is still dragging herself around in a circle, like a clock completing a rotation.

The playground is silent now, except for a teacher's voice drifting from the open classroom windows. He looks back at the building, but the door is still closed. One of the windows on the far edge of the building is broken, the glass jagged like a tooth. The way he's squatting, he feels like a bird about to lay an egg.

Juliana-Melissa, he could say, imitating the director's stern tone. *Get inside now.* If she were to ask why, he could resort to the inevitable, irrefutable answer: *Because I said so.* The director's infamous, well-worn catchphrase, echoing in the hallways, the classrooms, the office.

"Well," he says instead. "I guess I'll just have to leave you out here for the rest of the day, then." He tries to make his voice sound as confident as possible, like a lead stormtrooper giving orders. "How boring. I sure hope it doesn't rain."

Julisa doesn't say anything. He turns his body sideways so that her knees don't brush against him.

She's never aggressively rude. That's the problem! It would be so much easier if she were, in a way. She's not one of the swearers—not like Douglas, who threw a chair at his head last week while screaming, "You're the worst staff ever," or Ramón, who will return tomorrow from a weeklong suspension after twisting his teacher's nipples, or even Frank, who is apparently unable to get through a lesson without flicking water at people. She hasn't ever approached him the way Eva and Victoria have, giggling behind their hands as they ask, "So does your penis ever get hard? Do you have hair down there?" He hasn't caught her smearing a shit-covered hand over the sign that says PLEASE REMEMBER TO FLUSH on the bathroom wall, or casting a sly glance across the room as her hand skitters forward, sneaking coins out of a classmate's pocket.

Nothing like that. Just this lying here. The scrunched, shut eyelids. A painful reminder of the daily question, thudding in his gut: How is he supposed to do it? To be kind and understanding in the face of the annoyingly defiant?

"You," he says suddenly, "are not having a very good day."

She's come to a full stop now, letting her legs flop over to the side. She starts rolling her head back and forth on the dirt, like she's massaging the back of her skull.

He fiddles with the buttons on his shirt, runs his fingers

through his hair so that it's wilder than ever. They're the only two people in the courtyard now, but eventually the candy vendors will arrive for the eleven A.M. rush, wooden trays hanging from their necks by thick leather straps, rows of lollipops and battered red packets of Marlboros and plastic packets of thick yellow chips so sharp-edged they'll split open your gums. A cigarette, quite frankly, is suddenly seeming pretty good to him.

"If you come inside," he says, trying to sound calm, scientist-style, like he's giving directions in one of those apocalyptic American movies he loves to watch, or like a gangster boss icily issuing ultimatums to his mortal enemies, "that would be a very—very—big favor to me. It'll make me look like a good teacher in front of the director. Like I actually know what I'm doing. Could you do that for me, Julisa? Would you?"

No response. She's still rolling her head back and forth, one ear touching the earth, then the other. If she starts puffing up her cheeks like a fish, that's when he'll know that he's officially lost. Done for. Her rebellion complete; his negotiation process failed. It's the one expression that's one hundred percent effective at driving Julisa's classroom teacher out of her mind, reducing her to a state of tight-lipped irritation that culminates with her arm jerking in the direction of the director's office. Is that what he'll have to end up doing? Heading back inside and staring at the floor of the office, sheepishly mumbling as the director coldly blinks at him: "Juliana-Melissa . . . she's, um . . . she's . . ."

Wonderful, he thinks. *Juliana-Melissa is wonderful.*

"You know what?" he says suddenly. "Maybe you can help me with something."

He glances at the door again. Then he scoots forward, leans toward her as close as he can without tumbling over, face-first, into the ground.

"Tell me," he says in the most dramatic whisper he can manage. "You've seen them too. Right?"

Julisa doesn't open her eyes. But she stops rocking her head.

"Well, have you?" He makes his voice sound like it's trembling. Even though she can't see him, he darts his eyes around nervously, as though whatever it is he's talking about, it's everywhere. Surrounding them, inescapable, undeniable. He makes his arms tremble; he's practically giving himself goosebumps. He wraps his arms around himself to keep from shivering.

"You have to help me," he whispers. "We're going to have to find a way to escape."

She opens her eyes.

"We can't just abandon the others, though." He wipes his forehead with the back of his hand, as though he's dripping with sweat. "Maybe we can take them with us."

Julisa blinks.

"I think," he says, fixing his face into a grim expression (Al Pacino confronting Fredo! Mad Max gazing at the desert horizon!), "that I need to ask you to stand guard for me. I'm going on a quest, and I need you to watch the playground while I'm gone. This school is in *great* and *terrible* danger."

"From what?" she says. That deep, raspy voice of hers

never fails to take him slightly aback. The Pacific coast accent, the mumbling of vowels, her run-on sentences that smear into one another, so different from the musical lilts of his own cadence, Medellín-born and bred. Like most of the children, she's not from here, a recent arrival to the city who tumbled into the classroom ragged and thin and gray like shredded plastic bags hanging from barbed wire. Different slang words, different songs, different football teams to root for. Bewildered expressions, dazed eyes.

"Escape from what?" she says again, pushing herself up on her elbows. Her sudden attention feels like the thinnest of spider threads settling momentarily on him, capable of being blown away at any moment by any ill-chosen or misspoken word. The options flash across his mind in an urgent sequence: Ghosts! Demons! Devils! *La patasola,* hopping around on her single foot and drinking men's blood! *La llorona,* wandering the streets and weeping copiously for her lost children! Scarfaced ghosts banging on doors, ready to sweep you away and make you disappear, never to be heard from again! What's a scene from a film he can borrow? What's a Hollywood moment worthy of her attention? He rubs his hands together frantically as though starting a fire.

Before he can answer, though, she says, "Don't worry."

She scrambles to sit on her bottom. She is hunched over, her fists still clenched in her lap. She speaks in a hushed whisper that nevertheless sounds dramatically loud: "I can protect us."

She's opening her fist, fingers fluttering open. She's extending her hand, she's leaning forward, and without thinking Eduardo opens his palm and accepts what she drops into it.

It's a rock—a plain one. No sharp or jagged edges. No glimmering shards of color, no distinguishing features to speak of.

"This," she says, "is the Guardian. He'll keep us safe."

He stares at it. He can hear the capital letter in her voice. Before he can ask the questions that are already forming on his lips (*What do you mean? What is this for?*) she's dropping another object into his palm. This one's a black elastic hair band, covered in faint silver speckles.

"This," she says, "is the Gatekeeper. She'll keep us strong."

She's sitting upright now. Straight and tall, terribly solemn, as serious as the director when he leads the singing of the national anthem. Eduardo suddenly feels like he could bow to her, lower his forehead to the ground to pay respects. It's like watching Don Quixote defeat giants as opposed to windmills.

"Last of all—" Julisa opens her clenched fist one more time.

It's a stick. More of a twig, really. Any of the ordinary kind you can pull off an old tree or find in a patch of dirt on the hillside. She holds it in her palms like she's cradling it. If he didn't know any better, he'd think she was about to start rocking it, lullaby-style.

"This one's the most important," she says. She hesitates for a second but still drops the stick into his hand. Even after barely a second of holding it, it's already smudged dirt across his fingers.

"Who's this, then?" Eduardo says, holding it carefully alongside the other two objects.

Julisa raises her chin. "She's my favorite."

Eduardo wraps his fingers around it and holds it up like a wand, or maybe a sword—it could be anything, really, that you wanted it to be. "Yes," he says reverently. "I can see why."

Julisa grins.

Behind them, the school doors swing open. Both their heads turn: The director is strolling toward them, dark-faced and thin-lipped. "Juliana-Melissa," the director is saying. "Get inside. Now."

Eduardo stands up as fast as he can, shoving his hands into his pockets: "It's fine," he says. "It's under control—" But the director is yanking Julisa up by the elbow, pulling her roughly into the building. "You are *not*," the director is saying, "following instructions right now!"

She's taken to class, where she'll stay during recess and copy out psalms from the Bible. If she asks any questions, the director will answer, *Because I said so*. Eduardo is sent to help the third graders with their reading. He sits in on the fifth graders' English conversation class, drills the second graders in subtraction, plays football with the boys, and turns the jump rope for the girls.

It's only hours later, back home at his kitchen table, flipping the pages of his economics textbook while his mother cooks rice on the stove, that he puts his hands inside his pockets and realizes what he's kept.

Julisa doesn't show up the next day, or the one after. This in itself is not a cause for concern. It is normal for children in this neighborhood to attend school regularly for weeks, months, even years, then suddenly never be seen again. Gangs move in with their extortion taxes, families move out with their cardboard boxes and flour sacks filled to the brim, and on and on it goes. New students arrive to replace the old, streaming in endlessly with their new accents: Northern Antioquia, Chocó, the Pacific coast. This is just the way things are. What happens outside its brick walls is not the school's business.

Eduardo knows this. And yet. He brings Julisa's three items to work every day for a week. He scans the playground every morning for her small dark head, searches the hallways for a glimpse of her defiantly raised chin.

Other things happen too. Through a friend of a friend he learns the dates of the next protests and writes them down in his calendar. He joins a group that sends weekly letters to newspapers, letters that list members of army-endorsed death squads, first and last names. He impulsively writes an article for the university newspaper, something he's never done before, an article that criticizes the State's refusal to consider the ideological positions of the insurgents. (Every time he writes the phrase *the State*, he can't help but think of the director's inflexible, grimly set face, the sharpness with which he yanked Julisa to her feet.) He gives it to his editor friend Sergio: *Publish this if you dare*. Sergio raises his eyebrows but says nothing, as though phrases like *Are you sure about this?* or *So is this a risk you want to take?* are too painfully obvious to be said aloud.

And then Eduardo manages to get someone from Julisa's class to tell him where she lives: a girl who claims she went there once with her evangelical church. It's not an exact address (it never is). More like general directions.

"I didn't like it," the classmate says, blowing a bubble with her gum and immediately popping it. "It was weird there."

"Weird how?" he asks, but she gazes out over the dirt basketball court and doesn't answer.

He walks there by himself one Saturday afternoon, leaving more than enough time to get home before dark. It's farther than he expected—up a steep hillside, past withered groves of banana trees, telephone poles scarred by graffiti, signs in faded letters that say DUMPING IS PROHIBITED.

Julisa's house ends up being over an hour from the school, the dirt road twisting away from the faded wooden fence post as if frightened. The house huddles atop a muddy slope, a dusty plastic tarp yanked over the roof. There's trash scattered up and down the hillside, flattened pieces of cardboard and overturned buckets, the plastic kind you'd buy in supermarkets. It's hard not to feel like an astronaut on a strange planet, or Mad Max entering hostile territory. On the front porch a broomstick leans at an awkward angle against a refrigerator full of holes.

Eduardo stands there for a minute, holding his elbows. He takes a deep breath, but he's only taken a few steps in the house's direction when he stops again.

He's just spotted the burrows.

They're dug all over the hillside. The children are coming out of them, one at a time. They push aside the flattened cardboard, the planks of wood, the black plastic bags. Things he thought were garbage, discarded pieces of rubble. They crawl out of the shallow holes and stand before him, staring. Ten of them, a dozen. They don't speak. They're still in their school uniforms and they're all a bit muddy—cakes of dirt on their skirt hems and trousers, shirts faded, cheeks smudged, hands dirty—but otherwise nothing is out of the ordinary. There is no screaming or running around, no pointing. No wiggling or pinching, no high-pitched shrieks of *He hit me, it's not fair, I hate you, when can we play football?* If they were at recess, it'd be the most respectful behavior he's ever seen.

The children just stand there, not speaking. Somehow he finds it within himself to jerk his head in the house's direction. "Where are your parents?" he says.

None of them answer. One of the girls turns and presses her face up against another girl's shoulder.

"Wait here," he says. He heads up the hillside and bangs loudly on the rickety door—it's a wonder he doesn't cause the entire house to come tumbling down. "Hello?"

Nobody answers, but he still has the unmistakable feeling that somebody is on the other side, pressing their face against the wood, holding their breath. He glances over his shoulder— the children are all watching him. He knocks again, as hard as he can this time, then turns abruptly away as though seized by the uncontrollable need to stare out into the distance toward— what? The rest of the city spread out before him? The school with its tall brick buildings? His university library with its books and shelves?

By the time he's walked back down the hill to where they are standing, some of the children are already beginning to turn away. "Julisa," he says. "Is she here?" He reaches into his jacket and pulls out the items one at a time. Stone, hair tie, stick: the Guardian, the Gatekeeper, the one that was her favorite.

The girl with her face buried in her friend's shoulder closes her eyes. But one of the boys says, "Julisa's gone."

The girl whose shoulder is being leaned on says, "I can keep those for her."

Eduardo hands them over. The girl takes them from him with an alarming quickness, snatching them from his palm, clutching them to her chest. He opens his mouth to ask: *Is Julisa okay? Did she go, or was she taken? Is she safe; is she strong?* In the back of his mind, an unspoken question flickers, one for himself: *Do I really want to know?* He abruptly shuts his mouth, the questions dying on his lips. He instantly knows he has made a terrible mistake.

The children haven't noticed: They're already turning away from him, crawling back into the burrows. As he walks away they're raising the cardboard and pulling it down over their heads.

He never mentions what he's seen to anybody. He's careful not to talk about it—not to bring it up in staff meetings, not to think about it while studying his economics textbook in the evenings, or when pitching stories to Sergio about the link between death squadrons and the government, or among the jostling shoulders of the crowded university protests.

And then there's the night he's yanked into a deserted alleyway by three men with close-cropped hair, their motorcycles humming in the distance. They pull machetes out of the waistbands of their trousers. *You've been publishing the wrong kind of articles,* they say before bringing a blade down hard on his right hand.

If he tries hard enough, the memory might just start to fade. With enough time, and a little bit of luck, it might be like it never happened at all.

Armadillo Man

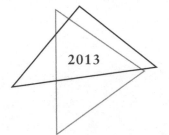

2013

NARIÑO

The Armadillo Man is watching her. She can tell by how quickly he lowers his face when she abruptly turns toward her bedroom window. He's sitting in his usual spot, on the white plastic chair beneath the grapefruit tree, walking stick leaning against his knee, hands folded in his lap. She raises her arms and jumps up and down, letting the towel drop. The wind sways the grapefruits above his head; his eyes stay resolutely fixed to the ground. She spins around, does jumping jacks, turns and bends over so that her hands lie flat on the floor. She wiggles her rear end and begins writing the alphabet in the air with it, spelling one letter at a time in long, lazy arcs. She gives him a good show—the best she has to offer.

———

Later that morning they go for a walk. They take shortcuts by crossing through people's yards, stepping over the collapsed portions of walls blown apart by grenades. They cut directly through abandoned houses, walking around shattered glass, splintered furniture, and piles of cigarette butts. There are never any lightbulbs or electric cables, no taps in the sinks or handles on the toilets. She leaves the doors cracked open for stray cats.

In Hortensia's old garden, they find the body of a drowned chicken in the fishpond. He surprises her by handing over his walking stick and getting down on his knees. He fishes the body out with his bare hands and tosses it into a nearby bush. When he stands up again (slowly but still surely), the knees of his blue jeans have transformed into muddy brown eyes staring mournfully back at her.

"What should we do with it?" she says, circling the bush warily. The water drips from its feathers and runs down the leaves of the bush, forming tiny rivers in the dirt below.

"Leave it," he says. "The other chickens will eat it."

"What!"

"You haven't seen them? Even the chicks will join in." He shakes his wrists up and down, splattering water on her shirt. "Pick the bones clean," he adds.

"That's disgusting!"

"Why?"

"Is that what you want to happen to you?" Her voice keeps rising, getting more high-pitched.

"What I want," he says, "is nobody's business."

She keeps looking at the bush. If it wasn't for the chicken's swollen claws and cloudy eyes, it could just as easily be sleeping.

"Or if you'd like," he says, "we could dig a hole."

"That's stupid." She's already walking away. So he leaves it there, propped up on the shelf of branches, where, she hopes, the beetles and ants will get to it first.

She dreams about sitting in church. On the ceiling are dozens of arms and legs, layers deep, sticking out like prickles on a cactus. As she stands and walks down the aisle, they keep brushing lightly against her hair: the wrists and heels, elbows and toes. As she approaches the door she begins to stumble; looking down, she sees fingers growing out of the floor, springing up between the tiles like weeds. The air is filled with smoke and smells like rotten eggs. Something thick and squishy is lolling around in her mouth, but no matter how hard she pushes it against her teeth with her tongue, she can't spit it out.

When she opens her eyes in the dark bedroom, her pillow is on the floor. For a second she thinks she can still smell rotten eggs, that the dream is a memory that never ended, an event that's still taking place, but she's able to take a deep breath and swallow hard before the pounding of her heart gets any worse. The sky outside her window is dark blue, and somewhere inside the room a cricket is singing. She picks up the pillow, flips it over to its cool side, and pulls her knees as close to her chin as possible.

When she's not taking him on walks or completing basic household chores, the main part of Sofía's job is accompanying the Armadillo Man on daily house calls. Three months ago, a few days after she and her aunt had returned from the morgue, he knocked on their door and said, "You know, now that I'm a retired man, I've been thinking I could use some help." It only took the first few hours for her to realize that he didn't actually need a caretaker, that he didn't need any help, period—from her or anyone. But she's never brought it up, neither to him nor to her aunt, so every evening the same ritual takes place: He gives her some crumpled brown bills in the kitchen and she walks next door to press the money into her aunt's hands.

That morning they go see Pastora. Her mustard-colored house looks bright against the rolling fields stretched behind it, the land brown from the government fumigations. Even the bananas in the front yard hang black and heavy, the large leaves wilted and discolored. In the kitchen Pastora bustles busily about, serving them overcooked rice mashed with white bread and sugar. Sofía manages a few bites before sculpting the mush into a smooth white mountain in the middle of her plate, making it look as though she's eaten more than she really has. Pastora and the Armadillo Man talk for hours, with Pastora saying things like "the taxes the guerrillas charged were much less" and "dressing dead civilians in rebel uniforms—shameless, utterly shameless." In his unmistakable Bogotá accent, with its calm, straightforward steadiness, the

Armadillo Man mostly responds with things like "Animals, animals," or "That's how it goes—they'll just keep going."

Sofía drinks her coffee in silence. She flips her arms over every few minutes, studying the different patterns the scratchy tablecloth has pushed into her skin. Every once in a while she sneaks a glance at the Armadillo Man's hands—even after three months as his caretaker, it still feels like an act she needs to get away with. Something sneaky, undercover. The skin on his hands morphs into different colors: patches of red in some places, brownish yellow in others. There's a bloated purple bump near his ring finger, engorged like a mini head. On his face the skin is white and flaky, like a tree trunk covered in lichens, with the patches in the middle parting in opposite directions, as if his face is trying to peel itself open.

"Six months and nothing," Pastora says loudly. "Not a word about a ransom. Not for the husband, nor for the son." She thumps her hand against the table, rattling the cups. "Eugenia is going out of her mind."

"I guess she didn't have a deal with the cartels after all," the Armadillo Man says.

"Don't you mean the guerrillas?"

"Maybe," he says. "Or I could mean the army. Or the paramilitaries. Does it make a difference?" He places his hands on the table, palms facing upward, as though offering her something invisible.

It still shocks her sometimes, looking at him that directly, in a room like Pastora's kitchen where plenty of light trickles in through the high windows. She keeps forgetting that he's not an old man. His eyes are watery but clearly belong to someone her uncle's age (or how old her uncle would have been), and the morning light as it hits his face makes his gray eyebrows turn white. She slurps the last of her coffee and wonders (not for the first time) if there's a scar somewhere, a pair of faded red blemishes or a single dark puckered hole, where the jungle parasite first entered his body. How would it have happened? It would have been five years ago: The Armadillo Man, who back then would have just been the Professor, a teacher originally from Bogotá who'd been teaching at the town's high school for years. Marching through the jungle, men with rifles and camouflage pants walking steadily beside him. Black rubber boots with yellow bottoms. A metal collar around his neck, attached to a chain. Once the Professor, now the Armadillo Man.

At what point did he realize what was happening to him? Did he figure it out for himself, or did the guards point it out? What part of his flesh began to rot away first?

"It was the Necktie cut that they used," Pastora says, brushing her fingers lightly across her throat. "Heads off. Genitals in mouth."

"That's not the Necktie," the Armadillo Man says. "That's the Monkey. The Necktie is when they pull the tongue through the jaw. And not all of them had their genitals in their mouths, just one."

"You can't pull out a tongue with a chain saw," Pastora says.

The two of them suddenly look at Sofía, as if only just remembering her presence.

"So nice to see there are still young people left in this town,"

Pastora says in a voice that sounds more angry than glad, and Sofía pushes away her coffee cup, hiding it behind the bag of sugar.

Next is a winding road up the mountain to Ramiro. His house is the one with a corrugated tin roof and a giant plastic tub sitting on top to capture rainwater. When they reach the front yard there's a goat tied to a stick bleating menacingly. It has the bushiest white eyebrows she's ever seen. She stops in her tracks until the Armadillo Man says, "That's enough, David." When Ramiro comes out of the house to greet them, she thinks, *David?*

Ramiro's back garden is filled with dead cornstalks and yucca plants. The narrow trunks of two papaya trees reach skyward, their leaves hanging limp on top. They walk on the path through the cornstalks, following Ramiro until he leads them to a field of coca bushes, the leaves browning and dry. Beside her, the Armadillo Man's breath sounds a little ragged, but when she offers him her forearm he shakes his head.

"See this one?" Ramiro says, pausing and kneeling beside a bush. He uses his machete to point at the roots, where there are still some green leaves left. "Still alive and fighting." His grin is a shelf of fuzzy yellow teeth. "That's a personal trick of mine—if you cut off the tops just after they've been sprayed, the roots don't die. That way, the bush can regrow. How about that?"

"Amazing," she says, scratching her arm. She doesn't have the heart to tell him that Yaison, twenty minutes away, does the same thing. She glances at the Armadillo Man, who's looking expressionlessly around the field, blinking slowly, sweat glistening in the cracks in his forehead. Ramiro pulls off the greenest leaves and sticks them behind the elastic band of his sweatpants.

On the walk back, Ramiro uses his machete again to point out several lines of holes in the dirt, several inches deep, surrounded by empty shell casings. "American helicopters!" he says, sounding almost happy, as if flattered that they even bothered. At his house he takes them on a tour of his botanical garden: bromeliads and orchids, ficus and ferns. The pots are lined against every wall space available, so she can't walk anywhere without a branch brushing against her arm or face. *Ten years ago,* she thinks, *this house would have been perfect for playing Tarzan.* Six years old, playing with her uncle: She would crawl around on her hands and knees, the jungle canopy overhead, monkeys whooping and jaguars growling in the distance. Her uncle always played the part of Cheetah the chimp, dragging his knuckles on the living room floor as she leaped from couch to chair, beating her fists against her chest. She swallows and roughly pushes a bougainvillea vine away from her face.

At one point Ramiro takes her aside, pulls the leaf off a nearby plant, and tells her to rub it against the yellowing bruises on her upper arm, faint stains left over from the last time her aunt pinched her. "It's also a cure for AIDS," he says, pressing a handful of leaves into her palm.

As soon as he's out of earshot, she says in a low voice to the Armadillo Man, "I have AIDS?"

He covers his mouth with his hands as though cupping his laughter. A warm feeling spreads through her chest like spilt water, and she takes a deep breath.

Ramiro puts the coca leaves into a brown paper bag. "Five minutes without boiling over," he says, handing it to the Armadillo Man, who passes him some bills in return. "That'll take care of any aches and pains!" He winks at Sofía, who smiles stiffly back.

"Bye, David," she says to the goat.

As they walk down the hill he says, "Oh my, my."

"Why 'Oh my, my'?"

"Every human being has to make his own mistakes," he says. He suddenly sounds impatient, striking his walking stick forcefully against the ground, so she doesn't speak again until they're back in town.

Their last visit of the day is to the municipal building in the town center, where they're greeted at the door by Márquez, the ex-sacristan. Márquez is from a Venezuelan border town. He speaks with a stutter and always stares directly at Sofía's chest when saying hello. It makes her uncomfortable enough to not feel bad about being rude to him and abruptly charging into the building without offering him a cheek to kiss first.

For the past two months the mayor has let people use the first floor of the building as a church space, until the archbishop in Bogotá sends funds to clear away the last of the rubble and rebuild. "It's going to happen soon," Márquez says, his voice cracking with a squeaky enthusiasm that Sofía finds profoundly irritating. "I really think he means it this time—I do!" The Armadillo Man nods and flips through important-looking papers while she wanders around the room.

The rickety metal tables are covered with remains salvaged three months ago from the debris: fragments of Jesus and Vir-

gin Mary statues, a dirty silver chalice. Splintered wooden
boards are stacked against the walls. She looks at everything
closely but doesn't touch. Three months since they lined everybody up in the church plaza. Three months since she and
her aunt visited the morgue. And this is still all that's left. The
longer she looks at everything, the harder her heart pounds,
until she has to wrap her arms tightly around herself, as if
afraid of losing her balance.

The next morning at breakfast her aunt says, "Be careful."

"What?"

"You know." Her aunt stirs her coffee rapidly, the spoon
clinking against the glass, the liquid transformed into a whirl-
pool. Sofía watches carefully to see if any liquid sloshes over
the side, but it never does. "He's a man."

"He's the Armadillo Man."

"Still a man," her aunt says. "And don't call him that. It's
disrespectful."

"But he came up with it himself. He says that being called
Professor makes him feel old."

"Shouldn't you be eating your breakfast instead of talking
back?"

Sofía looks down at the rapidly cooling arepa on her plate.
She slowly picks it up and stuffs it into her mouth whole,
barely chewing, holding her breath to keep the nausea from
rising. When she smiles at her aunt, all that shows is a mass of
white corn mush.

"Don't be an idiot," her aunt says. "I know you've barely
been eating. God knows he's been a help—your uncle would

have surely appreciated it." Sofía looks away. Her aunt's eyes have filled with tears, but with a shaky breath she's able to keep talking. "But all I'm saying is pay attention to how he looks at you. And God help us if you end up catching what he has."

She spits out the blob of unchewed food into her palm. When she swallows, a lump of warm saliva burrows down her throat, pushing down the sentence *Scars aren't catching.*

When she wakes that night, sweating and shaking, the disembodied arms and legs are still brushing against her forehead, as lightly as Ramiro's leaves, flitting at her hair like birds. She gets out of bed and heads to the window. She can see over the shrapnel-pocked wall into his yard: the back porch and potted geraniums, the grapefruit tree and empty soap dishes filled with water for stray cats. The white plastic chair is sitting in the same spot, empty. The door is shut and no lights are on, so if she didn't know any better it would look like nobody was home. She stands as close to the window as possible, pressing her bare skin against the glass.

The bruises don't fade, but the leaves cause a prickly red rash to appear. "Maybe I didn't rub it in hard enough," she says in the kitchen the next morning as she shows him her arm. He doesn't touch her as he looks, but all of a sudden she's conscious of the sweat stains in her armpits, of how she's holding her arm in the same position as Rose in the *Titanic* drawing scene. He drinks coffee at the table and listens to the radio as she washes the dishes. When she bends over to open the cupboard beneath the sink, she wonders how high her shirt rises on her back. She arches her spine slightly, feeling her hip bones push up against her jeans. It makes her stomach feel quivery, as if she's drunk too much coffee. She almost starts swaying her butt, spelling out the letter *A,* but stops at the very last second, quickly reaching for the rags. When she stands up she tries to make out his reflection in the kitchen window, but in the glass he just looks like a ghostly blur.

That day they go somewhere new: a house with metal sheets for walls, nearly a fifty-minute walk down the main road. The inside of the house smells like a mixture of must and salt and has a dirt floor. The furniture is four plastic chairs spaced evenly around a wooden table with a scratched surface. Each chair is occupied by a small child: three girls, and a boy with a shaved head. None of them can be more than ten years old. They swing their legs, staring at Sofía and the Armadillo Man as though they've been sitting there all morning just watching the door, awaiting their arrival. Their flip-flops are repaired with gray plastic threads she recognizes from sacks of flour.

He surprises her by insisting on doing the cooking himself, untying the knots of the plastic bags they've brought along. "Talk to the children," he says, slicing the plantains rapidly. As he drops the yellow circles into the spitting-hot oil, she kneels next to a girl cradling a gnawed corncob in her arms like a baby.

"What a pretty doll!" she says, lightly touching the girl's hair. Even from high up she can see the silver specks of lice eggs clinging to the roots.

The girl says, "It's a piece of corn."

Thankfully he cooks fast. She helps him spoon the food out evenly onto a stack of cracked plates that still have ancient grains of rice clinging to them. When the Armadillo Man passes her a plate, she quickly shakes her head, pressing her lips together.

"Don't worry, it's not for you," he says. "This way." He jerks his head toward the scratched-up wooden door behind her, hanging halfway off its hinges. While the children eat, she follows him into a dark bedroom, where the musty smell is so pungent she nearly stops breathing.

"Lunch, Gregorio," the Armadillo Man says, and in the bed what she thought was a bunched-up pile of sheets begins to stir. It's a man dressed only in shorts, propped up on a pillow, both arms ending in shiny pink stumps.

"Here," the Armadillo Man says, patting the edge of the mattress.

She spoons the rice into Gregorio's mouth while the Armadillo Man hovers nearby, chatting cheerfully about that morning's news. The government is offering a cow and barbed wire to everyone who uproots their coca bushes and plants *lulo* trees instead, and the Soldier for a Day program will soon be coming to town, so children can go and get camouflage makeup painted on their faces. Every once in a while he reaches out to brush off the grains of rice that have fallen on the sheet. Gregorio's face, chest, arms, and legs are covered in raw red sores shaped like cockroaches, some of which are bleeding. She alternates between holding her breath and breathing through her front teeth, which makes a faint whistling sound she prays no one can hear.

"Anything else, Gregorio?" the Armadillo Man says when the plate is empty.

Gregorio opens and closes his mouth. "No," he finally whispers.

When they walk out the door ("See you next week," he tells the children, who don't look up from the last grains of rice they're shoveling into their mouths), she can't help herself. She takes a deep breath and rubs her hands up and down her arms, as if suddenly chilled despite the bright sunlight.

"Do you want to know what happened?" he says after a few minutes.

"No." It's true too. She couldn't be less interested.

While they are walking along in silence she amuses herself by picturing the second half of the Armadillo Man's story. One scene follows another in her head, almost comfortingly, like images from a bedtime story, or a soap opera on TV. The Armadillo Man, escaping his kidnappers by throwing himself off a cliff. Crouching in a riverbank hole for days before deciding that his only way out of the jungle was following the river. Meeting illegal loggers who helped lead him back to town, how Dr. Ortiz barely managed to save the last of his skin from falling off his face. Her uncle told her the story, waving his cigarette around as if painting pictures in the air with the smoke; he not only made it seem as if it had happened to him personally but as if he'd enjoyed it.

"That Professor," her uncle said, flicking the ash of his Marlboro into the grass. "He's seen it all. Lived through it too."

She knows they're getting close to town when they pass a row of recently abandoned houses, the ones with no roof tiles or windows, the street crisscrossed with mossy electric cables. On one of the house walls, someone's spray-painted the initials of a paramilitary group in black capital letters. On another wall, the letters are separated by two painted hands with clawlike fingernails, each cupping a skull. Underneath the hands it says *IN DEATH WE ARE ALL EQUAL.*

That night in the dream she's able to spit it out. She's made it as far as the church door, her hand hovering over the wooden handle, when it falls from her mouth and hits the tiles with a squelch. The air is still smoky and sulfurous but she's able to see what it is without kneeling. A man's finger, the dark knuckle hair flattened by her spit, a crescent of black dirt beneath the bitten yellow nail, skin the color of egg white.

She stays in bed for a long time that morning, neither awake nor asleep. Her aunt enters the room without knocking. "Go away," she says without raising her head. "I think I have a worm."

"The things you come up with." Her aunt opens the curtains with a quick flick. "If you actually ate something besides coffee you'd feel fine."

"I mean it. My asshole is burning."

"My God, Sofía!" Her aunt's earrings, enormous silver hoops, swing as she shakes her head.

"I can feel it down there. Poking around."

"Then I guess we'll have to take you to Dr. Ortiz and have him take a look."

"Good luck with that." Ortiz was one of the lucky ones. Instead of getting him in the church three months ago, they left him on his doorstep, wrists tied behind his back with a shoelace and a slice in his torso from the base of the neck to the belly button.

The way her aunt's face crumples, it makes her wonder for a second if she had really forgotten—or if she hadn't wanted to remember.

"Okay, okay," Sofía says. She uses her hand to steady herself against the mattress as she swings her feet onto the icy floor.

In the kitchen, she stares at her wavering reflection in the cup of coffee before slowly walking over to the sink and pouring it down the drain. Her tongue is fat and hot in her mouth, squished behind her teeth. Her aunt remains seated, calmly peeling an orange with her sharp fingernails.

When she picks up the bucket of cleaning supplies, her aunt says, without looking up, "Make sure you get rid of that ass-face before you head over there."

"This is my normal face," Sofía says. "Is my normal face an ass-face?" She pulls the mop roughly away from its resting place against the wall.

"Oh, Sofía," her aunt says, placing the last of the orange segments on the plate as Sofía heads toward the door. "Try asking yourself sometime—are you acting in a way that would make your uncle proud?"

The harder she presses her lips together, the less chance there will be of it all coming out. Spilling everywhere. Splattering.

Instead of following the usual route to the Armadillo Man's door, she keeps walking down the mountainside until the grass becomes knee-high. When she comes to a wooden bench she sits down heavily, letting the bucket drop and roll across the dirt. Her uncle built the bench as a place to sit and sharpen his machete before heading into the forest below to clear away the underbrush. When she was little, she used to sit with him in the evenings as the sun set, and he'd point out the fireflies. There used to be hundreds of them before the pesticide sprayings, they would light up the dark silhouettes of the surrounding mountains. "Do you think they're more like stars?" he once said, gesturing expansively at them, as if he could sweep them all up into the palm of his hand. "Or Christmas tree lights?"

"They're like the eyes of angels!" she answered. "Or the lights of alien spaceships!" Her uncle stared at her for a moment before beginning to reverently applaud, as if awed by the scope of her imagination.

If he were to ask her now, she knows exactly what she'd say. *They're bugs, Uncle. It's silly to pretend that they could be anything else.*

When she sits here now, what she often sees are the lines of people draping over the mountain as they walk the winding trails. Pulling wagons, pushing wheelbarrows. Mattresses balanced on heads, cows and pigs in tow. Horse carts moving at a fast clip, people clutching baskets with legs dangling over the rims, entire families crowded onto a single motorcycle. Heading out, moving forward. Medellín, Bogotá, Cali— anywhere but here.

She exhales. The smell of rotten eggs is back, filling the back of her throat. She turns her face away from the bench and vomits up a thin stream of brown liquid—it's always brown first thing in the morning, but by evening it will be pale, transparent, the color of nothing. She wipes her mouth off with the back of her wrist. "There, there," she says. Wraps her arms around her rib cage, pulls herself close into a hug.

When she finally feels it, she doesn't need to open her eyes to know what it is. Scratchy and rough, like the back of a new sponge. The Armadillo Man's hand, resting on her forearm. She opens her eyes and looks at him. He looks right back, the peeling skin beneath his eyes trembling.

"Let's go," he says.

She's never sat in his living room before. Mopped and dusted it, yes, pushing a broom beneath the couch and running a wet rag over the windowsills, wiping the dust from the fogged-up frames of his university diploma and teaching certificate from Bogotá. Until now, though, she never actually dared to lower herself into the leather armchair, the cushions sighing beneath her as they release high-pitched exhalations of air.

He brings her a mug of steaming-hot water from the kitchen. Without his stick he walks stiffly, swinging his knee as though it is an ax chopping the air. When she brings the mug close to her face, she sees dark green coca leaves swirling at the bottom.

"Have you had any lunch?" he says, lowering himself into the plastic white chair. "If you're not careful, the wind's going to blow you away any day now."

"You sound like my aunt," she says, in a voice that's meaner than she intended. The curtains are wide open; anybody walking by in the street could look through the window and see them, stop and stare. She has a crazy, shaky feeling inside her chest, as though she's swallowed a tiny animal that's now frantically dancing around. She checks the water in the mug to make sure her hand isn't trembling.

He reaches for the brown paper bag sitting on the table, slowly turns it upside down, and pours out the remaining leaves. "You know," he says, picking up a leaf and twirling it around, "when I was in the jungle, I used to count these."

"The jungle?" It takes her a second to figure out what he's referring to: the Armadillo Man, who back then was the Professor. A chain around his neck and rubber boots on his feet, a tiny speck in an ocean of green.

He holds the leaf between his index finger and thumb. "I'd start with the ones on the ground, the brown ones. Then I'd move on to the tree branches, the green ones. Last of all would be yellow—there were never that many yellow ones." He brings the leaf to his face and touches it to his lips, as if smoking it.

"That sounds . . . awful," she says. She almost says *boring,* but manages not to.

"Oh, you know," he says. "It could have been worse. They never blindfolded me." He lowers his hand back to the table. "You'd always hear things—stories and rumors from the guards. Apparently there was an American prisoner in another camp somewhere. He started talking to the trees as if they were people." He stares at the leaf for a moment before slowing closing his fingers over it.

"I'm glad you escaped," she says, saying the words carefully, as if they're water she's afraid of spilling.

He makes a fist, and she hears the leaf crunching.

"You're not going to believe this from an old man like me," he says, "but I've been very fortunate. And so have you."

His face is close enough for her to touch, if that's what she wanted. If she asked him about that night—the time he watched her through the window—what would he say? Did he care? Remember, even?

"I'm going to Cali," she says abruptly. "As soon as my aunt lets me."

He looks at her.

"I'll work in a house there," she says. "I'll be good at it—don't you think?" She can picture it too, like something that's already happened. Her sandals in the hallway, propped up beside the door. A brand-new washing machine and a shiny modern kitchen. Giant TV screens to dust, DVD films to organize, shelves of brand-new American toys. She'll do the dishes every evening, the ones stacked in the sink and crusted over with lentils and rice; she'll scrub them clean with bright yellow gloves and sponges that are constantly replaced. She'll sweep the floors, punch the pillows to fluff them up, take out the garbage and cook things like lasagna, food from places like America or Italy, recipes she's only ever seen on TV soap operas.

She can't wait.

"Sofía," the Armadillo Man says in a careful-sounding voice, as though afraid his words might break something, "you're good at more than just that."

"Like what?" She abruptly pulls her hands into her lap.

He whispers something, mouth barely moving, so she has to lean across the table in order to hear him.

"Teach," he's saying. "You could be a teacher."

She stares at him like it's the stupidest thing she's heard in her life. "Professor," she says, and it's only when she says the words out loud that she realizes it's the first time she's called him that since he escaped. "I can't even read."

He looks down at the leaf pieces in his hand, the shredded fragments. "I could teach you."

She shakes her head.

"I could marry a narco trafficker," she says. "Or an army general. Which do you think my aunt would prefer?"

His lips twitch strangely and it takes her a second to realize that he's trembling. The cracks in his face look deeper and darker than ever. He leans forward and sprinkles the leaf pieces on top of her head.

"Well," he says. "A crown for your wedding day. You say what you think at the moment you think it, don't you?"

"My aunt says it's because I never helped out at the altar when I was young." She can feel the leaf pieces resting lightly on her hair, trembling like insects clinging to grass stalks.

"You mean," he says, "you're not young now?"

She slips her foot out of her sandal and places her bare foot on top of his leg, near his inner thigh. He stares at it.

"You're not old," she says. "Not really."

He doesn't answer.

She blows her nose on her shirt, a loud honking noise. "You're the same age as my uncle," she says. "Do you remember my uncle?"

He looks at her. She starts coughing so hard it almost turns into a gag.

"I keep thinking I can feel the pieces," she says when she is finally able to speak, "in my mouth."

She presses her fingers against her lips.

"Everyone was splattered," she says. "Everywhere."

She wants to tell him that in the morgue three months ago, her first thought was *At least chain saws make burials easy.* The laughter came out of her in a high-pitched burst, and both her aunt and the mortician turned slowly toward her, half-bewildered, half-appalled. Why couldn't people just disappear? Vanish into thin air, leaving nothing behind but shoes in a hallway, shirts in a closet, a dusty framed photograph on a bedside table? Wasn't it better to not have an explanation, a clear cohesive picture of what happened? Nothing like what the morgue had. Not at all.

He stands up abruptly, pushing the chair back behind him so hard it topples over. Her foot slides off his leg and smacks loudly against the tiled floor.

"Do you know," he says, "the best way to cook a chicken?"

Her hands move down from her face and begin squeezing the T-shirt cloth in front of her chest, her fists tightening into balls.

"The trick is," he says, "to cook it in the oven. No more than an hour and twenty minutes, exactly. It's not as fast as frying, but worth it." He's heading into the kitchen; he's opening the pantry door. He takes out three onions, a carrot as long as a witch's finger, garlic cloves with wispy skins, leafy stalks of celery. "You can cook it by itself, if you want," he says, opening a drawer and taking out a knife and a cutting board, "but you look like you need some vegetables. Vegetables and gravy."

She's still twisting the cloth of her T-shirt, as though wringing an animal's neck. He opens a cupboard, reaches down into a cloth sack, pulls out a handful of small yellow potatoes. "Fresh herbs also make a big difference. I bet that your aunt grows some in her garden, doesn't she? Do you recognize these from Ramiro's?"

He's moved to the windowsill now, is pointing at a row of small black plastic pots. Her hands are still clenching her shirt but her knuckles are no longer white. She shakes her head, nose dripping all over her chin and chest, but she doesn't make a move to wipe it off, and he doesn't offer her a kitchen rag.

It takes hours but she waits for him. She lets him take his time and do it the way he wants to: properly and slowly. She doesn't ask him questions like "Are you done yet?" or "Is it ready?" Instead she's patient, even as the house fills with a rich, salty smell and the sky outside the window darkens. She doesn't move or stir from her chair while he wipes off the counters and sweeps the floor, stiffly yet steadily. He makes a salad in a wooden bowl with lettuce leaves and olives from a dusty jar. She doesn't act annoyed or confused when he lays out a tablecloth or when he warms the plates and cutlery in the oven just before serving. He cuts off an enormous slab of meat, right from the center of the chicken, before passing her the plate.

"Here," he says, watching her take the first bite. He was right about removing the aluminum foil for the last ten minutes. The chicken skin is evenly browned and perfectly crisp, the meat so moist it almost feels like liquid in her mouth. She takes one bite, then another. He sits there watching, his hands folded on the table, fingers interlinked. She only opens her mouth a crack at first; then slowly but surely her bites get bigger, lips opening wide. Grease drips down her chin and stains her shirt but she keeps raising and lowering her fork. Her mouth fills with juices; she can barely move her tongue. She swallows.

It's even better than what he promised. Better than what she could have ever imagined.

Beyond the Cake

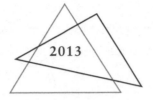

2013

CAUCA–VALLE DEL CAUCA

When Mariela invited us, we all got to go. This was back when kids were expected to invite every single person in the class for their birthday parties. It added up to something like eleven or twelve parties a year for me. I never got to go to any summer ones because I always went to D.C. to visit relatives. Plenty of us had ranches of our own outside the city, of course, but nothing like that. Not like hers.

It was a pretty great party. Instead of a piñata there was candy thrown out of the window, which everyone screamed and fought for in the grass, and gift bags filled with whistles and sticker sheets, and a pony we could ride around the yard, led by a man in a black-and-white straw hat. I didn't ride it because I was scared of the way its ribs curved out. We ate hot dogs with black char marks from the grill and chased around baby ducks and chicks that had been dyed pink and purple. There was a monkey that could kick a football, and fuzzy white rabbits with giant pink eyes, and a lion cage that we weren't allowed to approach, no matter how much we begged the gardener for permission. We went swimming in a pool with blue tiles and dived for the little frogs clinging to the drain covers. And then Sebastián left a brown turd in the corner of the shallow end, and we all jumped out of the pool screaming like a shark was chasing us.

Then it was time for Mariela to open her presents, which I couldn't bear to watch. My mother was the one who bought the presents for me to take to all those parties. She must have gotten pretty sick of it. For Mariela, she wrapped up an Eric doll. You know, Eric, the prince from The Little Mermaid. *That was a damn ugly doll. His face was all puffy and out of proportion to the rest of his body, like he was recovering from the measles. I felt so humiliated at the prospect of giving such a thing to Mariela, who I always thought was the smartest girl in kindergarten. It didn't help that there were girls there like Penelope, who had long eyelashes and two Ps in her name, and her best friend, Stephanie Lansky, who had hair down to her waist. The thought of girls like Penelope and Stephanie staring at that dumb-looking doll made me sick to my stomach. So when the moment came that Mariela started unwrapping it, I had to leave the room and ask one of the maids to call my parents to come pick me up. I couldn't bear the thought of watching it happen. I was a fairly anxious child, you know.*

———

"No kidding," he says. "And then what happened?"

"Well, that was it. I didn't even get a slice of cake."

It was a sponge one too—her favorite, the kind with strawberry jam in the middle. She saw it from a distance, set up behind the pile of presents.

They've been in the Popayán hotel room all day. "When the cleaning staff come," she tells him, "they're going to think the room was attacked by an eighties rock band." She's not exaggerating: bloodstains on the sheets from her period, shit smears on the heavy wool comforter (now crammed in the corner by the dresser) thanks to a misguided attempt at anal sex, crusty vomit on the carpet from where he leaned over the edge of the mattress and vomited up the aguardiente they'd stayed up all night drinking, up on the rooftop with the Australian tourists.

"No way," he says. "Just blame it on Mouse Pilot." This is one of several imaginary alter egos he adopts around her: a dapper World War II, Han Solo–esque fighting ace. It consists of him sputtering his lips (in imitation of a biplane engine), swaying his head around in slow circles (in imitation of legendary maneuvers made by first-class, world-famous pilots), and bringing his still-sputtering lips close to her body. There was maybe a specific reason why he chose to call this persona Mouse Pilot, as opposed to Fox or Deer or Rabbit, but it was so long ago she no longer remembers. This time around, he chooses to land his biplane lips on her neck.

"Not on the face!" she says. Even after two years together, she is still ticklish to the point of peeing herself. She covers her mouth and tries not to laugh.

They eat the rest of the birthday cake he bought her yesterday, one piece at a time. The disappearing slices transform the cake into a tiny Pac-Man, opening his mouth wider and wider. The cake is chocolate with vanilla frosting just the way she likes it, a thin coating rather than a thick slather. She eats the chocolate sprinkles first, picking them off one at a time, while he crams the entire piece into his mouth. He scrapes hardened crumbs off the cardboard with his index finger and lets her slurp down the remaining mush of frosting and cake.

"I feel sick," he says.

"Like vomiting sick?"

He shakes his head and pulls his knees into his chest, curling up beside her like a prawn. "More like sick in the head." He buries his face in the crook of her arm.

"Mouse Pilot," she says. "What have we done to ourselves?"

They take a shower together in a pitiful attempt to eliminate their headaches. He stands under the trickle of lukewarm-bordering-on-ice-cold water with his eyes closed, while she presses herself against the tiled wall with her arms crossed over her chest, covered in goosebumps.

"Ugh, freezing," she says

He leans in to kiss her and knocks over the tiny bottles of shampoo and conditioner.

"Eduardo," she says. "Be careful."

She ends up shaving her legs with his razor in the sink. "Me too?" he says, climbing out of the shower and standing beside her, still naked and dripping wet. "Please?"

He points at his face with his right hand. Water trickles off the stumps where his fingers should be: second, third, and pinkie.

She shaves him carefully, running the blade down his neck and cheeks, the same way she's done it countless times before. There are many things he can do just fine with his left hand (play basketball with his contemporary Latin American economics students, slice tomatoes for pasta night), but for whatever reason, shaving is not one of them (volleyball, turning certain doorknobs, and playing musical instruments are others).

Back in bed, wrapped in towels, he works on his paper for the upcoming conference while she watches a tennis match on TV. His left hand picks at the keyboard, thudding out one word at a time. "I should have finished this days ago," he says, face creased in misery. "What was I thinking?"

"Can you get an extension?"

He sighs. The way his hair is drying right now, standing up in fluffy patches, he looks like a balding mad scientist that's just been electrocuted.

"Well," she says. "Let me know if I can help."

"No one can help me." He pauses, as though contemplating his next statement deeply. "I," he says very seriously, "am totally fucked."

She pushes the empty aguardiente bottle off the mattress with her feet. (Did they really sleep with it in bed all night, like the saddest stuffed animal ever?) It lands on the carpeted floor with a thud.

Despite the very best part of herself, the part that allows her to be the calmest and most considerate of girlfriends, a lovingly present and forgiving partner, it's times like these when the thoughts come, sneaking across her mind. Army-style, crawling doggedly along on their bellies. Thoughts like: *We've been planning this trip for months. Why didn't you just finish it before we left D.C.?* Or: *You always do this. You always leave things till the absolute last minute.*

"Betsy?"

She turns her head. His eyes are wide and worried, his Adam's apple trembling as though there's something alive hiding in his throat, a tiny animal tucked away and quivering in fear. "Can you write for me?"

She types on the laptop, taking dictation as he wanders around the room, arms crossed behind his head, talking slowly, stating one painstakingly formed sentence after another. Paper Title: "The Possibility of Peacetime Economics in Colombia." Abstract: *How the potential end of the decades-long conflict and transition into economic stability is a model for other countries to follow for years to come.*

"Um," she says, fingers skittering over the keyboard. "A bit long."

"Write it down," he says. "We'll fix it later." He's using his teacher voice with her, the one he uses with his undergrads, mastered long ago during his days as an elementary school teacher, high up in the Medellín hills.

"Whatever you say, *profe*," she says, hitting enter on the keyboard, and on the far side of the room he grins.

On the television, the tennis match ends and turns into the news: It's a story about the peace negotiations in Havana. Senators in white shirts walk over to a table of seated men wearing camouflage pants and black berets. Everyone's shaking hands and smiling.

—

"All right," he says the next morning at breakfast. "Next stop, Cali. What's the plan?"

The hotel they're staying at is the classic kind, old and fancy, one of those colonial houses that was once a convent or a seminary; she can't remember what this one was—there's a bronze plaque on the wall somewhere that explains it. The courtyard has giant, lumpy cobblestones that make her feet feel like they're getting massaged every time she walks across them in flip-flops. Popayán has been blessedly quiet, perfect for getting a good night's sleep and thus worth every penny of the nightly fee ("practically East Coast prices," he moaned in English at the front desk that first night, yet still handed over his credit card). In the center of the courtyard is a fountain with a statue, some saint or famous monk, presiding worriedly over the mossy water and slimy-looking goldfish. The only other guests sit at the far end of the courtyard, a German couple with enormous backpacks resting near their ankles like loyal dogs, both wearing beige zip-off pants.

"I already told you," she says, ripping a croissant in half. "Remember?"

She shows him the pictures on her phone again. They're from the blog of a Norwegian photographer, who in addition to shooting abandoned houses in Detroit and Chicago has documented a series of abandoned drug cartel houses—crumbling mansions in Tijuana, empty Mexico City apartments filled with automatic weapons and junk food, Escobar's infamous ranch on the outskirts of Medellín, with its abandoned giraffes and hippos. And this one.

"Can you believe I went here as a little kid?" she says, scrolling rapidly through the photos. The stone walls with jagged glass, the ridiculously huge automatic gate, the skinny eucalyptus trees extending their thin branches on the other side of the wall like nervous hands. "Isn't that crazy?"

"Why crazy?" he says, using his teeth to tear open a packet of salt, which he then sprinkles over his chunks of pineapple. "You didn't know what kind of place it was."

"Well, of course not. None of us did." There are no photos of the house's interior, but there's one of a dirty patio patterned with dark circles of pavement, evidence of long-gone orange flowerpots, which hid the tiles from years of sun. She recognizes the monkey bars and slides, remembers the yellow butterfly eggs dotting the handlebars. She shows him the rusted drainpipe where they would have waited for the candy to be thrown from the window, taps her fingernails against the abandoned swimming pool, now an empty concrete hole. She holds the phone so close to his face that it almost touches his nose, but he doesn't flinch. "So that's where Sebastián pooped," he says calmly, mouth full of bread. "And where Mariela had her cake."

"That's right." She looks down at the fruit salad. A wave of nausea has just washed over her—is it possible that she could still be hungover?

"That's where I want go," she says. "I want to see it."

A sparrow lands on a nearby cobblestone and immediately flies away as Eduardo sighs heavily through his nose. "Lover," he says. "You haven't been here since you were nine. And you want to see *that*?"

"Eight." She was actually ten—ten years old, fifth grade,

standing in line with her parents at the American Airlines counter. The contents of their entire house had already been shipped ahead in the belly of an enormous steel shipping container, their new address in D.C. scrawled out in black permanent marker across the cardboard boxes. In college, she sometimes told people that she'd left when she was even younger—five years old, four, sometimes even three. *Yeah, I was really young when we moved to the States. That's why my Spanish isn't so good anymore, ha-ha. I know, what a shame, right?*

She never wonders what it would have been like if she'd stayed. What would be the point?

"Well," he says. "You're lucky it's your birthday."

She stabs a piece of melon with her fork. "Still?"

"You didn't know? With me, holidays last at least a week. Even Christmas."

"Lucky me."

His hands rest calmly on the table: The left is wide and strong, the palm capable of wrapping around a basketball and shooting a three-pointer with his fingertips. On his right hand, the nubs of his missing three fingers are bulbous and red, like thick tree stumps, the only things left standing in an apocalyptic wasteland. The morning light as it hits his face turns his gray eyebrows white. Even though he's only eight years older than she, he could pass for a lot more, as though the strain of learning English at community college night school had led to premature aging. Another army-style thought abruptly enters her mind, marching across in heavy boots: *Who is this old man having breakfast with me? How on earth did I get here?* She chases the thought away by filling her mouth with the last of the pineapple. Chasing away unwanted thoughts is one of her best skills, along with staring down people in bars who make racist comments or ask if Eduardo is her father. In a bar in Columbia Heights, a man once half-teasingly asked her, *So, does your dad always buy you that many tequila shots?* She just smiled at him, her lips still stinging from salt and lime, and said, *Only when he wants to fuck me from behind.*

"Okay," she says, pushing her chair back. "I'll look up directions for how to get there."

As they walk past the German couple, he tells them in English, "Welcome to Colombia!" They look up quickly, flashing brief smiles that are half surprise, half alarm, as though taken aback by his twitchy expression.

Packing up, she realizes she has some kind of yeast infection. Bacterial, vaginal. Maybe an allergic reaction to the shitty cheap tampons. She tries to hide it but of course it's impossible. "What's that smell?" he says, raising his head from in between her reluctantly open legs (*"No, baby, not right now, I'm really not in the mood, you know?"*). Mad Max (his favorite film ever) blares away on the TV as he reaches for the laptop and tells her to Google *fishy-smelling vagina.* "Okay, so these are the antibiotics you need to take. Are you writing this down?" He makes her check three different websites, eyes flickering only occasionally to the screen to watch trucks turn over and explode in the Australian desert. "Be sure to write

this down. We'll take you to the pharmacy; there's one at the bus station, I remember seeing it. And look, it says no dairy for the next couple of days."

He lowers his face back toward her crotch and kisses it, her tampon string tickling his nose. "Amazing," he says, inhaling deeply. "How did you know that fish is my favorite?"

She covers her face with her hands but can't help it; she's smiling.

Later he roams around the room as she's trying to get dressed, whipping his towel, pretending to kill imaginary enemies, *Street Fighter*–style. He's deep in what she likes to call his *"Mad Max* persona," smiling with a crazed glint in his eye, prowling around the bed. "Bam!" he says, snapping the towel sharply by her hip as she struggles to hook her bra. "Got the bastard. Take that."

With the next flick, he accidentally hits her full-force on the vagina, a direct bull's-eye. She immediately collapses on the bed and bursts into tears.

"Oh my God," he says immediately, dropping the towel and kneeling. "Lover. I'm so sorry." He wraps his arms around her and holds her tight. Even though to be perfectly honest it didn't hurt *that* much and the stinging sensation is already starting to fade, she still keeps crying hysterically, as though something inside her has suddenly burst, cracked wide open.

"Fuck," she says. "I don't want any drama. I just want to be on vacation. Is that too much to ask for?"

"No drama," he says. "Just vacation."

She wipes her nose with her bare arm. "Now we're going to miss the bus."

He raises his chin defiantly, as if he's challenging not her but the notion of time itself. "No, lover," he says. "We're not."

By some miracle she manages to finish getting dressed while he crams the rest of their clothes into the backpack, smashing down his pages of field notes and interview transcripts with peasant farmers, people whose entire families were slaughtered by paramilitaries as suspected Communists. The two of them are the last passengers to board, him banging on the closed doors and shouting at the driver ("Open up, *parcero!*"), but they make it just in time: her clutching the white paper bag of antibiotics, him with a plastic bag draped around the crook of each elbow, filled with burning-hot *pandebonos* and napkins already stained with grease.

"What did I tell you?" he says, heading down the aisle. Another couple is sitting in their assigned seats, eating plantain chips and scattering crumbs everywhere, so they take the last two empty seats at the back. A rumble begins beneath their feet and the bus lurches forward like an animal finally being released from a chain. Once they're on the highway, the wind whipping through the windows makes their hair fly back, like they're models standing in front of a gigantic fan.

He is careful with her during the journey, tentative and considerate, saying things like "Would you like a sip of water?" while she responds with "Oh, yes please. Thank you very much." She puts in her earplugs so she can nap and he buys, through the window, a packet of sugar-covered nuts (her favorite) from a street vendor. She wakes up during a traffic jam, and he passes the time by asking her question after question about the books she'll be teaching her fourth graders this year.

"And then what happens?" he says over and over, until she's basically summarized the entirety of the Narnia series, from the pond-hopping bits in *The Magician's Nephew* to Aslan's final onion-world monologue in *The Last Battle*.

When they're an hour away from Cali, she's already asked him to explain yet again how everyone in *The Godfather* trilogy is related to one another (one of his favorite topics) and to tell her for the umpteenth time his first thought when he met her, at a mutual friend's house party two years ago ("I thought, *Who is this beautiful Colombian girl, and how do I get her away from the guacamole dip and talking to me instead?*"). They talked together all night, sharing anecdotes, scooping tortilla chips out of the bowl until only tiny broken shards were left. She told him about how back in Cali, her father had received kidnapping threats while serving on the school board, and Eduardo nodded and said, "Most likely from the police." "Yes!" she said, so excited, she accidentally spilled wine over her arm. "That's exactly right!" He seemed so serious and intense, staring at her unblinkingly with his bushy mad professor eyebrows, and yet when they walked back to her apartment together, he linked his fingers with hers at the traffic light (his left hand, of course, never his right). Tugging at her insistently like a little kid who needed help crossing the street. She couldn't help but laugh at the time, but there was something sad about it too.

That's what being with Eduardo seems to bring out in her, more than anything else. Laughter and an ache.

"Lover," she says. "Tell me a story. The one about the protest?" This one is from when he was a university student, the time he got arrested because he mistook a policeman's van for a rubbish truck and jumped into it to escape the tear gas. There's another story she likes, where his brother pooped out a tapeworm and blocked the toilet in their one-bathroom house, and their mother had to fish it out of the pipe with a clothes hanger (this anecdote is inevitably one that makes her squirm with both delight and horror, as he luridly describes the floppy way the tapeworm dangled, exactly like wet spaghetti). Or the story in which his mother gave him condoms before he flew to D.C., telling him, *If you're moving to America, it's better to be sinful and practical than holy and diseased.*

Instead of retelling any of these, though, Eduardo shakes his head. "No stories," he says. "Not right now." His lips pull thinly inward in what might be a smile but might be something else.

She looks down at the dirty bus floor. "I'm sorry," she says, though she isn't exactly sure what she's apologizing for. He squeezes her arm, but it still feels like she's done something wrong.

(She never asks him about the time he took his university girlfriend to a polo match and the girlfriend's father told him, *I won't have any daughter of mine sitting with a renowned Communist.* Or about the morning his editor friend Sergio was found tied to a post, a bullet hole behind his ear, fingers severed, and one eyeball carved out. Or about the night with the men in the alleyway, and the motorcycles, and the machete blades. There are certain stories Eduardo will never tell more than once.)

"Do you ever think about it?" she says suddenly. "About what it would have been like if you'd stayed?"

He's craning his neck, still looking out the window, as though there's something behind his shoulder he needs to see before it fades out of sight.

"No," he says. "I don't."

In Cali they stay at a student hostel in San Antonio, a hip young neighborhood popular with tourists and backpackers. It's highly rated on TripAdvisor, which emphasizes its "quiet and peaceful atmosphere," perfect for "a great night's sleep." The reception area is decorated with soccer memorabilia, scarves and shirts and framed photographs of Colombia's national team. "Excellent decorations," Eduardo says to the young man at the front desk, and they beam manically at each other as though exchanging a vital secret.

As they hand over their passports, the loudspeakers begin playing a samba song at top volume. "No!" he shouts, almost making her drop her passport. "The music is too loud for *la señorita*! She won't be able to sleep!" She frowns at him, embarrassed that he's making such a fuss on her behalf, but later, as they walk up the freezing-cold stairwell, the samba abruptly stops and is replaced by a lower-volume song, a salsa cover of "Smooth Criminal."

"Thank you," she says, rubbing his back.

While he takes a shower she opens his laptop. The Word document for his paper is still open, filled with notes. A section in the middle of the page catches her eye:

"picar para tamal"—*to cut up the body of the living victim into small pieces, bit by bit*

*"bocachiquiar"—to make hundreds of small body
punctures from which the victim slowly bleeds to
death*

Eight-year-old schoolgirls raped en masse

*Unborn infants removed by cesarean section; replaced
with roosters*

Ears cut off

Scalps removed

Include statistics for forced disappearances?

She reads it one more time. She bites her lip. Then she clicks the little yellow button to minimize it and logs in to his Gmail account. She searches for the name of his ex-girlfriend, a Spanish architect who broke up with him in a tent on the Parque Tayrona beach, but thankfully the last email is from eight months ago, a cordial update she's already read. *Things are going well, thanks. So nice to hear from you.* She opens Facebook and types out a name in the search box, then immediately deletes it. She types it out again more slowly, as though that will somehow make it feel less like an irresistible compulsion: *Stephanie Lansky.* As usual, none of the faces that appear look even remotely familiar, and there are no mutual friends in common. It's the same for *Mariela Montoya*, who has never been mentioned in any of the articles she's read about the house, not even in passing. If you didn't know any better, you'd think Mariela and Stephanie had never existed at all—that they'd simply vanished into thin air. Her fingers hover over the keyboard, but that's as far as she gets—what was La Flaca's real name?

Instead of checking LinkedIn or Instagram, she deletes her browsing history and then heads downstairs. She sits on the couch and looks at her phone, reading the Cali Wikitravel page and Lonely Planet forums, scrolling, scrolling. She tries to find more high-quality photos of the house on Google Images, but the Norwegian blog is still the best source. She clicks on the photo of the ashy hole in the ground, what must have once been the barbecue pit, surrounded by the hunched-over grapefruit and droopy-leafed papaya trees. She copy-pastes a chunk of text into Google Translate and is able to decipher that the Norwegian blogger suggests that renting a motorcycle rickshaw for the day is the best way to get there, as opposed to taking a cab.

When he finally comes downstairs, her eyes feel cloudy, as though they're still blinking away pop-up ads. She tells him that according to Wikitravel, the foreigners who teach at the international private schools in Cali tend to live in this neighborhood, the kind of people who would have taught her in kindergarten: Canadian hippies, recent American college graduates on the lookout for a cushy job abroad. There are also a lot of hipsters, DJs, university students, and punk rockers. Maybe the local bands could even include some of her former classmates, transformed from happy-go-lucky fifth graders into bespectacled hipster musicians.

"Do you think there's a chance we'll run into someone you know?" he says.

She shakes her head just a little too quickly. "No," she says. "That's not possible."

They go for a walk. They wait for ages to cross the high-way, women on motor scooters threading through traffic in semitransparent blouses and super-short shorts, helmeted sol-diers staring down from the overpasses. They weave their way through a construction site, the road blasted apart in thick gray chunks, and she tells him that they're building a special lane for the buses that will speed by the jammed-up regular lanes, just like the ones they have in Europe. "I swear to God," she says as they pass a grove of trees with white Xs spray-painted on their trunks, "they started building that damn lane the year we left and it's still not finished."

"Nice," he says. "What else looks different?"

"How would I know?" she says in a voice that is maybe a little too loud. He frowns, so she makes an effort, says lightly, "I guess there's more malls."

They climb up the hill, passing a gray stone church and plaza filled with families pushing strollers, and cut through the park with its uneven cobblestone path, crushing tiny white flowers beneath their shoes. He borrows her phone and takes carefully framed photos of the surrounding mountains, the twinkling lights of the tin-roofed neighborhoods, the giant crosses on the summit lit up like air traffic control signals for UFOs. When she teases him about being a technology addict he looks genuinely wounded. "They're memories," he says solemnly in the professor voice she imagines he uses in lecture halls, "for our children."

"Our what?" she says, instantly hating the way her heart flutters. If she were watching from a distance, she'd want to punch herself in the face.

They sit on a bench by the *artesanía* marketplace and watch the vendors sell their little *chiva* magnets, the flag-colored T-shirts, the fuzzy tapestries of rural village scenes. He uses her bottle of water to take a painkiller; the ache in his stumps is bothering him again. She tells him that they're vaguely near the Baptist church that her family used to attend—she'd slump down in the seat and amuse herself by staring out the window and pretending to be Macaulay Culkin in that one scene in *Home Alone,* sliding along the telephone wires, hanging on to a clothes hanger.

"I used to do something similar on the bus," he says, "except I'd just imagine myself running really fast, smashing through anything that got in my way—dogs, telephone poles, parked cars." He plants his lips on her chin and sputters gently, Mouse Pilot–style.

A little kid is staring at them, mouth half-open, while his mother examines a row of dangling earrings. It takes all her energy to restrain herself from frowning back at him, scrunching up her face into a rude monster expression, maybe even saying loudly, "Didn't your mother teach you it's not polite to stare?" Somehow he's sensed it, that inexplicable air around her that screams foreigner, even though she didn't become a U.S. citizen until she was eighteen years old. What if she were to pull out the battered red Colombian passport in her purse and flap it in his face like a crazed butterfly?

"Maybe we should travel in the U.S. next summer," she says to Eduardo. "What do you think?"

He pauses from nuzzling her neck.

"We could rent a car and do American stuff. See the fireworks in Philadelphia. Go to Gettysburg for July Fourth."

"Gettysburg?"

She tries to explain it as the dim streetlights around them slowly flicker on. The reenactors dressed up in their blue and gray uniforms, the slow march across the field, the cannon-balls, and the tents and umbrellas the website recommends you bring to protect yourself from the sun.

He straightens up, frowning. "What makes you think I would want to see that?"

"Because it's historic. It was the most important battle in the history of the United States."

He shakes his head, picking at the splintered wood on the bench. "I've seen enough battles."

They start walking back before the sky becomes com-pletely dark. Across the street from the hostel is a parked car with the doors wide open, blasting Pitbull at top volume. A group of young men (boys, really) are standing around talk-ing, sitting on the edges of tires, smoking cigarettes, dented cans of Poker beer scattered on the surrounding sidewalk. They're baby-faced, smooth-skinned, only a few years older than her fourth graders back in D.C. Green-and-red soccer team shirts, caps on backward, shaved heads with black-ink tattoos on their necks and wrists. The volume of the music is turned up so loud her eardrums are already aching. As they pass the car Eduardo speeds up, quickening his pace, but she stops and turns toward them.

"Excuse me," she says in Spanish. "Would you mind turn-ing the music down? The guests staying here aren't going to be able to sleep."

They stare at her. She can sense Eduardo standing slightly behind her, torso close, arm hairs brushing urgently against her elbow as though sending her a secret message.

"Whas yo' problem," one of the guys says in English, in an exaggerated American accent. The others laugh.

"Wow, so polite," she says as Eduardo begins tugging at her wrist, softly at first, then harder. "Is that what your parents taught you? To be polite like that?"

They stare back at her, the bass still thrumming away. She can feel it deep in her belly, like a pulse. "Fuck America!" the same guy says, and they all laugh again.

She can still feel their eyes on her as she turns and walks toward the hostel steps. Eduardo follows behind, calling out over his shoulder toward the car: "Sorry, so sorry!" As she reaches the hostel door she hears the group burst into laughter, calling out and whooping, stray phrases following her inside. *Hey gringa, hey beautiful, come back!* By the time she bursts into their room her lips are trembling, but she still hasn't cried.

"Thanks so much for that," she says as he sits on the edge of the mattress. "I mean, wow. You were really there for me when I needed you. God, I felt so supported."

He's resting his arms in his lap. Pressing his wrists together.

"Yeah, really supportive." She opens her purse and shakes it up and down, scattering her makeup, her hand sanitizer, the silvery packets of antibiotics.

"Give me my phone," she says. "I'm going to call the police."

He's rocking back and forth. "Please don't do that."

"If you don't give me my phone, I'm going to go downstairs and ask the front desk to do it."

"Lover," he says. "Please don't create trouble."

She heads downstairs and waits at the desk while the expressionless teenage boy on duty rings the police station three times. Every once in a while she wipes her shaky palms off on her jeans.

"I left them a message," the boy says, hanging up. "They should be here soon."

She sits on the couch for thirty minutes, staring at the shelves of abandoned books and magazines on the opposite wall. Nobody comes.

When she finally heads back upstairs he's working again, left hand tapping at the keyboard, papers scattered around him. The sight of him typing away fills her with the angriest feeling she's had all night, as though a cloud of red has just descended over her eyes.

"You," she says, "are a coward."

He looks up from the screen.

"I needed you. I needed you to be there for me and you weren't."

He shuts the computer and scoots over to her.

"Why didn't you stand up for me? Why didn't you say anything?"

"Betsy," he says, and there's something steely in his voice now, a tone she hasn't heard before and doesn't recognize. "You don't understand what it's like here. Things are much better now—safer—but people are still used to solving their problems differently. They solve them with weapons. You think I want to risk that?"

"I know all that." She can hear her voice getting more high-pitched and shrill; she sounds as if she's on the verge of shrieking. She hears the way she sounds to him too: the typical voice of a naïve and deluded American demanding her so-called rights as a citizen, as irritating and ridiculous as a pair of beige zip-off pants, but she doesn't even care at this point. "You're talking like I don't understand how things are—like I live in some dumb, pretend fantasy world. You're making it sound like I'm the one who's done something wrong, when you're the one who's being passive."

He's waving both hands in the air now, gesturing emptily. The stumps of his missing fingers look redder than ever. "You think I like this?" On the street, the music has been turned up even louder and the flimsy windows of their room are shuddering from Sean Paul's thunderous raps. "You think I don't want it to be quiet, like it is in the States? You think I don't want the laws here to work?"

"They were laughing at me," she says. "All of them. And you didn't say anything. You didn't even try." Her hands are trembling. He stares at her. She heads to the bed and roughly snatches up the pillows, not leaving any for him, yanks the comforter up and gathers it in her pillow-filled arms. The laptop falls with a clatter onto the floor, but he doesn't make a move to catch it.

She heads to the bathroom, doesn't look back as she closes the door. She dozes on the floor, curled up on the tiles, waking up every hour or so. At four A.M. a neighbor starts playing Christian sermons on the radio and pouring buckets of water into the street. She cries for a bit, then wipes her nose off on the pillowcase. Runs her fingers through her hair and looks at the strands she's gathered in her palm, as though wondering what to do with them. In the end she rubs them into a giant knot between her thumb and index finger and throws it into the toilet, flushing it away.

When she opens the door she heads straight for the bed, leaving the comforter and pillows behind in the bathroom. He's lying on his back like a corpse, staring up at the ceiling. She slides her icy-cold feet up his legs. Tucks the back of her skull beneath his chin, as smoothly and easily as a key inserting itself into a lock.

"Do you want me to get a pillow?" she whispers.

His chin scrapes against her hair as he shakes his head. Or maybe he's just shifting his position, making room for her on the mattress. Not answering.

As the room slowly fills with light from the rising sun, she tells him the rest of it, the part she left out. How the very best thing about Mariela's birthday cake, what everyone most looked forward to (even more than the candy), was the rumor that there was a coin hidden deep inside, buried under the frosting. A silver two-hundred-peso piece, or even the five-hundred-peso one with its shiny golden tree. They all whispered about it together, nudging each other by the swimming pool, murmuring under the mango tree. It was a custom that they'd only ever heard about at Mariela's party, never at any of their own. They all wanted to be the one to find it—pick their slice apart with their plastic forks and spoons, search through the mess of crumbs, prove that it was really there and not just a rumor, not just a lie. She never found it, though. She never even got a chance to try.

So today's the day she'd like to do it. Her birthday outing. They have one full day left in Cali before their flight back to D.C., so today is basically their only chance. Despite what the Norwegian blogger recommends, she thinks that taking a cab will be easiest. She can cover most of the cost herself by going to the ATM and withdrawing more pesos with her Bank of America card. The drive shouldn't take more than two hours; she'll take some Dramamine to make sure she doesn't get carsick on that endlessly winding road; he should remember to bring his painkillers in case his stumps start bothering him in the heat. It will be an amazing trip, the opportunity of a lifetime. Seeing a place like that in person, with that kind of history. Seeing it with their own eyes.

"That's good," he says. "I'm glad, lover, that we'll get to do something that's so important to you."

He's still staring at the ceiling. She waits with bated breath.

"I'm the worst person," he says, "in the world."

"No."

"Yes. I didn't protect you. I can't protect anybody." He closes his eyes.

"Mouse Pilot," she says, "that's not true."

"It is," he says. "And don't call me that anymore. I'm not Mouse Pilot. I'm nothing."

He shuts his eyes even tighter, as if that will prevent the thoughts from rushing in. The wave of feelings that she can't keep him safe from.

"Eduardo," she says. "You're not the worst person in the world. I saw somebody way worse under a bridge in D.C. He was picking his nose and smearing his boogers against the wall, and when I walked by he catcalled me and said, 'Hey, pretty flower, why don't you give me a smile?'"

He's silent for a beat. "He does sound worse," he admits. "Who else?"

She thinks about it. "In third grade," she says, "my friends and I were mean to this girl in our class." She hesitates. "Mariela."

"The birthday girl?"

She nods, even though his eyes are still closed. "I think we were maybe a little afraid of her. She was really smart, even if she was a bit intense. We started teasing her—we got everybody in the grade to start calling her Fatty." She doesn't say anything for a moment, then says the next part in a rush, as though she can't help it: "She wanted to be our friend, and we wouldn't let her."

He opens his eyes. "Lover," he says. "That doesn't make you the worst."

She looks down at his chest, at that space of skin she's come to know so well, every patch of hair, every blemish and freckle. "It was a wrong thing to do," she says. "And we shouldn't have done it."

He tucks his hand down the skirt she still hasn't changed out of, pressing his stump against her crotch. She hasn't changed her tampon in hours; she could be leaking blood all over him. *Disgusting,* he could say. *That's gross.* He could push her away, frown at her: *I can't believe that you did that. That you're like that.* But he doesn't move away, and neither does she. Instead he says, "Tell me someone else. One more."

This time she's ready. "Anybody who didn't support the peace negotiations."

When he laughs his mouth fills with her hair. "Can't beat that," he says.

She wraps her arms around him and squeezes as hard as she can.

"Just pretend," she says, "that it's all going to be fine. What's the harm in pretending?"

He wraps his other arm around her and hugs her back, so forcefully that she momentarily loses her breath.

"None," he says. "No harm at all."

"I'll call the cab," she says. "We'll leave as soon as you finish."

"Yes," he says. "When I finish."

I went on vacation with my family once in Abejorral, where my mother's sister's family lived. Tierra Caliente, the land with all the hot springs and not-quite-extinct volcanoes, and the only peak in the country to have snow on it year-round. We had to make part of the journey on mules. And when we arrived at her house, there was no electricity, and the only light we had came in through tiny windows. If you wanted to, you could stay shut in there for days and never see the light.

One day the whole family went down to the river to swim. My brother impressed everyone by catching a fish with one hand. He was always very agile like that.

What were you like?

Very reserved. Believe it or not, as a child I was very reserved. Then when it was time to walk back to the ranch, it started to get dark and we got lost. "Uy," my aunt and uncle said. It was a witch who made us lose our way, the one who roams the woods crying, holding her still-bleeding stomach from where the paramilitaries cut out her baby. For whatever reason, in those parts it was typical to always blame getting lost on that one witch. But if you didn't acknowledge that she was there—or worse, if you ignored her cries, pretending that she didn't exist—then that was just asking for trouble. It was better to know about her and accept her than to not.

So I remember walking through the jungle on a tiny path in the pitch black. I couldn't see what was in front of me and I couldn't see where I was coming from. When I closed my eyes there was hardly any difference from when I had them open. Every time I brushed against a tree branch, a bush, or a vine, it felt like the hand of the witch or even the trees themselves, reaching out to grab me and pull me toward them, hold me tight. It was the scariest thing that had ever happened to me up till then. I was convinced that I was going to get lost and disappear into the blackness, and that no one would ever find me; no one would even remember my name. The only way I could keep myself going was to pretend I was a knight. Thwack! I cut the branches back with my sword. Bam! I drove the witches away with my shield. One step at a time, I kept moving forward.

And then finally we made it back to the house. As soon as we got inside, the first thing we did was light a candle. I remember that the flame was orange. Flickering. It made it seem as though the air in the house was moving. Of everything that day, it was the strangest thing I saw. I'd never thought of air like that before—as something that was around you all the time, without you ever feeling it or noticing that it was there. I'm so glad that I saw it—that I took the time to look and see.

———

"That's a good story," she says.

"I know." He leans in to give her a wet kiss just above the collarbone.

"I'm glad you guys found your way back."

"I know," he repeats. "Isn't it crazy to think that it could have been different?" He laughs so hard she can see the yellowish stains on the backs of his teeth.

He types for the rest of the day, barely stopping until evening, only pausing to drink papaya juice out of a giant Styrofoam cup, to eat french fries and fried chicken out of a greasy white paper sack that she brings from the food stand across the street. Sometimes he squeezes his stump and winces, but whenever she asks if he needs a painkiller he always shakes his head. Maybe they'll still be able make it out to the ranch in time and see it again. Maybe they won't. But the moment he finishes his paper, he reads it out loud to her: every undeniable statistic, every irrefutable graph. He quotes testimonies, lists percentages, stabs his finger in the air when he wants to indicate parentheses. It's the best story he's told her yet, the one she's been waiting to hear for years without even knowing it, filled with so much truth and fantasy it's hard to know which is better. His paper patiently explains (with precise terms and specific examples) how in present-day Colombia, the decades-long conflict has finally been successfully resolved. Land reform has been carried out in a fair and effective manner, hostages have been released, refugees resettled. Genuinely alternative leftist political parties have been established; union leaders, journalists, and priests can freely express left-wing dissent. Corruption has been eliminated, the War on Drugs considered ineffectual and brought to an end, the wealth of oligarchies and monopolies redistributed. Paramilitaries disarmed and disbanded. Guerrilla fighters reintegrated and forgiven. If a party were held tomorrow, everybody in the entire country would be invited, not a single person made to wait on the other side of a locked door.

Betsy will be there, of course: offering her cheek to everybody who wants to kiss it, never turning away without a greeting. *Hi, Stephanie—Flaca—Mariela. It's so good to see you; it's been so long. How are you doing; how have you been?*

He looks up from the laptop. "What do you think?" he says.

"Perfect," she says. "Don't change a word."

ACKNOWLEDGMENTS

Muchísmas gracias:

Clare Alexander, Anna Stein, Cindy Spiegel, Annie Chagnot, everyone at Spiegel & Grau, Trezza Azzopardi, Andrew Cowan, James Scudamore, Jean McNeil, everyone on the UEA MA workshop, *Lighthouse* literary journal, Daunt Books, *The White Review, The New Yorker,* Lauren Rose, Rachel Mendel, Ph.D. Babes, Emily & Laura, Pansy, Nick for MP.

Biggest thanks to my family, especially my parents: without their love and support I never could have finished this.

Thank you to the following books:

Out of Captivity (Marc Gonsalves, Keith Stansell, and Tom Howes)

Long March to Freedom (Thomas R. Hargrove)

Law of the Jungle (John Otis)

My Life as a Colombian Revolutionary (María Eugenia Vásquez Perdomo)

My Colombian War (Silvana Paternostro)

The Dispossessed (Alfredo Molano, Aviva Chomsky)

Beyond Bogotá (Garry Leech)

Law in a Lawless Land (Michael Taussig)

Los ejércitos (Evelio Rosero)

El olvido que seremos (Héctor Abad Faciolince)

ABOUT THE AUTHOR

JULIANNE PACHICO was born in Cambridge, England, and grew up in Cali, Colombia. She currently lives in Norwich, England.

@juliannepachico

ABOUT THE TYPE

This book was set in Sabon, a typeface designed by the well-known German typographer Jan Tschichold (1902–74). Sabon's design is based upon the original letter forms of sixteenth-century French type designer Claude Garamond and was created specifically to be used for three sources: foundry type for hand composition, Linotype, and Monotype. Tschichold named his typeface for the famous Frankfurt typefounder Jacques Sabon (c. 1520–80).